Compliments of Grumman

P9-DTS-554

To: Cdr. R.F. Aumack

D.V. Gallery

NOTE: Any resemblance to actual
persons, etc etc is purely
coincidental (It says here!)

DVG.

Stand By-y-y
to Start Engines

Also by Daniel V. Gallery

CLEAR THE DECKS
TWENTY MILLION TONS UNDER THE SEA
NOW, HEAR THIS!
EIGHT BELLS, AND ALL'S WELL

STAND BY-Y-Y
TO
START ENGINES

By Daniel V. Gallery

NEW YORK

W · W · NORTON & COMPANY · INC·

In Memory of
Commander M. L. Horner, U.S.N.R.

CONTENTS

FOREWORD

It is unfair to struggling authors to lend books.

If you like this one, after you have read it, lock it up in a safe place or burn it. Then tell your friends about it, and direct them to the nearest reputable book shop.

D.V.G.

Stand By-y-y
to Start Engines

CHAPTER ONE

Hanky-Panky Aloft

LIEUTENANT COMMANDER "Curly" Cue, cruising at 10,000 feet, sang softly to himself as he led the Navy's famous Blue Angels stunt team down the West Coast toward San Diego.

> We're intrepid birdmen who roam thru the sky,
> We fly 'em down low and we fly 'em up high,
> We spin 'em, we roll 'em, we fly upside down,
> We never drink likker except on the ground . . .

Curly was, of course, an ace blowtorch jockey. The only thing he would rather do than fly was to play harmless practical jokes on all who came within his orbit. At least Curly thought they were harmless. Like the time he smeared a little glue in the foam rubber lining of a friend's hard helmet just before a four-hour flight. When they got back the doctors had to trepan the helmet and shave his pal's head. Or when he put a small box of bumblebees in the cockpit of a squadron mate's jet plane, the box being rigged so it would pop open when the plane was catapulted. Flyers get extra pay for hazardous duty, but all Curly's shipmates figured they were doing *extra* hazardous duty.

The six Blue Angels were flying what was, for them, a loose formation, cruising between two layers of cloud. For many miles along the coast that day there was a high overcast and low undercast separated by about 6000 feet. Between layers, horizontal visibility was ten miles. But you were on instruments in there because the layers seemed to merge in the distance and there was no horizon whatever. You were flying in the center of what seemed to be a huge gray sphere that looked the same in all directions.

Suddenly Curly's roving eye spotted a big Navy seaplane some miles ahead and several thousand feet lower, coming in the opposite direction. Curly had been hoping they would meet somebody coming the other way that morning. The prevailing weather suggested to his alert mind the possibility for an interesting psychological experiment.

He squeezed the button on his stick and said into his microphone, "Wake up, you guys. There's work to be done."

His five teammates all waggled their wings, showing they had shifted their brains out of neutral and were no longer asleep.

"We are going to inverted flight for a while," announced Curly. "Rolling to the right. Acknowledge."

Five matter-of-fact "rajahs" came back, indicating only mild surprise. When you flew behind Curly anything could happen, and usually did. And, of course, the Blue Angels are just as relaxed upside down in formation on instruments as they are any other way. As the last "rajah" came in, Curly and his boys rolled bottoms up and flew that way for the next few minutes.

We take you now to the cockpit of the patrol plane. In the co-pilot's seat is Rear Admiral "Windy" Day, old-time Navy pilot who had been one of the best in his younger days and was still pretty good. The pilot's seat is empty at this moment, the pilot having just gone aft to the gents' can.

The plane was on autopilot and the Admiral was scanning the instruments with a practiced eye, noting that all was well. Every now and then he scanned the sky around him, too, as all alert flyers do, especially older ones.

He spotted the approaching jets when they were still mere specks, noted that he was headed right at them, but they would pass several thousand feet overhead. The jets were much smaller than his plane, so he didn't see them until nearly a minute after

Curly had spotted him. The planes were closing at almost nine miles a minute.

Soon Admiral Day began to have an uneasy feeling. There seemed to be something funny about the formation ahead. All of a sudden it hit him—they all *looked* as though they were flying upside down. *By George, they were flying upside down* . . . or else HE was!

Day shot a glance at his gyro horizon and saw no sign that it had tumbled. Instinctively he looked out to check the horizon and, of course, there wasn't any. True, he should have realized he was not hanging in his seat belt, but when the vertical seems to have suddenly flipped 180°, you don't always think logically and clearly.

In that empty gray sphere there was no way whatever to tell which way was up except by the gyro horizons of the various planes. Squadrons of jet fighters don't usually cruise around upside down on instruments, so the Gallup poll on "which way was up" seemed to be 6 to 1 against him. Admiral Day suffered a brief attack of the screaming meemies and his own personal vertical tumbled.

He slapped the autopilot switch to the "off" position, grabbed the yoke, and began trying to horse that big flying boat over on its back to match the vertical indicated by the jets. In just a few seconds the first pilot came scrambling back to the cockpit, hauling his pants up as he ran, took over the controls and resumed level flight.

Meantime Curly's formation, now flying right side up, circled the patrol plane, waggling their wings in a friendly manner and doing a slow roll to salute their big boat compatriots before buzzing off to the south.

As they disappeared, the pilot said to Admiral Day, "The Blue Angels, sir. Their leader, Lieutenant Commander Cue, is quite a practical joker."

"Harrumph," said Admiral Day, and tacked on a string of pithy observations which cannot be repeated here.

Of course the story was all over North Island minutes after the Blue Angels landed there. It didn't suffer any in the telling, and although the flying boat never got more than about 45° off the vertical, Curly and his boys had it doing snap rolls all over the sky. Immediately after the seaplane landed in San Francisco, the pilot, to protect his professional reputation, flashed word south through the fly-boys' underground that the Admiral was at the controls when this incident happened. That made it all the better. It became a permanent part of U.S. Navy folklore.

Next day Curly and his boys flew back to their home base in Pensacola and things went back to normal on the West Coast for a while.

A week later high over Pensacola four training planes droned back and forth doing some simple maneuvers. Three cadets were sweating out their final check in formation flying. The cadets were in a loose V, and the fourth plane, flown by an instructor, was tagging along not far behind.

These lads had only about two months' flying behind them and were pretty green. For them each flight was still an adventure. In the chase plane behind them the bored instructor told them by radio what to do and what a sloppy job they made of trying to do it.

The cadets were having a Bad Time this morning. They always did when Lieutenant Percy Peabody was in the chase plane. Student pilots are bold, eager lads who accept the risks of learning to fly for a paltry 50 percent extra pay and the coveted gold wings they will get if they make the grade. But they all figured they ought to get a campaign ribbon too whenever they went out with Lieutenant Percy Peabody.

Percy was a frustrated jet pilot who thought it was a sad waste of flying talent for him to be teaching kindergarten classes. He came to Pensacola for shore duty from a fighter squadron expecting to join the Blue Angels, and figuring this would be a big break for that famed elite group. But for one reason or another (mainly because he was Percy Peabody) he got thumbs down from that famous Navy team of precision stunt pilots. Instead, he wound up instructing cadets in primary flight school. This is a terrible comedown from performing amazing feats of airmanship and being wined and dined all over the country as the Blue Angels are. It rankled what Percy had where his heart should have been. As a result he hated cadets as a hen hates sharp-cornered eggs, and vented his spleen on them whenever he got a chance. He was at his nasty best this morning, and his pupils were being brainwashed.

"Come on there, No. 3," he sneered into the mike, "close up. You're twenty feet too far out. Whassa matter, sister? Ya scared? Get in there where ya belong."

"Roger. Wilco," replied No. 3 and eased in a little closer to the leader.

"Aw right now," growled Percy when No. 3 was in position. "Lemme see you go into right echelon."

The leader rogered, made a hand signal, and when his pals had acknowledged, wiggled his wings in the execute signal. Number 2 plane slowed down, pulled up a little, slid over to his right, and dropped into place on No. 3's starboard quarter, putting the three planes in a diagonal line to the right. It was a well-executed maneuver. Not even Lieutenant Peabody could find anything wrong with it.

But the Lieutenant had to have something to squawk about, so he set a booby trap. He squeezed his mike button and said, "Make a ninety-degree right turn."

"*Right* turn?" asked the leader.

"That's what I said," replied Percy.

"Roger," said the leader, and banked gingerly into a shallow turn to the right.

Turning right, against the echelon, No. 2 and 3 planes began to close in on the leader and had to throttle way back and slow down to avoid jamming up.

"Straighten out! Straighten out!" snarled Peabody as No. 3 began to wobble on the verge of a stall. "What the hell's the idea of turning against the echelon? Any dumb cluck oughta know better than that."

"But, sir, you told me to," said the leader.

"So what?" demanded Peabody. "Don't alibi. If I told you to fly into a mountain, would you do it? When guys like you crack up, they find blood all over in the crash but no brains. *Never* turn against the echelon. If you wanna go right, put 'em in left echelon before you start the turn. Were you just born stupid or did **you** have to study to get that way?"

And so it went for the next half hour, with Peabody hazing his pupils real good, and keeping them on the verge of what he called "nervous prostitution." By the time they landed the three angry, sweating cadets were almost ready to forget about flying and put in for submarines.

Going back that afternoon from Corry Field to the BOQ at Main Side, Percy spotted a car on the road ahead, driven by a sailor, with the Blue Angels insignia on it. A gleam came into the Lieutenant's eye as he throttled down to stay behind. He trailed the car for a while, checking its speed carefully and hoping the unsuspecting sailor would do something wrong. But he didn't. Finally Peabody gave her the gun, passed him, and shot a glance at the driver as he did so. Then he pulled over to the side of the road motioning to the sailor to stop.

The Lieutenant walked back to the sailor's car and said, "Lemme see your driver's license, sailor."

The sailor produced his license and said, "What did I do wrong, sir?"

Peabody ignored the question. He inspected the driver's license carefully, but could find nothing wrong with it. Then he said, "Kennedy, you're on the report for being out of uniform."

"I . . . I don't understand, sir," said Kennedy.

"Don't you know there's a station order out about wearing proper naval uniform whenever you're off station limits?"

"I *am* in uniform, sir," said Kennedy, unzipping the coveralls he was wearing and showing a blue jumper beneath.

"No, you're not," said Lieutenant Peabody "That coverall is uniform only in the hangar or on the flight line. You can't wear it off the station and a first-class petty officer oughta know that."

"But, sir, I'm just driving back to the barracks at Main Side," said Kennedy. "I been doing this every day for months."

"Then you've been out of uniform every day. You're on the report." Peabody scribbled the sailor's name and rate in a notebook, strode back to his car, and drove off.

Kennedy was stunned. Everybody wore coveralls driving to and from Corry Field. That station order was meant to apply only to men on liberty.

Of course "out of uniform" wasn't exactly a flogging offense. He probably wouldn't get anything worse than a warning out of it. But getting put on the report is always a pain in the neck. It means going through the rigmarole of appearing at mast with a lot of ne'er-do-wells who are always in trouble, and losing a whole day's work on your plane while doing it, to say nothing of losing maybe a week's liberty waiting to appear. And even a warning goes into your record as a black mark against you.

Kennedy sat there fuming until the Lieutenant drove off and then burst out with a blast of comments on Lieutenant Peabody's ancestry couched in language that it takes years of sea duty to learn. His observations cast serious doubt on the morals of the Lieutenant's whole family and indicated that he had probably sat in church scratching himself while his parents were getting married.

In the officers' club that night Lieutenant Curly Cue, and two of his Blue Angel teammates, Jim and Joe, were seated at a table swapping lies about their flying adventures. Curly was explaining a stunt he claimed he had performed recently which Jim and Joe knew very well was impossible even for Curly . . . or at least almost impossible for anyone except *maybe* Curly. Palms were extended and twisted this way and that, and elbows were cocked up as they always are when a group of pilots get 'em out of the hangar after hours in a bar. Curly had his right arm twisted like a pretzel and his shoulder almost out of joint trying to show how he had done a Cuban Eight with aileron rolls mixed up in it.

"Then I poured on the coal, kicked right rudder," he said, "and . . ."

At this point Lieutenant Peabody strolled up to the table looking like a cat full of canaries au gratin. "Hello, hotshot," he said. "What are you intrepid birdmen cooking up now? Something us ordinary flyers wouldn't even understand, I suppose."

"Hello," grunted Curly, who was one of the host of naval pilots who were rabid dis-admirers of Percy.

"You ought to take time out now and then from your looping, swooping, and sideswiping," observed Peabody casually, "and explain some of the facts of life in a military organization to that ragtime bunch of sailors you've got in your outfit."

"Whaddya mean by that?" demanded Curly.

"I had to put another one of your flathats on the report this afternoon," said Peabody smugly.

"Yeah?" said Curly. "Who? What for?"

"A first-class by the name of Kennedy for being out of uniform. He was driving back here from Corry wearing coveralls."

Curly's tailpipe temperature began creeping up into the red sector. "Hell, everybody does that," he said. "I should think you could find enough to do keeping your own people in line. Kennedy is my plane captain. Best jet engine mechanic in the Navy. Why don't you let me handle this?"

"Too late now," said Peabody. "I already turned in the report. Sorry . . . Well . . . I'll be seein' ya. Fly 'em low and slow and stay within gliding distance . . ." and he strolled off.

"That son of a bitch," said Curly fervently.

"Gutzon Borglum oughta carve that on a mountain," agreed Joe.

"That's about the sixth one of our people he's put on the report in the past couple of months," said Jim. "He does it because he's griped about not making our team so he takes it out on our enlisted men. One of these days I'm gonna put ground glass in his mashed potatoes."

"Yeah," said Jim. "He takes it out on the cadets too, especially on formation checks. Somebody was telling me the other day—"

"So, he's tough on formation checks, is he?" interrupted Curly with a shrewd glint in his eye. "That reminds me of a little hanky-panky I was thinking about some time ago. We might pull it on him."

"Oh-oh!" said Jim. "Fasten your seat belt, Joe. Here we go again." (Curly's hanky-panky always produced high blood pressure in its victims and, as already related, sometimes caused ace aviators to hit the panic button.)

"I wouldn't pull this on any regular guy," said Curly, "because it might put him in the bughouse. But that's where Peabody belongs anyway. It's a sure-fire way to drive a flight instructor plumb screaming crazy."

"With Peabody," observed Jim, "that wouldn't be a drive, just a short putt. Give out, Curly. What's the pitch?"

"I've listened in a couple of times on the voice radio," said Curly, "when Peabody was giving formation checks. He yells at the cadets like a big bad wolf, trying to show 'em how tough he is. But actually he's as oopsy as a mouse at a cat show up there. He's scared stiff that something will happen while he is responsible. He's trying to make admiral, you know. So he's a nervous Nellie when anything unusual happens. He don't give a damn how many cadets wind up in the meat wagon when they are on their own. But he don't want it to happen when *he's* in charge."

"So . . . where do we go from here?" asked Jim.

"Well, suppose he went out someday for a formation check with three cadets, and things got sort of out of hand. Suppose they started doing crossover turns, Dutch rolls, spinning in formation, and stuff like that there. That would shake him up, wouldn't it?"

"It would jar his dandruff loose," said Joe. "But it probably would splatter blood-guts-and-feathers all over the countryside, too. We would be shy three cadets at the next muster."

"Not if you pick the right 'cadets' we wouldn't."

"But those guys he checks are all brand-new primary students. None of 'em are good enough to do that kind of stuff."

"But *we* could do it. Couldn't we?" asked Curly.

"Sure. But what's that got to do with . . . hmmm . . . hah! . . . well, I'll be dipped in gook! Of course we can do it! Say hey!! Let's kick the idea around a bit."

"It will be as easy as a straight-in approach on the main runway with the sun behind you," said Curly. "After he gets through briefing his cadets for their formation check, we intercept them on the way to their planes and tell them to get lost. Then we get in the planes and give him the business."

"It will be wonderful," breathed Joe. "I can just see old Percy with his big mouth wide open and his eyes popping out like a tromped-on toad's. In five minutes we can have him crazier than a gooney bird. He'll blow his main gasket and pee in his pants."

"Not only that," agreed Curly; "we can have our boys tune in on our own ground radio and tape the whole thing. If it turns out the way I think it will everybody in the Navy will want a copy. It will be Number 1 on the hit parade. He'll never live it down even if he gets to be CNO."

Next day Peabody was briefing the three cadets he was about to check out that morning.

"Now you guys take off in V formation, head for Area B and climb to 6000 feet. I'll be right behind you and I'll tell the leader what I want you to do. You men in the No. 2 and 3 spots, never mind what I say. Just watch the leader and take your signals from him. Standard distance is two wing spans cockpit to cockpit. Don't try to pull any fancy stuff. Just plain, conservative, straightaway flying. *STAY OUT OF THE CLOUDS.* For guys at your stage of training, flying into a cloud can be just as bad as flying into a mountain. The leader is responsible at all times for avoiding other aircraft whether I see them or not. Also for not executing an order that would be dangerous. Any questions?"

There were none.

"Okay. Man your planes. Wait for me on the warm-up strip at the end of the runway—and try to show me that you're not as dumb as the three of you look."

A few minutes later three training planes manned by Curly, Joe, and Jim taxied out to the warm-up strip. The three Blue Angels ran through their checkoff lists and throttled down to wait for Percy. Presently he came rolling out and said on the voice radio, "Okay, mister leader. Get your aces up in the air."

Curly and his boys taxied out, assumed a loose V formation, and took off into the wild blue yonder, followed immediately by Percy.

It wasn't much of a takeoff. The two wing men straggled badly, and before long Curly was far ahead of them and there was no semblance of a proper V formation.

We shift now to the Blue Angels' mobile ground radio station, where a large group of pilots and enlisted men are expectantly gathered around a receiver tuned to the frequency on which Peabody will transmit. Soon after takeoff the following comes in:

PEABODY: "Come on, you guys. Close up. That was the lousiest takeoff I've seen in a long time."

(Curly keeps boiling straight ahead, climbing at full gun, and the others continue to lose distance.)

PEABODY: "Throttle down, No. 1. This isn't the National Air Races. How can these other guys catch up when you blast off that way?"

(Curly slows down, almost to stalling speed. The others pour on the coal and close in rapidly. But they overshoot him, and, to get back astern of him again, instead of throttling down, they go into 360° turns. Jim goes right and Joe left, thus scattering the formation all over the sky.)

PEABODY: "That did it! Now we got to take time out and rendezvous all over again. Hold your altitude, No. 1, and go into an easy turn to the left. Just keep on circling where you are until those other guys join up. All cadets acknowledge."

(Curly, Joe, and Jim roger promptly and for a minute the air is silent. Then the following comes in:)

"Number 2 to No. 1, Where are you?"

"Number 1 to No. 2, I'm over Corry Field at 5000."

PEABODY: "No, you're not, stupid. You're over Milton at 5500."

No. 2: "Oh, okay. I see you now. I'll join up right away."

(A minute later, No. 2 comes swooping down headed right at Peabody, chops off the gun at the last possible instant, fishtails violently, and drops into No. 2 position on the chase plane, which is tagging along a couple of hundred yards behind Curly. The slam-bang join-up nearly scared the drawers off Percy.)

JIM: "Number 2 joined up and in position now, sir."

PEABODY: "Like hell you are. You've joined up on *me*. Get out of here and get up there ahead where you belong . . . and don't do it like a bulldozer in a crockery store."

Jim: "Oh! Excuse me, sir. My mistake."

PEABODY: "Chase pilot calling No. 3. Chase pilot calling No. 3.

Come in."

JOE: "Number 3 to chase pilot. Hear you loud and clear. Go ahead, chase plane, sir."

PEABODY: "Just where in the wild hell are *you?*"

JOE: "Over the lighthouse, sir, at 6000 feet circling to the right. I can't see you anywheres."

PEABODY: "Over the lighthouse!! What makes you think there's a lighthouse at Milton? It's ten miles inland! Come on, now, get over here. We'll circle at 6000 and wait for you."

(There follows about a minute's silence and then—)

JOE: "Number 3 to chase pilot. Where is Milton, sir?"

PEABODY: "Good grief. Where is Milton? How long you been around here, mister?"

JOE: "I'm sorry, sir. I don't have a map."

PEABODY: "You prob'ly couldn't find it on the map even if you did have one! Everybody who isn't feeble-minded knows where Milton is. Can you read a compass, mister?"

JOE: "Number 3 to chase plane affirmative, sir."

PEABODY: "Then steer zero four five, that's northeast to you, for about five minutes, at 6000 feet. We will watch for you and try to take you by the hand and lead you into position."

JOE: "Roger. Wilco. Thank you, sir. Taking departure now from lighthouse."

(Five minutes later Joe comes barging up and joins the other three planes circling over Milton. He takes station to the right of Curly in the No. 3 spot, roughly abeam of Jim, who is flying in the No. 2 position—except that he is at a distance of about ten wing spans—much too far out. As Joe settles down in "position," the eager crowd in the radio shack hear the following from the loud-speaker:)

CURLY: "Number 1 to chase pilot. Section is rendezvoused, sir. Ready to proceed with check."

(By this time the crowd around the Blue Angels radio is almost rolling on the deck laughing at the comedy of errors coming out of the speaker. But one of the insiders on the deal remarks, "You guys ain't heard nothin' yet. The real act is just about to begin.")

PEABODY: "The hell you *are* ready to start the check. You're hardly within sight of each other. Close up."

(Joe and Jim cautiously close up to about nine wing spans.)

PEABODY: "Come on. Come on. Get in there where you belong."

(Joe and Jim gradually ease in to eight wing spans.)

PEABODY: "What the hell's the matter with you guys? Two wing spans is the right interval. Get in there goddammit."

(Jim and Joe now barge in on Curly and settle down with their wingtips almost touching his tail in the Blue Angels regular close-order formation in which a slight bobble would mean disaster.)

PEABODY: "My God . . . look out! . . . don't overdo it! . . . open out . . . open out!"

(Jim and Joe open out about half a wing span and stay there.)

PEABODY: "You're *still* way too close. Get back! Two wing spans is proper distance. Open out."

(Jim and Joe finally drop back to the proper interval and Lieutenant Peabody gets ready to go on with the business of putting them through their formation check.)

PEABODY: "Aw right now. Let's see if you guys can do anything *right*. Go into left echelon."

(Jim starts pulling up and sliding over to the right.)

PEABODY: "No. No. No. Hold it. I said left echelon."

CURLY: "I thought you said right, sir."

PEABODY: "No, I didn't. I said left echelon."

CURLY: "You want left echelon, sir."

PEABODY: "That's right."

CURLY: "Oh, excuse me, sir. *Right* echelon?"

PEABODY: "No. Negative. Dammit, get the feathers out of your ears and put your section in *left* echelon. Acknowledge."

CURLY: "Aye aye, sir. Left echelon. Wilco. Out."

(Curly gives the execute signal and Joe performs the maneuver very cautiously. He pulls up slowly about twenty feet, throttles down just a touch to lose distance gradually, and inches across to his new position at the end of the echelon. Before the maneuver is half over Peabody is yelling at Joe to speed it up, putting the blast on him in rather impolite language. Finally Joe makes it to his new position and, except for the snail's pace at which it was done, the maneuver was well executed.)

PEABODY: "You did that like an old lady crossing a slippery street on a windy day. Let's put more snap into it. . . . Now let me see a ninety-degree turn to the right."

(Curly goes into a very shallow turn to the right.)

PEABODY: "Come on. Bank it up . . . more . . . more . . . there, that's about right. Hold that."

(Curly keeps right on banking till his wings are almost vertical. The others stay with him in exact position. By the time the bank gets to 60° Peabody is screaming at Curly to come out of it.)

PEABODY: "That's too much . . . too much . . . level out."

(Curly straightens out on the new course. They are still in left echelon. At this point Peabody gets ready to pull his gambit of booby-trapping them into starting a turn against the echelon.)

PEABODY: "Aw right now. Mr. Leader, you're on your own now and you wanna make a ninety-degree turn to the left. Lemme see how you do it . . . but take it easy." (To turn left the leader should *first* shift the formation into right echelon.)

CURLY: "Ninety-degree left turn. Wilco. Out."

PEABODY (a few seconds later): "Good Gawd Almighty . . . look out! . . . holy cow!!"

(Curly had suddenly whipped into a vertical bank against the echelon and his pals had done a double crossover turn. In this maneuver the leader noses down and the others pull up to avoid hitting him as he crosses in front of them. As No. 2 crosses over the leader he whips around to the new course, and No. 3 crosses over both the leader and No. 2 before he does.

(This is a difficult and dangerous maneuver. Even good fighter pilots are apt to have a mid-air if their timing is just a little off. It was used in World War I but was abandoned afterwards. Pilots all agreed it was a hairy way to make a living and there was no future in it. But, of course, for the Blue Angels a double crossover is all in a day's work.

(In the time it takes to tell about it, the three planes were rolling back to level flight, 90° to the left of their former course, in perfect echelon formation but now [due to the crossover] right echelon instead of left.)

PEABODY: "Oh . . . oh . . . oh . . . [there followed a lot of language that cannot be repeated here and should never be used on the air] . . . You poor saps are lucky to be alive. Get that maniac out of the lead spot. Number 2 take the lead and No. 1 take No. 3 spot."

CURLY: "Roger. Turning the lead over to No. 2."

(The proper way to do this when in right echelon is for the leader to slide out to the left, slow down, and then ease over to the right, winding up in the tail-end spot of the echelon. The man who was No. 2 is now leading and No. 3 has graduated to the No. 2 spot. The way Curly did it was to haul back on the stick, going into a tight loop, sliding over to the right while upside down, and dropping smack into the No. 3 spot as he completed the loop.)

PEABODY: "No . . . no . . . NO . . . NO—"

CURLY (interrupting): "Sorry, sir. The stick slipped out of my hand and I lost control for a minute. I can do it better than that, sir, if you want me to try it again."

PEABODY: "Good Gawd, no . . . NEGATIVE . . . you'll *never* fead a lormation—I mean lead a formation—again if I've got anything to say about it."

CURLY: "Rajah, sir. Over and out."

PEABODY: "Now s-s-s-settle down, you g-g-g-guys . . . and don't g-get excited. See if you can't do things right in the time we got left."

JOE (who is leading now): "Rajah. Go left. Wilco. Out."

(They go into a normal 30° bank left turn.)

PEABODY: "Hell, no. I didn't mean *turn* left. I was talking about the time left. Straighten out."

(Joe rolls out of the turn headed straight at a towering bank of cumulus cloud about a quarter of a mile ahead. The base of the cloud is at 5000 feet. The formation is at 6000.)

PEABODY: "No! No! Keep going to the left. Stay away from that cloud. Go left."

JOE: "You were blocked out, sir. Please repeat."

PEABODY: "Go left. Go *left* . . . Stay out of that cloud . . . Oh migawd!"

(The three planes had just disappeared into the cloud.)

PEABODY: "Holy cow. D-don't get r-r-rattled now, you guys. All of you cold your horses—I mean hold your courses—till you clome out of the c-c-cloud. Fly straight ahead and d-d-d-don't . . ."

(At this point two planes fall out of the bottom of the cloud in tail spins.)

PEABODY: "B-b-bail   out!! Bail out! . . . MAYDAY . . . two crashes f-f-f-five miles north of . . ."

(The two planes, Curly and Jim, recover from the spin simultaneously 1000 feet below the base of the cloud, on the opposite course to the one on which they entered the cloud. They are abreast of each other on parallel courses. The third plane, Joe, comes diving out of the base of the cloud and drops into the leader's spot in front of them, making a perfect 3-plane V.)

PEABODY (after a string of incoherent obscene observations): ". . . Th-that's ENOUGH! . . . B-b-break up the f-formation and return to base immediately . . . *by yourselves.* Get on the ground as soon as you can."

JOE: "Rajah. Return to base at ground level. Wilco. Out."

(The formation breaks up and the three of them nose over and dive down to treetop height. They hedgehop back to the base, leaving Peabody screaming at them to get back to altitude all the way and falling far behind.)

PEABODY: "Corry Tower, Corry Tower, this is Lieutenant P-P-P-Peabody calling. Over."

CORRY TOWER: "Hear you loud and clear, Lieutenant. Go ahead."

PEABODY: "Three w-w-wild men are heading for your field. Get your trash-crucks out by the runway. Have the Marines arrest them as soon as they land."

CORRY TOWER: "Wilco. Out."

Back at the field Curly and his pals made normal landings, taxied up to the line, and beat it to the Blue Angels radio shack to hear a playback of the tape. There they were hailed as conquering heroes by a hilarious bunch of pilots and sailors.

Lieutenant Percy Peabody, as jittery now as a one-legged man trying to stomp out a brush fire in an ammo dump, fouled up his landing instructions from the tower and came in on the wrong runway, cross-wind. He ground-looped, blew a tire, knocked off a wing tip, and nosed up in the grass off the runway. The crash crews helped him out of the cockpit and towed the wreck in.

By the time Peabody got back to the line the story was all over Corry Field and everybody he met let him in on the secret. It didn't take him long to realize that the very best thing he could do about it was nothing.

That afternoon Percy was driving another instructor back to Main Side and explaining what had happened.

"Aw, I knew what the score was all the time," he said. "I was just playing along with the act. I'll bet those Blue Angel wise guys still think they fooled me."

"I wouldn't be surprised if they do," said his friend.

At this point a hotrod bearing the Blue Angels insignia roared past them at about 80 mph. There were three sailors in it wearing dirty dungarees. Peabody ignored them.

"How about that landing, when you sort of ground-looped a little bit?" asked his pal. "What about that?"

"The right brake grabbed on me," said Peabody. "Some dumb mech set it up too tight. If I hadn't of been on the ball it would of been a bad crash."

⚓ CHAPTER TWO

Loose Nut

A MONTH LATER Curly received orders to sea duty. He was to command a fighter squadron on the great new atomic carrier *Guadalcanal*, flagship of Rear Admiral Windy Day.

When Curly paid his courtesy call on the Admiral upon reporting he noted a certain reserve in the Admiral's manner. Even though Curly tactfully shunned any reference to inverted flight in big seaplanes, the admiral did not call him by his first name, nor did he slap him on the back and give him a handful of cigars, or urge him to stay for dinner in the cabin.

The Admiral was not an especially vindictive man, and Curly was a fine squadron commander. So for a while nothing happened between them. Curly avoided the Admiral whenever possible, but finally his past caught up with him.

One morning when Curly was scheduled to take off at 3 A.M., the call orderly goofed and didn't wake Curly up until two minutes before he was due in the ready room for briefing. Curly scrambled out of his bunk and instead of dressing fully he pulled on his G suit over his pajamas, put on his shoes, and hurried up to the ready room just as the briefing began.

"This is an exercise with SAC, to test our night fighter defenses," said the briefing officer. "The ship is 200 miles west of San Francisco. We are putting out a screen of 12 night fighters to intercept and 'shoot down' bombers which SAC will be sending out from 4 A.M. to noon. You people will be relieved on station at 0630 and will land aboard at 0700.

"Each pilot's station is shown on the blackboard. Just go to your station and orbit there until you spot a bogey or we vector you to one. Planes will operate singly, with 20-mile interval between orbiting points. Orbit at 60,000 feet, keeping radio silence until you make contact."

The pilots, wearing red goggles to protect their night vision from even the dim lights of the ready room, spent the next ten minutes working out their navigation, getting the weather dope, checking frequencies, calls, and codes, and doing other little chores that precede a night-flight operation. At 0240 the squawk box blared, "Pilots, man your planes," and they bounced to their feet and scrambled up to the quiet, darkened flight deck, ready for any emergency that might arise in the next four hours. Well, *almost* any, that is.

Curly buckled himself into his seat, hooked up his oxygen tube, and ran quickly through his checkoff list. His plane would be the first one launched and was already positioned on the catapult. The bull horns went through the regular preflight ritual: "Now check all loose gear about the deck. Stand clear of jet blasts. Stand by-y-y to start engines. . . . START ENGINES." The flight deck exploded with a great WHOOM.

Curly ran his engine up to full power, carefully noting the behavior of his rpm and tailpipe temperatures, throttled back, and stuck his fist out with his thumb up. Soon the launching light on the bridge went from red to green and the bull horns cut through the thunder of the jets, "LAUNCH AIRCRAFT."

The Catapult Officer gave Curly the highball, waving his lighted wands in circles overhead. Curly poured the coal on carefully, gave rpm and tailpipe temperatures a final check, put his head back against the rest, and brought his right hand up to the salute position, holding it for a second to let his jets develop full thrust. Then he braced himself, whipped the hand down, and grabbed the stick, and waited patiently for about half a second.

Down in the bowels of the ship a red light flashed to green, the catapult chief pulled a trigger and Curly went rocketing down the track, picking up 150 knots of airspeed in about $\frac{1}{10}$ of the time it takes to read this sentence.

As he hurtled into the blackness and felt the bridle get snatched off at the end of the track, Curly hauled back some of the stick to make *sure* he didn't settle, flipped the landing gear control up, and concentrated on his gyro and altimeter.

In a jet airplane at sea on a dark night, the first 500 feet are the hardest. The penalties for small mistakes below 500 are severe. Above 500 it's a milk run. As his altimeter wound up past 500, Curly relaxed and settled back, ready to deliver the milk.

During the next three hours a couple of the boys on the south end of the picket line had a little action with a SAC bomber trying to sneak out and clobber their ship. But nothing at all happened in Curly's sector. He just went round and round in a 10-mile circle, watching his radar and listening. Half an hour before he would be relieved, and as dawn started breaking, Curly was singing inside his face mask:

> The general public, now here's what they think—
>   We're a bunch of balonies addicted to drink,
> Our motors, they frighten their babies, they say-y-y,
>   They accuse us of leading their daughters astray,
> So, put on your tin bloomers, we'll . . .

At this point Curly's jet flamed out and so did the ballad. But a flame-out is just a flame-out even on a dark night. At 60,000 feet you've got time to tinker around, find out what's wrong and fix it.

You can't get a restart in the thin air above 30,000 feet, so there was no hurry. He had plenty of time to check and double-check every item on his restart procedure. Curly headed his plane toward the beach, flipped his throttle back to the starting gate, stuck his nose over, and held his speed high enough so that his jets wouldn't stop windmilling. He checked his gauges and fuel system methodically and found everything O.K. Nearing 30,000 feet he hauled the nose up at a sharp angle and held it there for a while to dump out any fuel which had accumulated in the tailpipes and make sure he wouldn't get an explosive start, which is regarded as very bad luck among jet pilots. Then he nosed over again, hit the restart button, and shoved his throttle forward. No start.

The old adage says, "If at first you don't succeed, try, try again." Curly tried and tried and tried, but he got no restart. He squeezed the button on the stick to tell the *Guadalcanal* he was having a little trouble but was working on it. His radio was just as dead as his blowtorch. He shot a quick glance over the side and noted with relief the line of surf far below, indicating he was crossing the coastline. At least he wouldn't wind up in the water.

You don't make dead-stick landings at night in rough country in jet planes. Approved procedure in the jet jockey trade, when you can't get the furnace going again, is to eject. Curly continued trying to restart but decided that his contract with the government to fly that airplane would expire at 10,000 feet.

At 15,000 a hydraulic line in the cockpit let go, splattering fluid all over Curly. In the forlorn hope that maybe only his earphones were out and the transmitter was still working, he squeezed his button and sang out, "This is Navy 7641, Lieutenant Commander Cue—Mayday—Mayday—Position 10 miles inland and 220 miles northeast of *Guadalcanal*—10 miles inland and 220 miles northeast. I am ejecting. Out."

Curly slowed down to as near stalling speed as he dared and pulled the safety pin out of the seat ejector. Then he tucked both feet up under the seat, flipped the switch that jettisoned the cockpit canopy, jerked his oxygen tube loose, and reached over his head with both hands. Getting a firm grip on the protective curtain, he yanked it down in front of his face, thus firing the ejector and blasting himself out into the night, seat and all.

Seconds later the seat flew apart and fell clear, leaving Curly tumbling end over end at a couple of hundred knots. Then the automatic ripcord puller acted, there was a sharp clap like a 40-mm gun as the chute cracked open, and Curly decelerated as if in a racing car with locked brakes.

As the drag of the chute checked his forward speed, Curly swept back and forth in great arcs under the chute like a kid in a swing. Gradually the swinging damped out and Curly floated through the darkness toward the good earth below, with the stars peering curiously down at him, and surrounded by the most awe-inspiring silence he had ever listened to.

His plane glided straight inland for about fifteen more miles and then nosed over and plunged smack into the middle of Clear Lake, a good-sized body of water in the mountains sixty miles north of San Francisco. Nobody saw it hit; it left no trace except a small oil spot on the surface.

So far so good. But Curly didn't have it made yet. The blackness below meant mountains, and parachuting into mountainous country at night is a tough way to make a living. For one thing, you can't tell which way the wind, if any, is blowing until you hit the ground and find out all of a sudden. You may get slammed against a cliff, dragged over one, or hauled over jagged rocks.

Curly had his usual luck, and though he came down in rough country, his chute hung up in a tree leaving him swinging ten feet above the ground, twenty miles from Clear Lake. Curly slid out of the harness, dropped to the ground, and noted by his watch he was due back on the ship in forty-five minutes.

It was a balmy night and his G suit was soaked with hydraulic fluid so he took it off and left it and his heavy crash helmet at the foot of the tree where his chute was. Then he started walking down the mountain just as dawn was breaking.

Soon he came to a paved road and took careful note of the spot so he could come back later and recover the government property that he was signed up for. Then he headed downhill on the road, confident he would soon find help.

Meantime, there was quite a flap on in the State Hospital for the Insane at Napa and all the surrounding area. A dangerous nut had bolted from the loony bin that night and was now at large. In his saner moments this screwball thought he was a space cadet and spoke the language of space and jet pilots fluently. But when he wasn't in outer space he tended to commit unprovoked homicides. He had blasted off from the bughouse that night in pajamas. All police in California had been alerted, given a description of him, and had been warned that he was dangerous. A statewide manhunt was now in progress for the loose nut. Heavily armed patrol cars were scouring the countryside and roadblocks controlled all key points.

At this time there was no excitement whatever on the *Guadalcanal*. Cue's group wasn't due back at the ship for forty-five minutes. The fact that they heard nothing from Cue was not alarming because he was required to keep radio silence until he had something to say.

Curly was right in his guess that he would find help soon, but you are entitled to your own opinion whether or not it was "help." In half an hour Curly spotted a police car coming up the road, took station straddling the white line in the middle, and waited.

He was puzzled when the driver slammed on the brakes and screeched to a halt fifty yards away. There was a pause while the occupants apparently held a brief conference. Then four state policemen, armed with shotguns, piled out, deployed across the road, and advanced, keeping Curly carefully covered all the way.

When ten yards away, the corporal in charge yelled, "Stick 'em up, mister. Don't make a move."

Curly dutifully raised his arms in deference to four double-barreled riot guns and asked, "Why all the excitement?"

"You other guys cover me while I frisk him," said the corporal, laying his gun down on the road, and advancing gingerly.

"What's coming off here?" demanded Curly as the corporal gave him a quick frisking.

"Okay, boys, he's clean!" yelled the corporal. "Bring me the handcuffs and leg irons."

"Wait a minute," yelled Curly. "What the hell do you think you're doing?"

Nobody answered this irate inquiry and, as the manacles were snapped on, Curly began to see red.

"Age 35, 160 pounds, 5 foot 10, and wearing pajamas," said the corporal. "It's him, all right." The other three agreed.

"You guys are nuts," Curly roared as they led him in chains toward the car.

"Oh," said the corporal, "so *we're* the ones who are nuts? How about yourself?"

"I am Lieutenant Commander Cue, United States Navy," said Curly with some heat. "I just . . ."

"Pleased to meetcha, Commander," said the corporal. "I'm Napoleon Bonaparte, and that there fella over there is Dr. Einstein. That's John Paul Jones over there, and—"

"Listen," roared Cue, "I just bailed out from a jet plane off the *Guadalcanal*. I've got to get word back to my ship."

"Hunh," said Dr. Einstein. "Used to be a space cadet but now he's only a Navy jet pilot."

This touched off a profane explosion by Curly and, as he started erupting, the Little Corporal said, "You guys keep him covered. He's dangerous. Look at his eyes."

There is no denying that by this time Curly had a wild look in his eyes.

"I been lookin' at 'em," said Dr. Einstein. "Anybody can see he's as crazy as a treeful of gooney birds."

"Yeah," agreed John Paul Jones, "and, like they said at the bughouse, he's wearing pajamas."

"I can explain the pajamas," Curly began. "I was called late . . ." Then he realized the utter futility of trying to explain pajamas when they wouldn't believe the other stuff, so he clammed up.

"Go ahead, Admiral," needled John Paul, "tell me about the pajamas. I was on the *Enterprise* during the war. Greatest ship in the Navy. We never went flying in our pajamas, though."

For the next hour, as they sped toward police headquarters, Curly alternated between heated repetitions of his story and torrents of abuse for the cops. He criticized their intelligence, character, performance of duty, and their parents' morals in language which can only be learned by long years of naval service. By the time they got to headquarters, each one of the cops wanted to beat Curly into a black-and-blue pulp. (But not with three witnesses present!)

Meantime, when the other planes returned, Curly had turned up missing in the *Guadalcanal*'s landing circle, and could not be found on the radar screen. The ship immediately broke radio silence, called the missing plane, and when repeated calls got no answer, Admiral Day canceled the exercise and launched an all-out search.

As they got out of the car at headquarters in Santa Rosa, Curly sneered, "You guys will get kicked off the force for this."

"We'll all get promoted, Buster," replied Napoleon. "Come on now. We're going to see the Captain."

The captain was a level-headed officer with long police experience. But his four irate cops were good men whom he had known for a long time. When they got through telling him about the prisoner's belligerent, uncooperative attitude, he was a bit prejudiced against the wild-eyed pajama-clad Curly.

"Okay," said the captain, when the cops had finished. "What's your story, mister?"

"Sir," said Curly, "my name is Lieutenant Commander J. C. Cue, U.S. Navy. I'm from the USS *Guadalcanal* which is now about 200 miles offshore. I took off from her on a night fighter mission at three A.M. this morning and had a flame out near the coast. While I was trying to get a restart, a hydraulic line busted and soaked my flying suit in fluid. Finally, I had to bail out and, after I got down, I took off my G suit and crash helmet and left them at the foot of the tree where my chute hung up. Now, please call Western Sea Frontier Headquarters immediately and tell them to notify the ship I'm safe."

"You see?" gloated Napoleon. "Just as crazy as a snowed-up hophead." The other three cops said, "Yeah."

"You guys let me handle this," said the captain. "I think you got the right guy all right. But we gotta be careful about not making a false arrest." Then to Curly he said, "How about them pajamas?"

So Curly explained the pajamas. But even he could see it wasn't very convincing.

"See?" demanded all four cops when he finished.

"Keep out of this, you guys," said the captain. Then he said to Curly, "If your story is true, we should of had a report of an airplane crash around here about an hour ago. We've had fifty prowl cars on the road all night checking in by radio every half hour and there's been no crash reported anywhere."

This news shook even Curly. "Maybe it hit up in the mountains where your men couldn't see it," he said weakly.

"A jet plane full of gas would torch when it hit," said the captain. "You'd see it for miles."

Curly had to concede the logic of this statement.

Just then low-flying jets became audible overhead. Curly looked out the window and spotted two planes from his squadron. "Look," he yelled triumphantly. "There are some of the *Guadalcanal's* planes looking for me now."

"Nuts," said Dr. Einstein. "There's a big Navy-Air Force maneuver today. I read all about it in the papers." The captain had read the papers too, and was unimpressed by the passing jets.

Curly noted a late model side band radiophone set in a corner of the captain's office. In desperation he asked, "Captain, can you come up on 7540 kcs with that set, sir? The *Guadalcanal* guards that frequency and we could settle this thing in short order and save you from a lot of trouble later."

"Seven-five-four-o kcs? Sure," said the captain. "Give it a try, Corporal."

This was a proposition that would cost the Captain nothing. He didn't believe a word of Curly's story but, in the unlikely event it was true, this call would save him from making a bad pinch.

Soon, in the *Guadalcanal's* Combat Information Center, a squawk box blared, "USS *Guadalcanal*, USS *Guadalcanal*, this is State Police Headquarters at Santa Rosa, California, calling. Answer, please."

A tense hush fell over the CIC room. The odds were about 6 to 5 and take your choice that the next message would report the finding of Curly's body. The operator squeezed his transmitter button and said, "This is the *Guadalcanal*, Santa Rosa. Hear you loud and clear. Go ahead with your message."

Santa Rosa replied, "We have a prisoner in our custody who claims he bailed out of one of your jet fighters this morning, that his name is Lieutenant Commander Cue . . . and that—!!!"

Cheers from all present drowned out the rest of the message. Among those present and cheering was Rear Admiral Windy Day.

When the cheers subsided, the operator said, "Santa Rosa, you were blocked out, repeat all after *and that.*"

"Santa Rosa repeating; and that he is a squadron commander from your ship. Please advise if this is true. Prisoner is in pajamas and fits description of dangerous maniac who escaped from asylum here last night wearing pajamas. Over."

One of Curly's squadron mates piped up, "He was called late this morning and put on his G suit over his pajamas. That's him all right."

The operator was about to pass this info to Santa Rosa when Admiral Day strode over and said, "Give me that microphone, son."

Then, with all ears in CIC cocked on him, the Admiral said, "Santa Rosa, this is Rear Admiral Day on the *Guadalcanal.* Is your prisoner injured?"

The answer came back, "No, sir. Not a scratch on him."

There were pleased smiles all over CIC.

"What did you say this man's name was?" asked Day.

"He claims it is Lieutenant Commander Cue, U.S. Navy."

"We have no one on board by that name," said the Admiral. "Anything else?"

"No, thank you. That is all. Out."

A flake of dandruff hitting the deck in CIC would have made an audible thud.

Day turned to the stunned Air Group Commander and said, "He's unhurt. We know where he is. We have no one on board, at this time, by that name. Recall your search." Turning to the ship's exec, he said, "Tell the Captain to bend on thirty knots, head for the beach, and when we're close enough, send your whirlybird to Santa Rosa and get him. We'll have him back by midafternoon."

"Aye, aye, sir," said the Commander.

"And," added the Admiral, "you had better send your legal officer and a doctor in too."

"They said he was uninjured, sir."

"I know," said the admiral. "But, send a doctor anyway—a psychiatrist. He may have to vouch for Cue's sanity or maybe try to restore it. This may even give Cue a new slant on practical jokes."

Admiral Day walked out of the CIC with a jaunty bounce in his gait, while admiring grins broke out on all faces (the upside-down episode being known to one and all).

⚓ CHAPTER THREE

Maniac at Large

BACK IN SANTA ROSA, as the outrageous denial of his identity came over the air, Curly's eyes bugged out like a surprised hoot owl's. His reason tottered and his usually nimble brain flamed out cold. He thought either he or all the rest of the world really had gone crazy.

"What do you say now, Commodore?" asked the captain politely.

Curly's jaws flapped up and down but the only words that came forth were "awk" and "eek."

"That squeaky noise you hear," observed Admiral John Paul Jones, "is a feeble mind trying to come unstuck and dream up another story."

"Are you ready to talk now, mister?" asked the captain.

"This is ridiculous," blurted Curly. "It's impossible. They must have all gone crazy out there."

"Yeah," said the captain, "but we're all of us a *little* bit crazy. Some more so than others, though," he added significantly. "Take him back to the bughouse, boys."

"Wait a minute," yelled Curly. "This is all a mistake. Call the ship again and let *me* talk to them."

"No-o-o," said the captain. "I don't hardly think I oughtta do that. You just heard them say they never heard of you. Now you want me to call them back and let an escaped nut ask them, 'Are you sure?' What kind of a sap do you think I am? Take him away, boys."

As the cop on each arm urged him toward the door, Curly lost his temper and lashed out at his escorts, to the extent at least that a prisoner in handcuffs and leg irons can lash out. An enthusiastic barrage of jolting jabs to the ribs and stinging slaps in the face soon brought Curly's temper back on the beam and they led him off to the squad car.

The first ten minutes of the ride to Napa marked the low point in Curly's life up to that time. Only two hours ago, when his chute cracked open, this had been a wonderful world and Curly rejoiced that he would get to spend some more time in it. Now he almost wished the chute hadn't opened.

But despair doesn't thrive on a nature like Curly's. After about ten grim minutes, his wits began to unscramble and come back to battery.

It just isn't so, he thought bitterly. The *Guadacanal* is the best carrier in the Pacific Fleet. Their air department and CIC crew are all sharp. They know exactly what the score is at all times. I'm two hours overdue. Within five minutes of the time I became overdue, CIC would start drastic action to find out if I was still in the air. Within ten minutes at the most they would cancel the exercise and lay on a search. Matter of fact, those low-flying planes passing over the police station prove that's exactly what has happened. But, why did the Admiral answer as he did?? . . . ADMIRAL DAY!!! . . . HAH!

The true state of affairs suddenly snapped into clear focus. *This was just the Admiral's idea of good, clean fun, paying him back for that harmless upside-down episode! There was nothing to worry about and a whirlybird was probably on its way in now to pick him up.*

"Well, I'll be damned," breathed Curly softly, in grudging admiration for the Admiral's crafty ploy.

"How about it, mister," demanded Dr. Einstein, "you ready to talk yet?"

Curly saw his chance to get some fun out of this himself now.

He hit the restart button and his brains lit off again. He shrugged his shoulders and said, "Okay, boys. I'll level with you now. You got the right guy all right. But you gotta admit I made a nice try."

"Hah!" snorted all four cops.

"We knew you wuz the guy all the time," said Napoleon. "Are ya ready to sing now?"

"Yeah," said Curly, and he launched into a lurid "account" of his adventures the previous night. He told of long months of careful planning. He described how he had outwitted the attendants, slipped past the inner guards unnoticed, and finally had popped over the wall right under the noses of the outer guards, and made a clean getaway. "Dopiest bunch of cops I've ever seen," observed Curly as he wound up this chapter of his saga. "And that includes," he added, "even you guys."

"Don't call them mugs at the nut factory cops," said Napoleon Bonaparte indignantly. "Those bughouse keepers are all half-nuts themselves. They *belong* in the bughouse, all right, but on the other side of the bars."

"You were only loose for about eight hours," observed Dr. Einstein. "How did you get all the way from Napa up near Clear Lake where we picked you up?"

"Hitchhiking," said Curly. "At least, it started as hitchhiking. An old lady in a station wagon picked me up. Looked like she was about eighty. But she was a nosy old battle-ax and kept asking me personal questions. When I asked her to take the back roads, she didn't want to do it. I had to put the slug on her with a wrench and do the driving myself."

Napoleon Bonaparte whipped out a notebook and started scribbling furiously.

"I dumped her out in a ditch about a mile back in the woods," continued Curly.

"Where?" demanded all four police officers.

"How should I know?" asked Curly. "I didn't have no road maps. It was just a mile or two back in the woods from some main road."

"Was she dead?" the officers asked breathlessly.

"No-o-o," said Curly judiciously. "At least, I don't *think* so. She was probably just knocked cold for a while. I didn't slug her very hard," he added deprecatingly.

"Where did you leave the car?"

"Way back in the woods. Ran out of gas."

Napoleon took time out from the grilling to call headquarters by radio and give them a flash on the facts so far established in the case of the little old lady so they could start a search for her body.

"After I left the car, I struck out through the woods," said Curly, resuming his saga. "After a while I came to a log cabin where a young fella and his wife lived. They looked like nice people but I didn't get along very well with them."

"Whaddeya mean?" asked the alert Dr. Einstein.

"They didn't seem to like me. They didn't want to let me come in the cabin and wouldn't open the door for me."

"What did you do then?"

"There was an ax on the porch, so I busted the door down with it and went in."

Bonaparte was scribbling away in his notebook again. "Oh, yeah?" he said. "And what happened then?"

"I don't know if I oughta tell you fellas this," said Curly, "but I'm going to be locked up again anyway, so I guess I might just as well."

"Yeah. Go ahead, pal," said all four.

"I kilt 'em both with the ax," said Curly, leering evilly at the law-enforcement officers. "Had to. What else could I do?"

Napoleon broke the point on his pencil. "Just where was this place?" he demanded.

Curly gave them a detailed description of the location of the tree where he had stowed his government property. "It wouldn't of been fitten to leave them laying there in the cabin," he added, "so I took 'em out and buried them in front of the cabin right alongside the path."

The excited corporal flashed this latest information back to headquarters, which sent another carful of cops flying over the road with siren screaming to find the scene of the crime and dig up the bodies.

"You officers will probably get a big reward for solving that case so fast," observed Curly. "How about taking these handcuffs off to show your gratitude?"

"Hah!" snorted all four cops. The bracelets stayed on.

But Curly's last remark started the officers thinking and pretty soon one said, "We oughta get *something* outa this. We make a clean pinch an hour after we're sent out on a job and we also discover and solve two unreported crimes. That's good police work. Even our captain oughta get something out of it, too."

By the time they got to the State Hospital at Napa, they had decided that the captain would be promoted to state headquarters, the corporal would make sergeant, and the other three would get corporals' stripes. They disembarked in a happy frame of mind, formed a square around Curly, and marched into the bughouse as smug as four cats full of canaries au gratin.

Arriving at the main office, the corporal announced to the head keeper, "Here's your man, Mac. The motto of the State Police is 'prompt and efficient service.' Call us any time we can help you. Sign this here receipt and we will be on our way." He placed the receipt on the desk and held out a pencil to the keeper.

The keeper looked Curly up and down and then said glumly, "It ain't him."

Now it was the cops' turn to be stunned. Eight eyes boggled and four jaws dropped.

"Wh-wh-what did you say?" the corporal finally managed to gasp.

"It ain't him," reiterated the keeper.

"Whaddeya mean, it ain't him?" demanded the corporal. "Age 35, 160 pounds, 5 foot 10 inches, and in pajamas. It's *got* to be him."

"But it ain't," said the keeper firmly.

"Why, he even *admits* he's the guy," stormed Dr. Einstein. "Cut out the comedy and sign the receipt."

"It ain't him and I ain't signing no receipt," said the keeper.

"How about it, Buster?" demanded Napoleon of Curly, "Are you the guy who escaped from here?"

"Of course I am," said Curly.

"There! Ya see?" chorused all four cops.

"I don't know what his angle is, but he ain't the right guy. I'll prove it with pictures and fingerprints." The keeper buzzed for an orderly.

The orderly soon produced pictures and fingerprints of the escaped maniac and an ink pad and cards to fingerprint Curly. While Curly was being printed, the cops examined the photos and had no trouble convincing themselves that they bore a striking resemblance to Curly.

"But it ain't him," said the keeper. "You know how these file mugs turn out. Everybody looks the same in them."

One look at the fingerprints convinced even the cops that they didn't check.

"Well, what the hell," said the corporal, "everything else checks. Age, height, weight, pictures, he's crazy, and he's wearing pajamas. You probably got his prints mixed up in the files."

"I've seen the guy every day for the past five years," said the keeper stiffly. "I *know* him and this *ain't him*. You guys just made a bum pinch."

Half a dozen other keepers verified his opinion and finally even the four angry cops had to admit that the best they could claim was a near miss. Then the sergeant said, "We're going to leave him here with you anyway. Sign my receipt so we can get out of here."

"You are *not* going to leave him here," said the keeper indignantly.

"Why not? He's crazy, ain't he? Crazier than all the rest of the nuts you got here put together. Crazy guys belong in the bughouse, so you gotta take him."

"You know just as well as I do," said the keeper, "you can't commit nobody without papers. Signed by a court. He's *your* problem now, not mine. Get him out of here."

After much legal wrangling, the cops had to admit defeat. They marched Curly out to the car and started back to Santa Rosa in cold fury.

"Now that I'm a free man," said Curly pleasantly, "you might as well take these irons off me."

"Free man, hell." snorted Napoleon. "You got two, maybe three murder raps against you!"

"Yeah," agreed John Paul Jones.

"Wait a minute," said Dr. Einstein. "Maybe he made that up too—like he did all that stuff about being a Navy flyer."

"We got plenty to hold him for anyway," said Napoleon. "Loitering, vagrancy, disorderly conduct, indecent exposure, interfering with police officers performing their duty, disturbing the peace. And, besides, he's crazy as a hoot owl."

The corporal reported this new angle of the case by radio to headquarters, and soon thereafter got word from headquarters that the actual maniac had just been recaptured close to Napa.

"Just who the hell *are* you, mister?" demanded Napoleon after getting this report.

"Like I said this morning, Bub," replied Curly, "I'm Lieutenant Commander Cue, U.S. Na—"

"Cut it out," snapped the corporal. "You heard us talking to the *Guadalcanal* on the short-wave phone. The Admiral hisself said he never heard of you."

"That old buzzard," said Curly, "is the worst admiral in the whole U.S. Navy, and that takes in a lot of ocean. He's so dumb he doesn't even know the difference between the port gossard and the starboard anchor. He couldn't navigate a cake of soap in a bathtub. I even seen him spit to windward the other day with twenty knots of wind blowing. Got it all right back in his face, he did."

"No admiral could possibly be that dumb," said Dr. Einstein scornfully.

"This one is," said Curly. "He probably never *will* find out I'm missing. He's almost as dumb as some of you cops." Then, warming to the intriguing task of doing justice to Admiral Day, he went on, "He's scared to death of airplanes. You couldn't drag him into one. Scared of everything, as a matter of fact. Goes to his cabin and locks the door whenever a little blow comes up at sea. He had a heavy cruiser during the war and ran like hell one day from a little Japanese destroyer."

"Then how did he ever make admiral?" demanded John Paul Jones.

"His political friends hushed it up," said Curly confidentially.

"He's a chippy chaser and fanny pincher, too, he is. And talk about a rumpot! He's drunk all the time at sea. Gets so blotto he can't tell the bow from the stern. . . . But I'm glad to see men like him make admiral. It means there's hope for all of us."

"Knock it off, mister," said John Paul Jones. "I was in the *Enterprise* in World War II. If a plane is missing, the Admiral knows it right away, no matter how dumb he is. The Captain tells him."

"That *Guadalcanal*," observed Curly, "is the most ragtime ship afloat. They never tell the Captain *nothing*. The main reason is that most of the time they don't *know* nothing. Nobody keeps track of how many planes they got in the air or where they are going. We lost two planes out in the middle of the Pacific a week ago and nobody noticed the pilots weren't around any more until yesterday. But it was too late to do anything then."

"Even if that was *so*, I wouldn't believe it," said John Paul Jones firmly.

"Lots of things happen on that ship that I wouldn't believe either unless I seen them," said Curly sadly. Two weeks ago up on the flight deck they taxied a brand-new jet fighter onto the forward elevator. The only trouble was the elevator was down on the hangar deck at the time. They had a bad time explaining that one to the skipper."

"That's enough of your fairy stories, Buster," said John Paul Jones, "Come on now. Level with us. Who are you?"

"Cross my heart and hope to die, I'm either Napoleon Bonaparte, Albert Einstein, or John Paul Jones. Guess which."

"Corporal," said Dr. Einstein, "when we get back to the station house, you get lost for about an hour and leave the three of us with this wise guy. We'll have him singing like a canary bird when you come back."

"Okay by me," grunted the corporal, "if I can clear it with the captain. But he's kind of narrow-minded, you know."

Curly took up the cudgels to defend the captain. "He's an efficient law-enforcement officer," said Curly indignantly. "He protects the constitutional rights of citizens from rock-headed cops."

Back at the police station the captain was conferring with the county attorney by phone. "You've got plenty of grounds for hold-

ing him," the legal beagle was saying: "obstructing justice, conceal-
ing his identity, suspicion of murder, and attempted assault on
four officers in the performance of their duties. And, from what
you say, a sanity hearing certainly seems to be in order. I'll send
my mental examiner right down. He'll be there in a minute."

When Curly was again escorted into the captain's office, that
official said, "Are you ready to come clean now and tell us who you
are?"

"Sure. The story I told you this morning is true. Every word of
it. I'm Lieutenant Commander Cue, U.S. Navy—"

"Wait a minute," snorted the captain. "The only trouble with
that story is the USS *Guadalcanal* says it ain't so and you heard
them say it. Remember, Buster?"

Curly stood there hanging his head for a minute and trying to
act as if he were going through an emotional struggle. Then he
said, "All right. I'm licked. Get the Russian consul in San Francisco on the phone. I want to talk to him."

"What the hell has the Russian consul got to do with this?"
demanded the captain.

"More than you think," said Curly, assuming a crafty, furtive
look. "According to your laws I'm entitled to a lawyer and the
minute the consul hears you've got *me*, he'll have the best one in
California on the way up here."

"Holy cow!" said Dr. Einstein. "A Soviet spy! He must of been
flying a Russian U-2!"

Visions of sugar plums began dancing in the corporal's head. He
could see banner headlines all over the country and his picture on
the front page as the alert police officer who made the pinch.

"Get Officer Zinkoff in here," ordered the captain. "He speaks
Russian as good as Krookyschuff himself."

Officer Zinkoff entered and undertook to check Curly's command of the Russian language.

It only took about four minutes to flunk him cold. Curly's entire
command of the language consisted of phrases such as "Ya vash
leblou" and "Ya hachoo vash selavatch," useful only in dealing
with inexperienced females who are willing and anxious to acquire
more experience.

After Curly had used these phrases alternately to answer the first four of Zinkoff's questions, the officer said, "This guy's about as Russian as Paddy's pig. Even his bedroom Russian has a Brooklyn accent."

The sugar plums in Corporal Bonaparte's head shriveled into prunes and the headlines faded away.

"Cap'n," said Dr. Einstein, "they've got this big Air Force-Navy maneuver going on now. Sometimes on these war games they are very mysterious about everything while the game is going on. A guy who gets separated from his unit has to tell a phony cover story until the maneuver is over. Maybe this guy is an Air Force pilot."

"What?" roared Curly. "Captain, I've never been so insulted in my life. He wouldn't dare say that if I didn't have these chains on. You cops have no right to insult law-abiding citizens and assassinate character like that."

"For the first time," observed John Paul Jones, "I'm beginning to think that maybe the guy *might* be in the Navy."

"Yeah," said the captain, "but not the *Guadalcanal's* navy anyway. That's for sure. And that's where he claims he's from."

"At this point the mental troubleshooter from the county attorney's office came bustling in. "Where is the patient?" he demanded in a businesslike manner.

"There he is, doctor," said the captain, pointing to Curly. "I don't think you gotta waste much time on *him*. He's crazy all right. He's not sure whether he's a Navy jet pilot, a Russian U-2 pilot, or the guy from the bug house. Confessed to a couple of murders, too. You better have some cops in the examining room with you, doc."

"Yes, good idea," said the doctor. Napoleon Bonaparte and John Paul Jones escorted Curly and the headshrinker to the back room.

"Siddown and relax now, son," said the doctor, "I'm not a policeman. I'm a doctor. I'm here to help you and try to keep you out of trouble. So, take it easy and just answer my questions as best you can."

Curly leered at the doctor and said, "Okay, doc. How about prescribing a big shot of hooch for me first? I need it."

"No," said the doctor, "not now. Answer the questions first."

Curly looked down at the front of his pajama coat and began brushing it with both hands and blowing at it.

"What's the matter?" asked the doctor.

"These feathers," said Curly. "The air was full of feathers above 5000 feet this morning, and when I bailed out I got 'em all over me."

"I see," said the doctor thoughtfully. "We are going to start with a word association test. I'll say a word and you must tell me as quickly as possible the first word that enters your mind. I'll write that word down and then give you another and you do the same thing. Do you understand?"

"Yeah," said Curly with a silly giggle. "This is gonna be easy, doc."

"Aileron," said the doctor.

"Brigitte Bardot," said Curly like a flash.

"Flame out."

"Brigitte Bardot."

"Mach number."

"Brigitte Bardot."

"Wait a minute," said the doctor. "Maybe I didn't explain very well. When I said, 'do the same thing,' I didn't mean give the same answer all the time. I meant you say the first word that pops into your mind after you hear what I say."

"That's what I been doing," said Curly. "*Everything* reminds me of Brigitte Bardot. I'm thinking of her all the time," he added with a sly smirk.

The Rorschach test produced no better results. On this test the subject is shown a group of inkblots of various sizes and random shapes. He is supposed to study these abstractions, give his imagination free reign, and tell the bug expert what mental pictures the blots conjure up in his mind. Most people can see animals, flowers, atomic explosions, cloud formations, or the like.

Curly positively identified the ugliest blot of all as being the headshrinker himself, the next as the corporal, and the rest as various other cops and police officials. According to his mental images,

as related to the doctor, they were all caught red-handed performing very reprehensible and unprintable acts.

"All right, son," said the doctor, "that's enough. Let's go back."

"Did I pass, doc?" asked Curly eagerly.

"I'll have to study the data before I can answer," said the doctor
evasively.

Back in the captain's office, the doctor shook his head at the
Captain and held out a fist with the thumb pointed down.

"Mister," said the captain, "if you won't, or can't, tell us who
you are, there's no use asking you any more questions. I'll just have
to lock you up."

"Well, sir," said Curly, picking imaginary butterflies out of the
air putting them carefully into his pajama pocket, "when you look
back on this thing later on you're going to have to admit I gave
you a hot clue about being a Navy jet pilot when I first came in
this morning. I have no fresh leads to offer at this time."

"I give up," said the captain. "Book him, mug him, fingerprint
him, and lock him up."

While Curly was being mugged, the captain got a phone call
from Clear Lake. The voice said, "I'm a skin diver. I saw an oil
puddle out in the lake this morning and I went down to see what
was making it. It's pretty deep there so I couldn't see too well. It
feels like a speedboat, but I've checked around the lake and no
speedboat is missing."

"Okay, thanks," said the captain, scribbling on his memo pad.
"We'll send regular divers down tomorrow and find out."

A small voice in the back of the captain's head was trying to
make itself heard but didn't quite get through.

A few minutes later the squad car that had gone out to dig up
the bodies called in. "That guy is the biggest liar in California and
that means in the world. There isn't a cabin within miles of the
location he gave. We searched the woods thoroughly. But we did
find a parachute hanging in a tree and some aviator's gear at the
bottom of it. We are bringing it back with us. No signs of the
flyer, though. That is all."

The little voice in the captain's head suddenly came in loud and
clear. "Corporal," he yelled, "bring that crazy blankety-blank pris-

oner back in here."

All the cops in the station house came trooping in to follow this latest development.

"Take off the cuffs and leg irons," ordered the captain, when Curly was ushered in.

"So you believe me now, sir, do you, sir?" asked Curly with mock courtesy.

"I'm not sure I do yet," said the bewildered police officer. "The *Guadalcanal* claims they never heard of you. How do you explain that?"

"Like I told your officers coming back here, she's not a very efficient ship. They're just a bunch of beatniks out there. They might not miss me till next payday. Why don't you phone them again about ten days from now and see what they say? They lose planes and pilots every day and don't find out about it for a week."

"That's a lie," snarled John Paul Jones. "I was in the *Enterprise* during the war and that's just impossible."

"Nothin is impossible on that bucket," said Curly. "One day they got the ventilating system of the garbage disposal cross-connected with the air conditioning for the Admiral's cabin. There was a big stink about that one."

"Hah!" observed John Paul Jones.

Curly glanced at his watch and said, "Commissioner, I am six hours overdue now. Maybe some sharp character may have noticed and started rumors going which might get to the captain about now. Why don't you phone them again now?"

"He's still lying," said John Paul, loyal to the wartime traditions of the *Enterprise*. "The ship would of called in and told us if they found anybody missing after our call this morning. Maybe he ain't even an Air Force pilot. Maybe he put that stuff in the tree to throw us off the scent and cover up something else he done."

"O.K.—lock him up," sighed the now completely befuddled captain.

As they were leading Curly away the beat of a rapidly approaching helicopter was heard. The whirlybird fluttered down on the front lawn of the station and disgorged the *Guadalcanal*'s legal officer and doctor.

They briskly identified themselves, vouched for Curly's identity, and began talking fast. The Navy doctor shook his head knowingly, made circular motions with his finger pointed at his temple, and gave his head-shrinking colleague a song and dance about oxygen anemia and high altitude bailouts. The headshrinker didn't know anything about oxygen anemia but nodded emphatic agreement with the finger signals. The legal officer spouted a lot of stuff about federal jurisdiction, the Universal Code of Military Justice, and the Attorney General of the United States—meantime producing a legal paper with the ship's seal on it acknowledging receipt of Commander J. C. Cue, U.S. Navy. At the end of his harangue he signed this document with a flourish, handed it to the captain, and before the flabbergasted cops could get over their flabbergast, he, the doctor, and Curly climbed into the whirlybird and took off for the ship.

As the blast from the whirlybirds takeoff subsided, all the cops looked at each other and said in unison, "Well, I'll be gahdam."

When Curly reported in to the Admiral back on the ship he was greeted at the cabin door with a big hello and a resounding slap on the back. "Glad to see you back, m'boy," said the Admiral. "Siddown, Curly. Have a cigar," and he thrust a handful at him.

"No, thank you, sir," said Curly, "don't use them. Admiral, I owe you an apology for some of the things I said about you to the State Police today."

"Forget it, m'lad, forget it," said the Admiral with a tolerant wave of his hand. "How about having dinner in the cabin with me tonight, Curly, and you can tell me the whole story?"

The dinner in the cabin that night was a hilarious one. In telling his tale, Curly thought it tactful to tone down a little on some of the details he gave the cops about the Admiral. But he gave him an uncensored account of all the rest of it and Admiral Day almost blew his main gasket laughing. Curly and the Admiral were bosom pals ever after.

A few days later the captain of the Santa Rosa police received a letter on two-star Navy stationery which took most of the curse off this episode so far as the police were concerned. It was a most flowery letter of praise, commending him for the efficient performance of his officers in finding and caring for the Navy's downed pilot. Enclosed was a copy of an even more flowery letter the Admiral was sending to the Governor of the state. It recommended that the Governor promote the captain and the four officers involved at the earliest opportunity.

But to this day the Santa Rosa police shake their heads sadly whenever the Navy is mentioned. They still cannot understand how the great U.S. Navy, which won World War II for us, could go to pot so fast and so far as it obviously had.

CHAPTER FOUR

Night Fighter

IN THE HEADQUARTERS of Patrol Wings Pacific Fleet, squadron commanders sat nervously around the conference table awaiting the arrival of their boss, Admiral "Bugler" Bates. The previous night a large-scale operation had been snafued by poor radio discipline and only a few days before Admiral Bates had issued an order saying that from now on radio discipline would be "excellent." So everyone expected him to lower the boom this morning.

When the Admiral strode in, his blood pressure was still in the emergency red sector of the dial from the previous night's performance. He glared menacingly around the table and said:

"I will not tolerate any more of this Flash Gordon stuff on the radio. In the kind of operations we're now doing, lives can depend on proper radio procedure—and we are going to have it. From now on I'm not going to bother with individual pilots but if there are any more violations I will hold the squadron commander responsible and suspend him from duty."

Bugler scowled. Each squadron commander glanced accusingly at each of his neighbors and at the same time assumed an air of injured innocence himself.

"So much for that," the Admiral continued. "Radio discipline will be especially important in the fleet exercise next week which all this is leading up to. In this exercise our job will be to defend San Francisco against an atomic attack coming in from a fast carrier task group at sea.

"The rules agreed on require the task group to launch its attack not more than 1000 miles from San Francisco. I want to 'sink' those ships before they can do this. Even after we locate the task group, it will take some time to get our attack organized and fly 1000 miles to sea, so we've got to find them at about 1500 miles. I am especially anxious to do well on this exercise because . . . because of its strategic aspects."

A squadron commander near the end of the table leaned over and whispered to his neighbor. "Nuts! Old Bugler wouldn't know a strategic aspect if he got hit on the head with one. He just wants to clobber Admiral Day's task group and make a bum out of his old rival."

Everybody in the Navy knew about the feud between Bugler and Admiral Windy Day—aided and abetted by a certain Lieutenant Commander Cue, known to all as Curly.

"Now you gentlemen get busy," continued Admiral Bates. "Figure out the details. I want an airtight search plan that extends out to 1500 miles for a sector from northwest to south—that's more than 3,000,000 square miles. I want to run a couple of preliminary exercises against our own shore-based fighters to find the best way for getting through the task group's fighter defenses . . . and remember, that fellow Cue who commands the fighter squadron in the task group is a shifty, underhanded individual. Don't let him suck you into any booby traps; don't jump to any conclusions about what he may seem to be doing."

There followed a lot of technical discussion about barrier patrols, scouting lines, and sector searches, plus much measuring of distances on charts. Radar bombing tactics, night intercepts, and evasive measures also were covered. Everybody knew that if they nailed the task group, Admiral Bates would be much easier to serve under, and if they didn't they might just as well all apply for transfer.

When details had been worked out the chief of staff announced: "In order to prevent collisions on these night intercepts, we have agreed with the task group that no intercept will be pushed closer than 500 yards and all planes must show navigation lights."

That same night, out in the middle of the Pacific Ocean, a task group consisting of the carrier *Guadalcanal*, a couple of heavy cruisers, and a dozen destroyers also was getting ready for the exercise. Lieutenant Commander Curly Cue, skipper of the *Guadalcanal*'s night fighter squadron, whooshed past the blacked-out bridge of the ship in his twin jet Banshee, singing softly to himself:

> Bell-bottom trousers, suit of Navy blue . . .

Curly flashed his lights in the breakup signal, peeled off, and tooled his Banshee around into the landing circle, dropping his wheels, flaps, and hook as he reached the downwind leg.

> He will climb the rigging like his daddy used to do . . .

The landing signal officer picked up Curly with a "roger" on his neon wands, gave him a "slant" signal to cock her up steeper—a "low"—an "agitated low"—a frantic "come on"—and then a desperate "cut."

> If it is a girlie, bounce her on your knee . . .

Curly sang as he whacked off the power and flopped on the deck, hooking No. 1 wire.

Curly lifted his hook as the arresting wires were lowered. He gave his Banshee a blast from both jets and scurried forward of the barriers.

> If it is a boy, send the brascal out to sea.

He braked his plane to a stop, cut the switches, and squirmed out of his harness, sighing philosophically, "You'll never get rich —but it's a living."

After the last plane had landed, the squadron commanders and senior ship's officers assembled in flag plot to discuss the night's operation with Admiral Windy Day and his staff.

"How goes it, Curly?" asked the Admiral.

"Pretty good, sir," said Commander Cue. "My fighters caught

nine out of ten bombers trying to sneak in on us tonight—and these little bombers of ours are much harder to catch than those big P2Vs will be. A few more sessions like tonight and we'll be ready."

"I think so, too," said the Admiral. "Of course Bates will try to clobber us before we can launch the attack, so I want to get that attack in the air right on the thousand-mile mark from San Francisco. We will make a high-speed run all night, and launch our bombers just before daylight. The whole show depends on what your fighters can do on the run-in that last night.

"We will cover about 400 miles between sunset and sunrise, but there will be a lot of P2Vs looking for us. You've got to find them before they find us, and put them out of action. We'll need a combat air patrol of twelve planes all night. Do you think you can handle the job, Cue?"

"Yessir," said Curly. "If the radar people can spot them for us and give us fifteen minutes' warning we can stop them cold."

"We'll spot 'em for you, Commander," said the Combat Information Center officer. "We'll have picket destroyers stationed about sixty miles ahead as early-warning stations. All you jet jockeys will have to do will be follow the directions of my controllers."

"Yeah, that's all," said Curly. "Except for such things as flying on the gauges for three hours, making intercepts in the dark, avoiding collisions, and landing on a blacked-out deck."

"Okay, Curly," said Admiral Day. "We know your boys won't just be sightseeing up there. It's going to be a busy night for the flight deck crews and hangar detail, too. They'll have to get the bombers up out of the hangar deck just before dawn—and they'll have to do it all blacked out. . . .

"Just remember, I want to get that attack off before they hit us."

Next night the *Guadalcanal* put up a combat air patrol of twelve Banshees, led by Curly, and sent out six of her own bombers to impersonate P2Vs. It was a black night under a solid overcast, and you couldn't tell which way was up. When catapulted into space, the pilots simply went on the gauges, following the dials to their assigned altitudes, and flew as the controllers told them.

Danny Deever, senior controller, seated at the master radar scope in CIC with his earphones and transmitter clamped on his head, kept a roving eye on everything happening in the task group. All six of his controllers reported their respective pairs of fighters under control, orbiting on station at assigned altitudes, and ready to intercept any incoming target picked up by radar.

Up in the darkness, Curly relaxed with his brains in neutral, his eyes scanning back and forth over the array of instruments on his panel. As he orbited waiting orders, he sang softly to himself:

Here we go round the mulberry bush, mulberry bush . . .

Tooling around in a single-seat jet fighter at night on the gauges is no bowl of strawberries. But for night fighter pilots like Curly and his boys it's all part of a day's work.

You can't see another plane very far on a dark night. So the whole thing is done by radar and radio. When the ship's radar spots an incoming bogey, the fighter director, hunched over his scope in the Combat Information Center, plots its track on the tube with a grease pencil. When he has it fixed, he "vectors" you out by radio to meet it. He brings you in two or three miles astern of the target where the two blips merge on his scope. There your radar gunsight should pick up the bogey and guide you in the rest of the way. You do all this on instruments, flying just the way the man below tells you to.

Soon the voice from CIC said, "*Guadalcanal* to Night Hawk One. Bogey bearing zero four five, distance fifty miles. Steer 050. Acknowledge."

Curly poured the coal on his jets, whooshed up to 600 knots, and answered, "Rajah from Night Hawk One. Steer 050. Wilco. Out." As his compass swung around to 050 he rolled his wings level by the gyro horizon and buzzed off to meet the bogey.

The fighter director, watching the blips on his scope, coached him out toward the bogey and then swung him around behind it as the two blips began to merge on the scope. Then he said,

"*Guadalcanal* to Night Hawk One. You are three miles astern of him now, on same course; he is 1000 feet below you. Take over and attack."

"Rajah. Wilco," said Curly, flipping his radar gunsight on and nosing down a little. Soon a small blip appeared near the middle of his sight. Curly moved his stick a little to bring the blip to the center, squeezed his mike button, and said, "Tallyho. Tallyho. Two miles dead ahead."

All he had to do now was to hold the blip from the target centered as he closed in, and squeeze the trigger when he got within gun range. If he was lucky he might be able to see the dark shape of his target when he got close. But it didn't matter if he couldn't. With his radar gunsight, he could shoot the bogey full of holes even if he didn't see it.

In wartime he would stay on the gauges all the way, holding his trigger down and the blip centered until the target torched in front of him. In peacetime, being a cagey character as night fighter pilots have to be, when he got in close he would let one eye work for the government on the instrument panel. The other would work for LCDR Cue, his heirs and assigns, looking out ahead to avoid collision.

Curly bored in to half a mile and then began peeking a little. Of course, bomber crews are cagey characters too. They listen in on the intercept, and know exactly where to look for the fighter. As soon as they spotted Curly coming in astern, the bomber pilot popped on his running lights. Bomber pilots acting as targets during an exercise don't trust night fighter pilots in close any more than night fighter pilots trust them—which is not at all.

When the lights came on, Curly sang out, "Okay, I see his lights. Bogey is a flamer. Request course back to ship."

Here Commander Deever cut in. "Disregard target's lights and follow your instruments. The enemy won't show lights in wartime."

Out of the blackness came a reluctant, "Rajah," as Curly went back on the gauges.

In the target plane the bomber pilot, who was eavesdropping on the fighter frequency, growled to his rear seat man, "These characters want to play for keeps. Keep a bright lookout for those guys coming in at us. I don't trust any blowtorch jockey too close on instruments at night."

Soon Curly and his partner whizzed past the bomber's tail from opposite sides and the squawk box in CIC said, "*Guadalcanal*, this is Night Hawk One. Splashed bogey. Am returning to ship."

"Roger," replied CIC; "any comment on that intercept?"

"Affirmative," said Curly, "you're damn right there is. I don't like this instrument stuff all the way in at night. I guess I missed him far enough that time, but I'd rather watch where I'm going."

Again the FDO in CIC took charge and guided Curly back over the darkened ship at 20,000 feet. Then he spiraled him down through the blackness until he had him at 2,000 abeam of the ship to starboard on a parallel course. Here the approach controller took over and brought him around as if it were soupy weather. Following his directions, Curly circled left ahead of the ship, let down to 1000 feet, and ran through his landing checkoff list. He lowered his flaps, dropped his wheels and hook, and throttled down to final approach speed, on the gauges all the way. He saw nothing of the ship on the black ocean and simply did as he was told.

As he was banking into his final, half a mile astern of the ship at 1000 feet, the ship popped its lights on (this being peacetime) and Curly came in the rest of the way using his good old Mark I eyeball. As he smacked the deck and felt his hook grab a wire, he sighed, "Another day—another dollar; it's a hell of a way to make a living."

At the critique in the ready room afterwards, Danny Deever, the CIC controller said, "How'd it go, Curly?"

"Well, it was no strain until you daredevils sitting on your cans in CIC began getting fancy and trying to bring us in close on the gauges. I didn't go for that much."

"You did fine, Curly," said Deever. "There's nothing to worry about as long as you do what we tell you to," he added smugly.

At this point, the communications orderly handed Admiral Day a dispatch which had just come in by radio:

From: Com Pat Wings Pac Fleet
To   : Com TG 81
During intercept exercises here last night jet fighter came too close and chopped vertical stabilizer off P2V. Jet pilot bailed out and was rescued. P2V landed safely. Propose increasing minimum allowed range on night intercepts from 500 yards to 1000 yards. Advise.

Admiral Day read this dispatch to the assembled group and said, "How about it, boys? How shall I answer it?"

"I suggest 'hell yes'. . . sir," said Curly Cue.

Admiral Day handed the dispatch back to the orderly and said, "Tell the watch officer to answer affirmative."

As indicated by this dispatch, the Pat Wings were busily preparing, too. Admiral Bates had his P2V squadrons up day and night, working with F-86 Sabrejets of the Air Force. The P2V gunners took miles of camera gun film and spent many hours studying the results.

The day of the big battle turned out to be hazy. This produced several snafus for Pat Wings Pac. Two hundred P2Vs scoured the Pacific looking for the *Guadalcanal,* and couldn't find her. The ocean is vast and a highly mobile task group is easy to miss on a hazy day.

At various times half a dozen P2Vs got within fifty miles or so of the *Guadalcanal,* with Banshees buzzing all around them, but they didn't find the ship. Finally, a cagey P2V pilot followed a Banshee that had to limp home on one jet and the elusive carrier was found.

Late in the afternoon the first wave of twenty-four P2Vs roared out from San Francisco, with Bugler Bates in the lead plane, headed for the *Guadalcanal*'s reported position. They climbed to 30,000 feet and settled down to cruise in formation until they reached the fan-out point several hundred miles from the target.

So far, things looked rosy from Admiral Bates' point of view. The *Guadalcanal* couldn't elude his gang now, and they would catch her about six hours before she reached her launching circle with all her bombers on deck. Their attack would be made in the middle of the night, and no matter how good her night interceptors were, some of the bombers were bound to sneak through undetected. Several scores of long standing against Admiral Day would be evened up by sunrise.

Shortly after sunset, disaster struck the task group in the form of dense fog. Carrier-controlled approach is O.K. in a pinch, if you've got some ceiling and maybe half a mile visibility, but in zero zero at night carriers just don't fly.

On the flag bridge of the *Guadalcanal* gloom was thicker than the fog. A P2V on instruments wouldn't be bothered at all by fog. With its search radar and radar bombsight, it could find and attack the *Guadalcanal* just as well as in daylight. It looked as though the task group was going to get knocked cold, and Admiral Day took a dim view of his next meeting with Bugler Bates.

The Admiral conferred with his chief of staff about the possibility of postponing the exercise.

"No chance at all, sir," said his chief. "We agreed to take the weather as it came, just as we would have to do in wartime. The P2Vs are probably on their way out right now, and I'm sure Admiral Bates won't let us get off the hook on account of the weather."

LCDR Curly Cue, who had been listening in, piped up, "Admiral, I've got an idea which might possibly get us out of this jam. It's one of those things that you might just as well try because we can't possibly lose anything and we might gain something."

"You can't put planes up in this stuff," growled the Admiral. "I wouldn't even think of it."

"But, sir," said Curly, "the P2Vs don't know what the weather is down here. I want to put some phonies up there and make the P2Vs think we're flying as usual."

"What good would that do?" demanded the Admiral. "You won't kid anybody except yourself." But Curly had a gleam in his eye. The Admiral saw it, and recalled some things that had happened in the past under similar pressure. "All right," he said. "Go ahead."

Curly adjourned quickly to the Combat Information Center and as soon as he got there barked, "Get the squadron commanders and about a dozen of their pilots up here right away. Man all

CIC stations for flight operations."

"Aye aye, sir," said the duty officer with a shrug, looking know-ingly at one of the radar operators and making circular motions with his forefinger pointing at his head.

When the jet pilots assembled, Curly outlined his plan.

"The idea is to put out the same line of chatter on our fighter director frequencies tonight as we would if we had a big combat air patrol up. Those P2V pilots are naturally going to listen in on our frequencies the same as we do on theirs, so let's give them something worth listening to.

"Each of you fighter directors pair off with about four pilots, hand the mike back and forth and make like you are actually run-ning intercepts on any bandits that appear. I'm going to turn the power way up on our transmitters so they can hear us a long way off and maybe we can make them think we are strafing hell out of them."

"So what?" asked Danny Deever. "They will get in their attacks anyway and we can't make any claims. We'll just have to admit they caught us flat-footed."

"You just watch and see what happens," said Curly. "I've got a few punch lines to stick into the script of this broadcast at the crucial points."

So the *Guadalcanal* went on the airwaves and "launched" twenty-four imaginary Banshees. The pilots "climbed" to altitude, checked in with the CIC controllers, and received their instruc-tions for orbiting until bandits were sighted, just as they would have done on an actual operation.

At this time the P2Vs were coming within range of the *Guadal-canal's* souped-up transmitters. There was no moon, and it was pretty black and hazy. Soon Admiral Bates' copilot said, "I hear 'em, Admiral. Sounds like they are just launching their planes."

The Admiral nodded and switched the plane's intercom to the task group frequency so the whole plane's crew could listen in.

Over the intercom came the word, "*Guadalcanal* to flights one, two, three, and four—report number of planes in company with you."

Each air patrol leader came back with the same report: "Six."

The copilot looked at Admiral Bates. "Twenty-four jet fighters up on a night like this?" he said. "They'll have trouble controlling them. I'll bet some will get in their own way."

"Yeah," said the Admiral pensively, "or in ours, maybe. . . . Flash your lights and start the boys fanning out."

Soon the picket destroyers, whose radars could see through fog, spotted the incoming P2Vs and flashed word to the *Guadalcanal*. In CIC fighter director officers went to work, broke off pairs of Banshees from each imaginary patrol, and started vectoring them out to intercept the various bomber groups.

It was easy enough for Admiral Bates, watching his own surface radar scope on which the *Guadalcanal* was now visible, to dope out that the pair of fighters vectoring 090 was the one trying to intercept him.

Soon the air was full of radio traffic. The picket destroyers spotted more P2Vs coming in from all directions, and fighter directors vectored more imaginary jets out to meet them. Despite the fact that they had to handle many targets and twenty-four fighters at once, there was little confusion. Six pairs of Banshees got their vectors, rogered for them, and were on their way without jamming the frequencies.

The copilot remarked to Admiral Bates, "They've got good radio discipline—these guys are professionals."

"Yeah, they're pretty good," said the Admiral, staring intently into the blackness.

Then the *Guadalcanal* ordered: "All fighter planes turn out your lights. We will make these attacks under war conditions."

"What the—?" growled Admiral Bates, stiffening in his seat. "Those guys must be nuts. It was agreed we *would* use lights. . . . Well, we've got ours on. If they run into each other it's their funeral."

The Admiral picked up his mike and broadcast to his group: "This is Admiral Bates. All P2Vs make sure your lights are on. Night fighters are coming in without lights."

Before he was half through, the *Guadalcanal's* direction finders, who had been waiting for the squadron commander to identify himself, pounced on the transmission and got an accurate bearing.

"Zero nine zero," they reported.

Over the intercom in the Admiral's plane the order came in: "*Guadalcanal* to cap four, vector four more planes 090. We will make a three-way split attack on target approaching on that bearing."

"Six of them coming in at us in this soup!" muttered the Admiral.

The *Guadalcanal* was still 100 miles ahead of Admiral Bates and the six jet fighters, according to the chatter on the radio, were converging on him at speeds as high as 600 knots—one mile every six seconds. Vectors to the fighters came fast now. Apparently the task group fighter directors meant to bring six Banshees in on one target almost simultaneously.

Then came a plaintive call from one of the Banshees. "*Guadalcanal*, this is Cap Four Baker—I can't see a thing ahead of me up here."

"Roger, Cap Four Baker. Keep going. Don't worry, we won't let you hit him."

By this time Admiral Bates and all his people in the P2V were in cold sweats. Suddenly there were six jubilant tallyhos over the radio in rapid succession.

The Admiral grabbed the mike and asked his tail gunner, "How close did those guys come?"

"Too close for comfort, Admiral," huskily replied the gunner, who couldn't see a thing but had heard every word over the intercom.

A few seconds later the following came in out of the night: "*Guadalcanal* from Four Baker, I didn't like that run. You brought me in too close. I almost chopped his tail off."

"*Guadalcanal* to Four Baker. Roger. Sorry. We'll be more careful next time. Rendezvous with your section leader for another attack."

That was enough for Bugler Bates. He made some blistering comments, winding up with "Let's get out of here while we're still in one piece."

Grabbing his tactical mike he broadcast: "This is Admiral Bates. Exercise canceled. All P2Vs return to base. Reverse course immediately and get out of this rat race."

The other P2Vs, who also had been eavesdropping, rogered promptly and cheerfully. The nearest P2V at this time was forty-five miles from the *Guadalcanal*.

Down in the *Guadalcanal*'s Combat Information Center, Curly Cue finally made himself heard over the jubilant whooping and hollering, and yelled: "Get back on those microphones, every one of you guys. We've still got twenty-four planes to bring down out of the soup. We can't just cut off the program and leave them—and our public—in the air."

As soon as Admiral Bates' plane rolled to a stop in front of the tower at San Francisco, the Admiral scrambled out and burned up the direct line to Radio Seattle with the following dispatch.

> To: Com TG 81
> On tonight's exercise I personally observed flagrant violations of safety rules by your planes. Fighters operated without lights and hazarded lives of P2V crews by making dangerously close passes. In two cases collision averted only by expert evasive action of P2Vs. Recommend drastic disciplinary action on offending pilots.

This dispatch was delivered to Admiral Day on the *Guadalcanal* just as she broke out of the fog an hour before dawn 1000 miles from San Francisco and started launching her bombers to attack the city. Admiral Day wrote his reply in high glee, checking the wording carefully with his legal officer, who was an expert at framing statements which, although literally true, could be a bit misleading.

> To: Com Pat Wings Pac Fleet:
> Replying to your message—believe there is some confusion about what happened last night. My planes did not operate with running lights turned out and careful questioning of all *Guadalcanal* fighter pilots convinces me that no planes from task group approached within 1000 yards of P2Vs. Respectfully submit your planes were not actually in danger.

As the last plane of the bombing attack rolled off the bow, Curly Cue said to Admiral Day:

"When Admiral Bates finds out what actually happened, I won't dare go ashore in Frisco any more."

"Okay, my boy, don't you worry about that," said Admiral Day. "Old Bugler ought to know by now that if you believe everything you hear when you're eavesdropping on a party line, you may get booby-trapped into jumping to conclusions."

Of course when the *Guadalcanal* got in to San Francisco the story was bound to leak out. Matter of fact as soon as the first liberty boat hit the beach it "leaked out" the way Old Faithful erupts at Yellowstone. Before long everyone in the Navy knew it and Admiral Bugler Bates had one more score to settle with his old rival Admiral Day.

CHAPTER FIVE

Rescue Mission

NEXT DAY the *Guadalcanal*, 300 miles offshore, plowed through dense fog heading for San Francisco. The fog gave all pilots a day off. The planes' crews were busy pulling engine checks and tinkering with their planes as they always do when they get a chance. In CIC the duty section relaxed at their stations with all except the lads on search radar and distress radio half asleep. The fighter director, his feet on a desk, pored over a paperback thriller. It looked as though it would be a dull watch.

Meantime a TransPac airliner, Flight 132, with 100 passengers aboard, was coming in from the west also bound for San Francisco. The airliner was at 20,000 on the gauges and was having a bumpy trip. The turbulent air was rough on the passengers, but it didn't bother the pilots. Thanks to radio beams and loran, they could stay on course and check their position just as well as if the sun were shining.

The whole West Coast lay under a thick overcast, and a blanket of pea-soup fog extended far out to sea. San Francisco Airport had a ceiling of 100 feet and the visibility was close to the landing minimum.

Flight 132 entered the clouds an hour out of Honolulu and had been there ever since. It was now well past the point of no return for Honolulu and was scheduled to land in San Francisco in about another hour. Salt Lake City was its alternate in case SF closed in.

SLC had 500 feet and three miles. In a few minutes it would be time for a routine position report to Air Traffic Control.

The navigator watched the dancing traces on his loranscope and twiddled the knobs till the traces stood still. Then he put down some numbers in his notebook, flipped a switch, and took another reading. On his loran chart of the Pacific he picked out a red line with the first set of numbers on it and ran his finger along until he came to a green line with the second number on it. There he pricked a small hole in the chart, looked at the clock, and wrote down the time. This gave him a pinpoint fix, like reading the signs where two streets intersect. He then drew a line joining this position with his last previous fix and checked to see that his ground speed and course were what they should be. They were—showing that the wind Aerology had given him was correct.

The navigator filled in his position report and went up to the cockpit. He reported, "450 miles to go, Cap'n. We are on course. Ground speed 410. You should be right on the Golden Gate beam when we pick it up."

"Umph," grunted the captain; "give radio the position report."

Turning to the copilot, he said "It's getting a little bumpier. We must be getting close to that thunderstorm area Aerology told us about." A couple of extra-heavy bumps confirmed this. A minute later the gray haze they were flying through began blinking with purple light flashes, and heavy rain set in. The pilot said to the copilot, "Get on the Golden Gate beam frequency and let me know when you pick it up." Then he flipped the autopilot off, took the controls himself, and settled down for a bit of serious work on the gauges.

Shortly after that there was a blinding flash as a bolt of lightning hit the plane just aft of the cockpit. Lightning seldom does much structural damage to a big plane, and it didn't do much this time. But it played havoc with the radios. Purple sparks flew all over the radio compartment, fuses blew, and the radioman nearly got knocked off his stool. When the sparks quit jumping, the cabin was full of smoke from burned-out wiring and all radio receivers were dead. So was the loran set.

The radioman grabbed his interphone to the cockpit and said,

"Radio to pilot—all receivers are knocked out." No answer from the cockpit. The intercom was out, too. He yanked off the headphones and staggered up to the cockpit. "All radios knocked out, Cap'n," he said.

"Okay," said the pilot, "get 'em back in again. Did you get the position report off?"

"Nossir. We got hit right in the middle of it."

Scanning his instruments methodically the captain said to the copilot, "Go back and see how much damage that bolt did. See what the engineer has to say about the power plants."

While the copilot was aft the pilot did some iffy thinking. If the radios were badly hurt, this situation could turn out to be a nasty one. An airliner on instruments depends absolutely on its radios. You can control the plane all right without radios. Your gyro horizon, compass, air speed meter, and altimeters enable you to fly safely as long as your fuel holds out. But without radio, when you are in the clouds, you can't tell where you are. Dead reckoning will give you a rough idea, but it's not good enough for a letdown through a low ceiling. To let down and land in bad weather you've *got* to have radio. If you try to do it on dead reckoning, especially in rough country like the West Coast, you're apt to splatter yourself all over a mountainside.

Flight 132 had fuel enough to reach Salt Lake City, plus some reserve beyond that. But S.L.C. is right at the foot of the Wasatch Mountains and a blind letdown there would be even more dangerous than at S.F.

Before takeoff Aerology had told him this overcast was thick and solid everywhere. There was little chance of finding a hole that would let him duck under it. He was well past the point of no return, and the soup was thick for 500 miles behind him, so there was no point in turning back. This *might* be a bad jam. The only answer was to keep going and get those radios fixed.

Soon the copilot came back and said, "No structural damage, Cap'n. Just the usual pinholes in the skin where the bolt hit. Engines are okay. But it sure made a mess of the radio shack. . . . Passengers are a bit worried and a padre back there is giving his rosary beads a workout. We got a General aboard, too. But what *he's* saying is no prayer!"

The radioman stuck his head in and said, "It looks bad, Cap'n. All my receivers are blown to hell . . . wiring burned out and guts all melted. Loran is shot. Main transmitter is gone too. Try your voice transmitter and I'll see if it puts out."

The pilot squeezed his mike button and said, "Flight 132 testing 1-2-3-4-5-4-3-2-1 Flight 132 testing." Nothing came back through his earphones, but the radioman popped his head back in the cockpit and said, "I think you're putting out, Cap'n. The ammeter says you are."

"Umph," grunted the captain. "We can't get beyond the horizon with voice, but it's *some* help anyway. Keep working on those receivers. We *gotta* have at least one beam receiver."

"Will do, Cap'n," said radio dubiously.

Turning to the copilot the captain said, "Go back aft and have the stewardesses get the rafts out and get ready just in case we have to ditch. Give the passengers a pep talk. Break it to them gently."

"Yeah," said the copilot, "how do you do that?"

"Tell 'em the company is embarrassed but I may have to land them in the water. Tell 'em the gals are getting the rafts out so everybody will be comfortable after I do."

"Okay, Cap'n," said the copilot and disappeared aft.

The captain picked up his mike, squeezed the button, and said, "TransPac Flight 132 calling any station. TransPac 132 calling any station. Mayday. Mayday. Have been struck by lightning 500 miles west of Golden Gate. Minor structural damage but all radio receivers and all transmitters but this one are out. I am sending this message blind hoping someone picks it up. More in a minute. This is TransPac Flight 132. Mayday. Out."

Meanwhile Air Traffic Control in San Francisco was getting a bit concerned about Flight 132. Radio had reported right away to the controller when Flight 132 broke off in the middle of his position report. After five minutes of futile calling and getting no answer, the controller alerted Air Sea Rescue and the Coast Guard and called the TransPac operations officer to the control room.

"What do you make of it?" he asked as the air ops officer came in.

"Could be a number of things," said Air Ops. "Number one, he has just lost his transmitters for some reason."

"Right," said the controller. "In that case we're not in any real bad trouble. He can let down and land okay except that we can't tell him anything about other traffic. I'll cancel all outgoing flights from San Francisco and divert the incoming ones, so he'll have the air all to himself and a clear field if he comes in."

TRANSPAC: "The next possibility is that he has lost *all* radios—in which case we got real trouble."

CONTROLLER: "Yeah. It's a solid overcast all up and down the coast. I don't know anywhere that he can let down safely. And the stuff is right down to the water, too, for a thousand miles to sea. Do you think he might try to let down here—on dead reckoning?"

TRANSPAC OPS: "Good God, no. Joe Tinker is one of our senior captains. He wouldn't think of it."

CONTROLLER: "So . . . what *will* he do?"

TRANSPAC: "I think he'll come straight in at 20,000 till he thinks he has crossed the coast, figuring that we will pick him up by radar. Then I think he'll go back out to sea until he either finds a hole he can duck down through or runs out of gas and has to ditch. If I know Joe he'll make it easy for us, and we will find him somewhere along the course on which we last saw him by radar not more than 100 miles off shore."

CONTROLLER: "Sounds logical. I've already alerted the early warning net and Fighter Defense HQ to watch for him on radar. I'll have all other inbound flights make a big circle, ten miles offshore as they come in, so radar can sort him out from the others when *he* comes in straight."

TRANSPAC: "The last possibility is that he's in the drink already."

CONTROLLER: "The Coast Guard has a cutter on the way to his last reported position right now. I'm also notifying Air Sea Rescue."

TRANSPAC: "That's it, then. There's nothing else we can do."

In the waiting room at the San Francisco Airport, the man on the bulletin board changed all scheduled departure times to "de-

layed" and all arrivals to "diverted." To anxious inquiries by waiting passengers and friends, he explained "weather." Experienced
air travelers could look outside and see that the weather wasn't
bad enough to cancel takeoff. They paced around muttering, "If
you've time to spare, go by air." Soon the board showed the new
destination for all the diverted flights except 132. To inquiries
about that one, the answer was "not decided yet."

Meanwhile the *Guadalcanal* plowed along about 150 miles east
of the stricken airliner. The radioman in CIC picked up the faint
test count from the liner after the bolt had struck, but this was
nothing to be concerned about. The CIC officer didn't even look
up from his reading when it came over the loudspeaker.

But when the Mayday came in a few minutes later all hands
scrambled for their stations. "Put that on our high-power radio
and relay it to San Francisco," barked the CIC officer. Then he
dialed the Captain's sea cabin and said, "Just got a Mayday from
an airliner, inbound 150 miles west of us, Cap'n. I'm relaying it to
San Francisco."

"Very well," came the reply. "Get the operations officer and Air
Group commander up to CIC. I'll be right down."

In a minute CIC was fully manned and the senior officers of the
Guadalcanal were gathered around the Air Situation Board to see
what could be done to help the distressed plane. The sailor behind the big plastic display board marked in the *Guadalcanal*'s
position 200 miles west of San Francisco, and the plane's reported
position 150 miles west of that, writing backwards on his side of the
board so it would read properly on the other. Radar operators
hunched over their scopes while the big dishes on the mast probed
the sky to the west searching for the liner. But the thunderstorm
area returned so much spinach that they couldn't find the blip
from the liner.

"He's in a bad jam," said the Captain, scanning the Mayday
message. "There isn't an airport this side of the Rocky Mountains
he can get into without radio."

"Right," agreed the ops officer. "If we could get him to ditch
anywhere near us we could probably save them all."

"But we can't," said the Captain. "We can't talk to him. And ditching in this fog would be tough anyway."

Here the loudspeaker cut in: "Flight 132 to any station. Mayday. I'm going to let down while I'm still over water and see if I can get under this stuff. I will broadcast every few minutes and let you know how I'm doing. Flight 132 starting descent from 20,000. Estimated position 350 miles west of Golden Gate. Mayday. Out."

"He won't get under it," said the Captain; "it's right down on the water everywhere," and all heads around the circle nodded grave agreement.

"You're relaying all this to San Francisco, aren't you?" asked the operations officer of the radioman.

"Affirmative," said radio.

In the next five minutes Flight 132 let down to 1000 feet broadcasting as he passed through each thousand-foot level on the way down. At 1000 he said, "I'm going to feel my way down slowly from here and see if I can get under it. If I can't, I'll go back up to 20,000 till I think I'm over the coast. Then I'll head south until I have to ditch. I will broadcast estimated position every five minutes. Flight 132 now starting descent from 1000."

"Have you got him on radar yet?" asked the Captain.

"Nossir," said the CIC officer. "We would have by now if he had stayed at 20,000. He's too low now. But I figure he is about 130 miles west of us."

All this time Curly Cue had been on the outskirts of the crowd around the plot board saying nothing but thinking hard. At this point he said, "Cap'n, if he doesn't smack the water trying to get under this stuff and goes back up again I can get him down safely."

All heads snapped around and the Captain said, "How?"

"As soon as he goes back up again we'll have him on radar. Launch me now and orbit me over the ship at about 20,000 feet. As soon as you pick him up on radar, run a controlled intercept on him. With my radar gunsight I can come right up alongside where he will see me. Then I will lead him in for a GCA at Moffet Field. Nothin' to it."

"Hmmm . . ." said the Captain. "Maybe you could . . . Anybody see any bugs in it?" he asked, glancing around the circle.

Nobody did. But the ops officer had to get in his two cents' worth, so he said, "Of course if anything goes wrong it's your funeral too. We can't get you back aboard in this stuff."

"That's okay by me," said Curly. "Nothing *will* go wrong."

"Let's go," said the Captain. "Tell San Francisco what we are doing. Sound Flight Quarters."

Ten minutes later the *Guadalcanal* blasted Curly off the catapult into the soup. He roared off wide open with the stick hauled back and climbed out of sight in the fog. Holding her in a stiff climb, he soon passed 1000 feet, giving him enough elbow room to be comfortable, and then went into a climbing spiral around the ship following orders from CIC.

As he was climbing through 6000 the ship said, "*Guadalcanal* to Flight Able. We have bogey bearing 270 distance 100 miles. We think it is TransPac Flight 132."

"Flight Able to *Guadalcanal*. Rajah. I'm climbing through 6000. Still orbiting. Out."

A minute later, "*Guadalcanal* to Flight Able. We have a good plot on TransPac 132 now. He is climbing back to 20,000. Steer 280 and climb to 20,000. Over."

"*Guadalcanal* from Flight Able. Steer 280 and climb to 20,000. Rajah. Out."

A few minutes later Curly reported, "Flight Able at 20,000, steering 280. How much farther to go?"

Answer: "About twenty miles. Start a standard rate turn to the left. Over."

"Wilco. Twenty miles to go. Starting standard rate turn to the left."

For the next five minutes CIC kept plotting the two blips to the west and turning Curly more and more to the left to bring him in astern of the airliner. Then the fighter director said, *Guadalcanal* to Flight Able. You are now five miles astern of airliner. His course is 090. He is cruising at 20,000. You should overtake him soon."

"Flight Able to *Guadalcanal*. Rajah. I am at 20,000. My course 090. I am turning on radar gunsight."

A few minutes later when the two blips had merged and were

nearly over the ship, a crisp "Tallyho" came out of the loudspeaker and cheers went up from the crowd in CIC.

Up in the air Curly throttled back a bit so as not to barge in on the airliner too suddenly and startle him. Keeping the blip centered in his gunsight, he closed the range slowly, darting a glance into the fog ahead every few seconds. Soon a dark area in the cloud took shape and there she was, 100 yards ahead. Curly eased over to the left, passed just over her left wingtip, and dropped into position a wing span away from the airliner on its port bow.

Meantime, in the cockpit of the airliner, the two pilots had their eyes glued on the instrument board, scanning methodically and thinking about the things pilots think about at a time like this.

"Have you ever ditched one of these ships before, Cap'n?" asked the copilot.

"No-o-o," said the captain. "But I had to put a B-29 in the drink on the way back from Tokyo to Saipan during the war. We all got out of it okay. A lifeguard submarine picked us up."

The navigator was standing between them peering grimly out into the soup ahead. Suddenly he gasped, "Gawdalmighty!" Then he tapped the captain gently on the shoulder, pointed out to the left, and said, "Don't look now, Cap'n, but we got company."

"Well, I'm a son of a bitch," breathed the pilot as he looked up and saw Curly. He relaxed back in his seat and added, "Good old Navy! This is the second time they've bailed me out, God bless 'em." Then he grasped one hand in the other, held them up over his head, looked over at Curly and shook hands with himself in the traditional gesture of a fighter greeting his fans.

Aviators the world over are adept at talking to each other in pantomime. Curly pointed at the airliner, patted himself on the head, crooked his finger in a beckoning gesture and then pointed ahead toward the Golden Gate. Any pilot would immediately translate this as meaning "Follow me and you'll live happily ever after."

The airline captain made a circle with his thumb and forefinger, held it up in front of his face, then made a fist and stuck his thumb up, nodding his head. To aviators of all nationalities this means "I understand, approve, and will do."

Then he turned to the navigator and said, "Get the name of that padre back aft. I'm going to join his church as soon as we land."

Curly squeezed his mike button and said, "*Guadalcanal* from Flight Able. Have airliner in tow at 20,000, course 090. Air speed 400. Everything lovely. Over."

Soon a jubilant "roger" came back from the ship, followed by "Hold your present course and speed. San Francisco early warning radars have been alerted to pick you up. When they do we will turn you over to West Coast Fighter Defense Command."

"*Guadalcanal* from Flight Able—rajah—standing by for Fighter Defense Command controller."

Curly put his plane on autopilot and the airliner settled down flying a tight formation on him.

Meantime things were happening in San Francisco. Air Traffic Control relayed all messages from *Guadalcanal* to Fighter Defense HQ. Fighter defense aimed their radars at the spot where Flight 132 should come over the horizon, tuned their voice radios to the Navy fighter band, and the controller sat with his pencil poised over his scope ready to take over. ATC got on the hot line to Naval Air Station Oakland, briefed them on the trouble, and asked, "Can you bring them in at Oakland by ground-controlled approach."

"Can do," said NAS Oakland. "Turn them over to our GCA controller at 5,000 feet over Golden Gate."

Up in the airliner a stewardess explained to the passengers that the pilot had changed his mind and was going to land at the Naval Air Station in Oakland.

"Well, I should think he *would* change it!" said a little old lady sitting in one of the front seats.

"You mean we won't have to get in those rubber things?" asked her companion.

"Not this time," said the stewardess.

The padre, who didn't want the Lord to get the impression that he took things for granted, started saying his rosary all over again. This time it was in thanks for blessings received.

At 150 miles out, Fighter Defense controller came on the air. "San Francisco Air Defense controller to Navy fighter. We think we have you on our scope now. How do you hear? Over."

"Loud and clear," said Curly. "I am at 20,000, on course 090, air speed 400."

A few minutes later ADC said, "We have a good solid blip now and we think it's you. Change course to the left ninety degrees for a check."

"Roger. Wilco," said Curly, banking into a gentle left turn and beckoning the airliner to follow. The beckoning was really unnecessary. He couldn't shake that airliner off now except by blasting off at war emergency power and running away!

Soon ADC said, "Okay. We have identified you. Come back to course 095 and descend to 5000 feet."

"Flight Able to ADC. Come right to 095 and descend to 5000 feet. Flight Able and TransPac 132 now leaving 20,000."

Of course, with all the electronic aids he had on his dashboard, Curly didn't need any help from the ground to find his way to the Golden Gate. He knew at all times which way it was and how far. As his distance indicator was turning up to zero, the FDO said "Nice work, Navy, you are over the Golden Gate. Switch to button three for your GCA controller."

Curly punched button No. 3 on his console, called Oakland, and a clear confident voice from the ground went into the familiar pattern. "This is your GCA controller. We have you now at 5000 feet four miles south of the station. Perform your landing checkoff list and report when completed."

Curly looked back over his right shoulder and made a series of gestures which to any ordinary observer might have indicated he was trying to show how to grind hamburger and catch flies. But to Joe Tinker it was, of course, obvious that he meant to lower flaps and wheels. They did this together, throttled back to approach speed, and Curly reported, "GCA, this is Flight Able. Checkoff list completed. Airliner has gear and flaps down too. Over."

Then the GCA ritual began:

"This is your final approach controller. . . . Do not acknowledge my transmissions from now on. . . . If you lose communication and do not hear me for ten seconds, pull up and go to 10,000 feet until communication is restored. . . . Come left to zero one zero . . . we will land you on runway ten . . . runway ten is 8000 feet long and the wind is zero. . . . Start your standard rate of descent . . . you are *on* glide path and starting in nicely."

Curly was all wrapped up in his instrument board now, holding his course, speed, and rate of descent exactly where GCA called for them. The chips were down and this was for keeps from here on in. The airliner stayed with him like a hip pocket.

"Going a little below glide path . . . bring her *up* . . . twenty feet below glide path . . . *pull up* . . . [Curly goosed his jets] . . . coming up nicely now . . . *on* glide path . . . the field is one half mile ahead of you . . . you are lined up with the runway and *on* glide path . . . one quarter mile to go . . . you are *on* glide path . . . you will break out soon . . . WE HAVE YOU IN SIGHT . . . take over and land visually."

Curly came up off the gauges and found he had just broken through a ragged 70-foot ceiling with the long runway looming up out of the fog dead ahead and nicely lined up. The airliner was breathing down his neck. Coming up on the runway, Curly eased his throttle forward to hold her off, then gave her the gun and took a wave-off, circling out over the bay and giving the airliner the whole runway to himself. As he swung around, lined up again, and plopped down on the runway, the airliner was just turning onto the taxi strip and heading for the control tower.

When he taxied up to the line Curly was greeted by all the operations personnel of the air station, the crew and passengers of the airliner, as well as Admiral Bugler Bates and most of his staff. When Admiral Bates saw Curly climb out of the cockpit he blurted, "Well, I'll be damned."

The airline captain made a little speech thanking Curly and the Navy on behalf of the company, crew, and passengers. Curly hemmed and hawed and said "Aw . . . it wasn't much." As the passengers all crowded around to shake his hand, Admiral Bates was one of the first to get to him. "Well done, m'lad," he said. "But if I had known it was *you* up there I'd have suspected there was a trick to it."

CHAPTER SIX

Ensign Willy Wigglesworth

A WEEK LATER as the ship was leaving San Francisco, Curly's executive officer said to him, "A new pilot reported to us yesterday. An Ensign William Wigglesworth."

"Good God," said Curly, "what a name for a fighter pilot. Willy Wigglesworth! Sounds more like a piccolo player or a ballet dancer than a jet pilot. Can he fly?"

"I suppose so," said the exec. "His log book shows he is checked out in everything, including night intercepts."

"Willy Wigglesworth," said Curly, shaking his head sadly; "what sort of a looking guy is he?"

"Just about what you would expect. Like a whiz kid or a choirboy."

"Where did we get him from?" asked Curly.

"From Naval Air Station Columbus. And there's something funny about that. He just finished a tour of sea duty in the Med on the *Coral Sea* and he went to Columbus for shore duty. He was there only about a month and now he comes back to sea again with us."

"Hunh," said Curly, "that's strange. I wonder why."

"So did I," said the exec. "But I couldn't get much out of *him* about it. He's not a very gabby guy."

"Send him around to see me," said Curly.

Later that morning a baby-faced ensign approached Curly timidly and saluted. He looked as though he would be more comfortable if his mother were holding his hand. "Ensign Wigglesworth reporting for duty, sir," he said.

"Haryah, Wigglesworth," said Curly, shoving his hand out. "Glad to have you on board."

"Glad to be aboard, sir," said Willy, wincing a little from the iron grip Curly gave him.

"I hear you're all checked out in these planes and ready to go," said Curly.

"Yes, sir. I flew them for a year in VF 102 in the Med."

"You didn't stay long on shore duty in Columbus after that, did you? Just a month."

"Yessir," said Willy.

"How come?"

"Well, sir, I received orders to come here and so I carried them out," said Willy.

"Well, now, that's fine," said Curly, nodding his head in mock approval. "I'm always glad to see young officers carry out their orders. That's the way to get ahead in this Navy. . . . Now let's cut out the horse crap . . . wha' hoppen? How come you got the bum's rush out of Columbus?"

"Well, you see, sir, the Pennsylvania Railroad runs right by there and I didn't get along very well with them."

"Oh-h-h, I see," said Curly. "But not very much. How does the railroad come into this thing?"

"The railroad owed me money and they wouldn't pay it to me," said Willy.

"Well," said Curly tolerantly, "it's always hard to get money out of a big corporation—lots of red tape and all that. You just have to be patient."

"I *was* patient," said Willy. "I wrote letters back and forth to their lawyers all the time I was in the Med. But finally I got fed up with their release forms and vouchers."

"So then what?"

"I wrote to the president of the railroad about it. I advised him to make his people pay up or it would cost him a lot more in the long run."

"I see . . . you threatened to sue the railroad?"

"No, sir. I didn't have the time or the money to do that. I just gave him some friendly advice about how he could save the railroad a lot of money by paying me promptly. But he didn't follow it."

"Maybe he thought he knew how to run his railroad better than you do. Sometimes these big executives are funny that way. But what has all this got to do with you getting shanghaied out of Columbus? I didn't know you had to be friendly with the railroad to serve on that station."

"You don't, really, sir. But the Captain knew all about my troubles with them and I think he began to get worried about it."

"What kind of a song and dance are you giving me? Why should the Captain be worried about your troubles with the railroad?"

"Well, sir," said Willy, "I don't think he was worried *too* much about the railroad. It was more about the FBI."

"Oh-h-h. Well, I can see why he *would* worry more about the FBI. . . . How the hell do they come into it?"

"They began snooping around town asking questions."

"They always do," said Curly. "That's their job. What has that got to do with it?"

"The Captain just didn't want me around if they began asking questions on the Air Station."

"Judging from what I've been able to pry out of you so far," observed Curly, "it wouldn't have done them a damn bit of good to grill *you* about anything. Come on, Mr. Wigglesworth. What's this all about anyway?"

"I think it was probably about the Twentieth Century Limited, sir."

"Oh-h-h. The Twentieth Century Limited . . . now we're getting some real clues. . . . What the hell about it?"

"It put on the brakes one night when it was making seventy miles an hour and flattened all the wheels. Cost the railroad a lot more for new wheels than it would of cost to pay me."

Curly's eyebrows shot up and he hastily revised some of his

opinions of the little man he was talking to. "What did you do?" he demanded. "Pull the emergency brakes on the Limited?"

"No, indeed, sir. I wouldn't think of doing such a thing."

"Well, who did, then?"

"The engineer," said Willy.

"Why?"

"Well, I really don't *know* why he did it, sir," said Willy, "but he claimed he saw another train coming right at him on the same track."

"Yeah," breathed Curly, "I can see why he would do it, if he thought that. But why did he think so?"

"I wouldn't know, sir. They tell me there were no other trains anywhere near that night."

"And where were *you* at this time, Mr. Wigglesworth?" asked Curly.

"I was out getting in some cross-country night flying time."

"Where," demanded Curly.

"Well, sir," said Willy, "it wasn't far from Columbus. I was following the Pennsylvania tracks heading east when the Limited came barreling out of a tunnel heading west."

"Hah!" said Curly, beginning to smell a smell. "What altitude were you flying at?"

"Not very high, sir. Only about ten feet above the tracks."

Curly's eyes popped and his jaw dropped. "Gawd Almighty! Ten feet! I don't suppose you had your big landing light turned on, did you?"

"Matter of fact, I did, sir. It was real dark that night, not even any stars, and I *had* to turn it on to see where I was going. When I noticed the Limited bearing down on me I turned it off and zoomed up out of his way."

"Well, I'll be dipped in lukewarm gook," said Curly. "I can see why your skipper wanted to get you the hell offa that station and send you far away."

"Yes, *sir*," said Willy.

"Uh . . . Mr. Wigglesworth," said Curly; "I hope no large corporations on the West Coast owe you any money, do they?"

"Nossir."

"And . . . if at any time you don't like the way I'm running this squadron and have any suggestions to make, please bring them directly to my attention. And please be a bit patient. Don't take any drastic action till I've had time to consider them."

"Aye aye, sir," said Ensign Wigglesworth respectfully.

Later that morning Curly met his exec, and said, "Joe, there's more to that young Wigglesworth than meets the eye."

"Could easily be," said Joe. "He doesn't look like much."

"Don't be deceived by outward appearances," said Curly. "The lad has good stuff in him. Matter of fact, if you're not careful he may get it all over you. He has firm ideas about some things . . . and he knows how to carry them out."

"Glad to hear that, Cap'n," said Joe. "I'll keep an eye on him."

"You'd *better*," said Curly cryptically.

During flight operations that morning there was a minor snafu that almost put one of Curly's planes in the drink. It was the guppy plane, which carries a big radar dish and can "see" much farther than the radars on the ship's mast, which go only a little beyond the horizon. This is a 2-seater propeller-driven plane with a radarman in the after cockpit.

On this particular morning Joe Bluberry, the radarman, made a booboo and gave the pilot a bum steer on the course back to the ship at the end of the exercise. The pilot, Lieutenant Potter, had flown the wrong way for half an hour before he caught the mistake, much to Joe Bluberry's embarrassment. When they got back aboard they were pretty low on gas.

As they taxied out of the arresting gear and Potter cut the switch, Joe popped out of the after compartment and scrambled up on the wing alongside the cockpit before the prop stopped turning. "I'm sorry, Mr. Potter," he said, "It was all my fault."

"Okay, kid," said Mr. Potter. "It's a good thing I sometimes check up on the idle rumors that come out of that after cockpit. Otherwise you and I would be paddling around in a rubber raft by now."

"Yessir," said Joe, who worshiped the very air Lieutenant Potter flew through, "It won't happen again, sir."

At dinnertime that evening Joe was standing in the chow line and had almost reached the serving table at the galley when a pal came by and said, "Hey, Joe, didja hear about Lieutenant Potter?"

"No," said Joe, "what about him?"

"He got knocked cold in a basketball game on the hangar deck about an hour ago. I thought he busted his skull wide open when he hit it on that steel deck."

Joe stepped out of the line.

"Where ya goin'?" asked his pal.

"Down to sick bay to see the Lieutenant."

"Oh. He came out of it okay," said his pal. "He wouldn't go to sick bay and he seemed to be all right when he shoved off for the officers' country."

Joe picked up his tray and started to take his previous place in the line.

A tough-looking first-class PO who had been right behind him in line sounded off: "Where the hell do you think you're goin', sailor? G'wan back to the end of the line where you belong. What's the idea of trying to muscle in at the head of the line that way?"

"I just stepped out for a second," protested Joe. "You know very well I was right ahead of you for the last ten minutes. Lemme back in my place again." Joe tried to push his way in.

The first-class resisted, a scuffle resulted, and Joe hauled off and busted the first-class smack in the nose. Other hungry sailors in the line pulled the battlers apart as the Chief Master-at-Arms swooped down on the fracas.

"Knock it off," snarled the Chief, "what the hell's comin' off here? Break it up."

Order was quickly restored. Joe was informed he was on the report for hitting a petty officer, and was sent back to the end of the long chow line muttering obscene comments about the injustice of life on this earth, particularly on board the USS *Guadalcanal*.

Next day the squadron exec sent for Willy Wigglesworth and said, "Mr. Wigglesworth, I've got a job for you."

"Yessir," said Willy.

"I'm going to make you personnel officer of this squadron."

"Aye aye, sir," said Willy.

"We've got a fine bunch of men in this outfit," said the exec. "But they have personal problems on which they need help and advice. Like taking training courses for advancement in rate, converting their insurance policies, extending enlistments, and getting emergency leave for troubles at home. They seldom get in trouble aboard ship, but when they do we need someone to advise them about their legal rights and so forth. I want you to help me out on this business. It will take a big load off my back if you can take care of those sort of things."

"Aye aye, sir," said Willy.

"Your first job is to see what you can do for one of our plane captains by the name of Bluberry. He's on the report for fighting, and he's usually a very peaceful kid. See what it's all about. And see if you can't take care of it so it won't go into his record."

Willy went right to work on Joe Bluberry's case. "What's this I hear about you being in trouble?" he asked when Joe reported to him.

"Yeah. That's right, sir," said Joe.

"Tell me about it," said Willy, trying to assume a judicial manner.

"I busted a first-class PO in the nose, " said Joe.

"Well, now," said Willy, "you shouldn't go around busting first-class petty officers in the nose, although sometimes it's hard not to. . . . Tell me how it happened."

So Joe related the incident in the chow line.

"Maybe I can talk to this guy's division officer," said Willy. "If you're willing to apologize, maybe we can get them to drop the charges."

"Not a chance, sir," said Joe; "he's a mean so-and-so, always earbanging with the officers. He'd never drop this report, and I've always hated his guts anyway."

"How come?" asked Willy.

"He took my job as movie operator away from me. That job got me twenty bucks a month extra pay and he did me out of it."

"I know how you feel," said Willy. "I used to run the movies on the *Essex* when I was a flat-hat before going to Officers' Candidate School. Nice work if you can get it. I had to do some wangling myself to get it on the *Essex*. How did this guy finagle you out of the job?"

"There used to be a lot of echoes in the hangar deck before we went to the Navy Yard and it was very hard to keep the volume control adjusted right. You had to fiddle with it all the time. This guy told the Commander it was my fault, and that he knew how to run the machine better than I did. Then we went to the Navy Yard, they put in those echo curtains, and now *anybody* could run that machine. But the exec gave this guy the job, and now he thinks the guy is a genius."

Willy pondered on this problem for a minute, and then said, "Bluberry, I'm not sure what we can do about that report against you. At least not right away. But I know how to get that guy fired from the movie operator job, and maybe you'll get it back. In fact," he added, "if things work out like I think they will the Commander might get so mad at that guy he will want to punch him in the nose, too."

"How can we do that?" asked Joe eagerly.

"I think the movie machine on this ship is the same as the one we had on the *Essex*," said Willy. "It had two volume controls. One next to the peephole where the operator looks out and one behind his back."

"That's right," said Joe; "you set the one behind your back where you want it before the show starts and then you monkey with the other one to adjust the volume during the show."

"Okay. We got it made, then," said Willy. "After the show starts you change the volume control behind his back. You turn it up or down, and he corrects it with the one next to his peephole. Then after a minute or so, you diddle with it again. You just keep turning the volume up and down and pretty soon the audience wants to lynch him. That's how I got the job on the *Essex*."

"Yeah," said Joe, "that's fine. Except that those volume controls are inside the booth and that place is too small for anybody to hide in."

"You do it from outside the booth," said Willy. "That's the beauty of it. He's the only one in the booth, so they blame it all on him. There are a lot of ventilating holes in the back of the booth. You get up on one of those big beams running under the flight deck behind the booth; reach in through one of the holes near the volume control."

"You can't reach the volume knob from outside," said Joe; "your arm isn't long enough."

"I had the same problem on the *Essex*," said Willy. "What you do is, you get a short piece of whip antenna and stick a piece of gum on the end of it. Then you stick it in through a venthole, shove the gum against the volume control knob, and twist it. One minute you can blast them right out of their seats on the hangar deck and the next minute they can't hear a thing."

"By golly, you're right. You *could* do it that way," said Joe.

"Just one more thing," said Willy. "If you really want to fix that guy up right, there's one more thing you can do."

"What's that?" asked Joe eagerly.

"The movie booth has got a sprinkler head in it and a thermostat near the back. After you have loused up the show enough, just stick a cigarette under the thermostat. When the sprinkler lets go it will drown him out and bust up the show and you might get your job back."

"Gee, thanks, Mr. Wigglesworth," said Joe. "I'll do it tonight."

The movie program that night was one that was long remembered by the 3000 officers and men of the *Guadalcanal*. The hangar deck was jammed for a hit film that night. Up front near the screen were several rows of wardroom chairs for the officers, with a special section in the center for the Captain, Admiral, and senior officers. Behind them were the chiefs and then row after row of mess benches brought up from the deck below, benches designed to seat six but each accommodating ten tonight. There were not nearly enough benches, so sailors were standing six deep all around the sides and back of the center hanger bay. The great I beams that run athwartships under the flight deck were festooned with sailors sitting on the flanges with their feet hanging down. Everyone was jammed in like sardines and no one could have left early that night even if he had wanted to.

Soon after the picture began the sound track petered out and became almost inaudible until the stamping, whistling, and ribald yelling stirred the operator into readjusting the volume. Then after a brief interval the loudspeakers erupted in a blast that almost blew the flight deck off. This was repeated a number of times, and prompted the Captain to inform the Executive Officer somewhat crisply that in a crew of several thousand men he ought to be able to find *somebody* who knew how to operate a movie machine. The Exec assured the Captain he would look into the matter first thing in the morning.

So far so good. Ensign Wigglesworth's plan to get Joe Bluberry's job back for him was working to perfection. The part designed to get him off the hook for busting the operator in the nose had not come to a head yet.

Standing on a beam behind the projection booth, Joe Bluberry and a couple of his pals were having the time of their lives playing with the volume control. After about twenty minutes, Joe lit a cigarette and said to his pals, "Watch this now. I'm going to stick this under that thermostat in there, drown that wise s.o.b. out with the sprinkler and bust up the show."

One of his pals, who knew a little more about the hangar deck sprinkler system than Joe did, looked at him in amazement for a moment with his eyes popping out. "Yeah-h-h-h," he said, "you'll bust up the show all right! I wouldn't do it if I were you. . . . So long, pal. I'm gettin' out of here." (NOTE: Whether Ensign Wigglesworth knew as much about the *Guadalcanal*'s sprinkler system as Joe's pal did, present deponent knoweth not.)

Joe stuck the lighted cigarette on the end of his whip antenna and carefully maneuvered it under the thermostat.

(It should be noted, at this point in our story, that when fire breaks out on the hangar deck of a big carrier you can't afford to fool around with it. You have to clobber the blaze quickly with plenty of water. "Sprinkler" system is really a misnomer for the fire-fighting equipment. "Flooding" system would be more accurate.)

When Joe maneuvered that cigarette under the thermostat, the Good Guys were in hot pursuit of the Bad Guys on the screen, to the noisy delight of the assembled sailors. Seconds later, after the cigarette had boosted the temperature enough, the thermostat closed an electric contact and a carefully predetermined chain of events began. It was like the cascade of events in the great power blackout in New York. Electric current shot through the circuit and actuated not just the solenoid in the movie booth but also a dozen others which tripped relays which started small motors which opened valves and spewed tons of salt water all over the center bay of the hangar deck. Disaster struck the crew of the *Guadalcanal* that night suddenly and without warning; and pandemonium broke loose.

It is a historical fact that there has never been a panic on board a U.S. naval vessel. True, there was some confusion on the *Maine* when she blew up in Havana; the crew of the *Oklahoma* were a bit upset when she capsized at Pearl Harbor; and things got a little out of hand when the *Franklin* was blazing from stem to stern and her own rockets were making a shambles of the hangar deck. Precise military drill procedure was not followed at all times while these things were happening. But there was no panic.

Nor was there any on the *Guadalcanal* the Night of the Deluge. There was a certain amount of yelling and shoving. The usual custom of letting officers leave the movie area first while the crew stands fast was not observed that night. The stricken area was evacuated by all hands with great speed. A certain number of wardroom chairs and mess benches got smashed up and had to be thrown overboard next day. Some heads were cracked and a number of ribs got broken.

But there was no panic. Matter of fact, as the Captain pointed out in his report of the incident, the damage-control party got the water turned off in half a minute, by which time all personnel had evacuated the affected area.

It didn't take the fire marshal and damage-control officer long after the water had been turned off to locate the active thermostat in the movie booth. When they found a burned-out cigarette stub sitting just beneath it, they both toyed seriously with the idea of securing an anchor around the operator's neck and heaving him overboard. The indignant protests of the operator were futile in the face of this damning evidence. He was seized roughly by the Master-at-Arms, dragged down below, and hurled into the brig. Matter of fact, he was glad to be put behind bars by the time they got to the brig, because on the way there plenty of dripping sailors offered to lynch him if the MAA would turn him loose.

Soon after the great exodus, Joe crept into the crew's bunkroom where his rack adjoined those of his pals who had been helping him at the movie booth. "Boy oh boy! You really fixed him up, didn't you?" said one of them, as Joe slid into his bunk. "He won't give you no more trouble in the chow line the rest of this cruise."

"I guess not," said Joe soberly.

"I like to busted a gut laughing," said his pal, "when I seen the Captain and the Admiral and all them officers jump up and start running. All the earbanging that movie operator's been doing ain't gonna pull him out of this jam."

"I guess not," said Joe; "but I'm afraid we're in trouble too."

"How come?" asked his pal. "We're just as clean as a couple of plaster saints. Nobody seen us up there."

"I know," said Joe; "but what do you think they will do to that movie operator? Do you think they'll bust him?"

"Hell, compared to the other things they'll do busting him ain't even a fart in a teapot. They'll throw the book at him. He'll get a general court, they'll bust him clear down to Wave Third Class and send him to Portsmouth until he's eligible to retire on thirty years."

"But that ain't right," said Joe; "they can't do that."

"You just watch and see if they can't," observed his pal.

"But we can't let them do it," said Joe.

"What do you think we can do about it? All the lawyers in the United States couldn't beat the rap for that guy now. He's just *had* it, that's all."

"*We* gotta take the rap," said Joe.

"What," asked his pal incredulously, "are you *crazy?* . . . And where do you get that *we* stuff anyway? Leave me out of this deal, brother. If you wanta take the rap that's your funeral. After all, I didn't have nothin' to do with it . . . you remember I *told* you you'd better lay off that thermostat."

"Okay," said Joe; "I'll leave you out. But if he gets a court I'm going to spill the beans. I wouldn't do a trick like that even to a Marine."

Next morning Bluberry came around to the personnel office to see Mr. Wigglesworth.

"Good morning, Bluberry," said Willy. "I spoke to the Chief Master at Arms this morning and he's going to withdraw that report against you for socking the movie operator; in fact, he said he'd like to bust him in the nose himself. So that's all fixed up now. If anything else comes up that I can help you out in, don't hesitate to call on me."

"Sir," said Joe, "I'm going to have to go to the Captain and tell him what really happened."

Willy looked at him in amazement, and then said, "Don't you do any such a thing! You'll never make chief that way! Why should you want to do a thing like that?"

"Because otherwise that movie operator will get crucified for something he didn't do."

"Well, now, that's just the way it goes in this Navy sometimes," said Willy. "Sometimes you get a medal when you don't deserve it. Sometimes you get hung on a bum rap. It's the same way in the Army—and everywhere else on this earth for that matter. I thought you said this guy was an earbanger. He prob'ly should of been hung for something else long ago."

"That's right, he *is*," said Willy; "but I just ain't going to let him get hung for something *I* did. I'm not built that way."

"Well, now, look, Bluberry," said Willy, "that's just a weakness of character that you *can* correct if you try hard enough. After all, it isn't your fault if you were brought up that way. But you can overcome it. And, besides, all *you* did was to carry out the advice I gave you. *I'm* the one who should have a guilty conscience—not you."

"Do you want to tell the Captain it was your idea, sir?" asked Bluberry.

"No, indeed," said Willy, "I d'ruther not! But if you're going to try to make a martyr out of yourself, maybe I'll have to."

"Why would *you* hafta do it? You just got through telling me I shouldn't."

"That's different," said Willy. "You prob'ly wouldn't understand, but sometimes officers have to do crazy things when their men are too dumb to help themselves."

The call to flight quarters interrupted this dissertation on ethics and Joe had to beat it up on deck and get his plane ready for the morning's operations.

On deck Joe climbed into the radar operator's cockpit of his plane and began a methodical check of all the switches, dials, and circuit breakers in the compartment. This compartment, located in the tail of the plane just aft of the pilot's cockpit, has no internal access to the cockpit. Carrier planes are small, and in the Douglas Skyraider the radarman gets in and out of his cubbyhole through a door in the side of the tail. He sits there watching his instruments, only a foot or so behind the pilot's back, and can peek around the corners of the pilot's seat and see part of the instrument panel. He can reach one arm around the side of the seat to hand the pilot a cigarette but he can't get into the cockpit.

After everything was squared away back aft, Joe climbed out of the tail, clambered up on the wing and got into the cockpit to adjust and test the automatic pilot.

When Lieutenant Potter came up to man the plane and get ready for the takeoff, Joe solicitously helped him get into the cockpit and adjust his shoulder harness.

"Good morning, Lieutenant," said Joe. "How's your head this morning? I hear you got quite a bump yesterday."

"It's okay, I guess," said Lieutenant Potter. "Keep that head of yours working this morning and don't give me any more bum steers."

"I won't, sir," promised Joe, as he jumped off the wing and crawled back into his cubbyhole.

So Joe and the Lieutenant took off into the wild blue yonder for what was scheduled to be a 4-hour flight.

One hour after takeoff the following message from Lieutenant Potter boomed in over the loudspeaker in *Guadalcanal* Combat Information Center:

"*Guadalcanal*, this is Four Sail One. I'm turning back. I will have to land as soon as I get there. Over."

"Four Sail One, this is *Guadalcanal*. Roger. What's the trouble?"

"This is Four Sail One. I don't know. Wait."

Combat Information Center phoned this news up to the bridge, and the flight deck was alerted for a deferred emergency landing.

A few minutes later Lieutenant Potter came through again: "*Guadalcanal* this is Four Sail One. I'm sick. I'm passing out. I'm putting plane on autopilot."

Guadalcanal's No. 1 fighter director barked at the radio direction finder, "Get on that transmission! Get a bearing!" Then at the radar operators, "Stand by to clamp on to this bearing!" Then into his transmitter, "Keep talking, Four Sail One, so we can get a bearing! Give us a short count!"

No answer from Four Sail One.

Meantime the Combat Information Center team hastily checked the flight schedule and determined that Four Sail One, accompanied by Four Sail Two, had been briefed to operate 200 miles northeast.

"*Guadalcanal* to Four Sail Two. Are you in company with Four Sail One?"

"Negative," the chilling answer came back. "He went down into the overcast five minutes ago and I lost him."

"Okay," said the Combat Information Center officer to his helpers. "Get a bearing on Four Sail Two. That will give us the general area. Plot everything around there and start eliminating."

He called the bridge and passed the word up: "Pilot of Four Sail One reported he was passing out. Estimate he is to northeast, within 150 miles. No radio bearings or radar fixes yet."

On the bridge the Captain changed course to northeast, bent on thirty knots, and said to the air officer, "Get four radar planes ready right away for a search mission. Have your helicopter ready to go on short notice."

As the *Guadalcanal* swung around to the northeast, the following came in: "This is Four Sail One, radar operator Bluberry speaking. Stand by for short count. One . . . two . . . three . . . four . . . five . . . five . . . four . . . three . . . two . . . one. How do you hear? Over."

The direction-finder operator announced, "Okay. I've got him bearing zero-four-six degrees. Got a good sharp cut on him."

"Got anything out there, radar?" asked the Combat Information Center officer.

"Yes, sir; we've got two plots; one circling at 110 miles, one coming straight in at eighty."

"*Guadalcanal* to Four Sail One. Is your pilot okay now?"

"Negative. He is slumped over on one side of the cockpit and appears to be passed out. I reached around, got hold of his microphone and pulled the cord back into the radar compartment. We are flying on autopilot now, and seem to be okay so far."

"Roger, Four Sail One. We have two plots on our radar scope. Are you flying straight or circling?"

"I can't tell. We are in an overcast and I can't see a thing outside. I can't see the compass or flight instruments from back here. Over."

"*Guadalcanal* to Four Sail Two. What are you doing now?"

"*Guadalcanal*, this is Four Sail Two. I'm flying directly back to ship on course 225, at angels twenty, estimated distance eighty miles. Over."

"Roger. Four Sail Two, we have you on our radar bearing zero-four-zero, distance seventy miles. Four Sail One is circling forty miles northeast of you. Go back and stand by."

"This is Four Sail Two. Roger. Wilco. You will have to coach me because he is down in the overcast."

On the bridge of the *Guadalcanal* a hurried conference was in progress. The Captain said, "He's got three more hours of gas left. If he keeps circling we can be under him in three hours. We can spread our destroyers out in a big circle, have the helicopters in the air, and maybe, when he runs out of gas and spins in, we can get to the spot in time to pull him out."

"That's right," said the air officer. "He might not spin in. That autopilot will hold the nose on the horizon, and depending on just how the plane is balanced, he may spiral down instead of spinning."

"There's about thirty knots of wind blowing, so a lot will depend on whether he hits heading into the wind or downwind."

"Meantime we've got to get that radar operator out of there. As soon as we get over to where he is circling, we'll have him bail out. The helicopter ought to be able to spot him coming down in a chute and fish him out of the water without any trouble at all."

Meanwhile, in the radar operator's compartment of Four Sail One, Joe Bluberry was sizing up his situation too. He could see the Lieutenant's head slumped over on the side of the cockpit, and could see that he was still breathing, although apparently out cold. Joe knew that as long as the autopilot was working he was in no immediate danger, and that they had several hours' gas left.

Soon came a message from the *Guadalcanal*. "To radar operator of Four Sail One. We have you on our scopes at 100 miles. You are flying in a five-mile circle and are perfectly safe as long as the autopilot works. We are heading your way and will be in your area in about two and one half hours. When we get there we will have you bail out and will pick you up. Meantime, take it easy and don't get excited."

In the next two and one half hours, while the task group raced northeast, Joe did some figuring and a little experimenting. He could see the controls of the autopilot up in the cockpit, even though he couldn't reach them. Lieutenant Potter had set the bank knob for a standard-rate turn to the left and the elevator knob for level flight. Joe arrived at the same conclusion that the conference on the bridge had reached—namely, that the plane might not spin when it ran out of gas, and that a lot depended on whether the plane hit the water heading into the wind.

Joe also found that by using a short length of spare whip antenna he could reach the bank-control knob. By twisting that knob a quarter turn to the right he knew he could level the wings, and thus set the autopilot for straight flight. As always, he had a big wad of gum in his mouth.

Just before noon the task group arrived under the spot where the radarscopes showed Four Sail One to be circling in the clouds. The *Guadalcanal* took station in the center of the formation several miles downwind of this spot, with the destroyers spread out in a 10-mile circle around her. Three helicopters were in the air and all lookouts in the fleet trained their glasses aloft to watch for a parachute emerging from the clouds. The task group turned downwind so as to stay under the plane until its engine quit, and word went out from the Combat Information Center: "*Guadalcanal* to Four Sail One. We are directly under you now, all set for you to jump. The instant your feet touch the water, slide out of your parachute harness, inflate your Mae West, and we will pick you up right away. Okay now. Bail out."

Out of the squawk boxes in Combat Information Center came the startling answer: "*Guadalcanal*, this is Four Sail One. Radarman Bluberry speaking. Negative. I'm sticking with the plane."

Everyone in the Combat Information Center goggled for a moment, and then the fighter director broadcast: "Don't get scared, Bluberry. There's no danger at all. The whole task group is right under you. We have three helicopters in the air; we will have you out of the water almost as soon as you hit. Just open the door and bail out."

"This is Four Sail One," said an obviously cool and unflustered voice; "I ain't scared, and I ain't jumping; I'm riding this plane down."

This unforeseen development made no sense to anyone in Combat Information Center. Neither there nor on the bridge could anyone see how Bluberry could do any good by riding the plane down. If he jumped, his chances of coming through O.K. were a thousand to one. If he stayed with the plane, they weren't much better than fifty-fifty.

Soon another voice from *Guadalcanal* came on the air: "Four Sail One, this is the Captain speaking. Do as you are told. That is an order. Bail out."

Back came the cool and positive reply: "Captain, sir, negative. I won't do it. I think when we run out of gas I can straighten this plane out and make it hit the water heading into the wind. I'm going to ride her down and maybe she will float long enough for me to pull the Lieutenant out of the cockpit after we hit."

The tense group in Combat Information Center mulled this one over incredulously. "Impossible" was the general consensus, but the fighter director officer said, "Maybe. All the control cables run through the radar operator's compartment. If he knows which ones are the ailerons, and if he pulls hard enough on the right one, at exactly the right time, he might overpower the autopilot and straighten the plane out. If he bails out, the plane might sink before we can get to it and pull the Lieutenant out. The odds are pretty long against this deal, but it isn't impossible."

This conference was interrupted by another message from aloft: "This is Four Sail One. I see other planes all around me on my radarscope now. When our engine quits and we spiral down out of the clouds, somebody is bound to see me. Let the first guy that sees me sing out on the radio and tell me when the plane is headed into the wind. I'll try to level the wings and hold them that way until we hit the water. Acknowledge. Over."

"This is *Guadalcanal*. Roger your last message. We advise you to bail out. If you refuse, we will do the best we can to help you."

While the circle of eyes in the Combat Information Center fixed on the fighter director began to light up with gleams of admiration, the fighter director officer muttered huskily, "That kid has a lot more guts than he has good sense."

Half a minute later: "*Guadalcanal*, this is Four Sail One. Engine just quit. Stand by."

Presently the squawk box in the Combat Information Center said: "Four Sail One is okay so far. . . . We are still in the clouds, but I think we have slowed down as much as we are going to and she hasn't spun yet . . . I think the autopilot may hold her. . . . If the cloud base is still at 3000 feet, we should be breaking out any minute now."

A dozen lookouts sighted the stricken plane as soon as she broke out below the overcast. Another plane only a quarter of a mile away came on the air immediately with: "Four Sail One, I have you in sight. You are in a normal left spiral and are headed nearly downwind now. Keep coming to the left and I'll let you know when you are in the wind. . . . Ninety degrees to go . . . forty-five degrees . . . twenty degrees . . . stand by . . . Bring her out."

While all hands in the task group watched prayerfully from below, Joe reached forward with his magic gum-tipped whip, gave the bank-control knob a flip into the straight-flight position and brought the plane into a normal glide headed smack into the wind.

Heading into a 30-knot wind, the bump when the plane hit the water was no worse than a hard landing on the *Guadalcanal*. Before the splash had subsided, Joe tore the door off his cubbyhole, scrambled up on the wing and pried the cockpit hood loose. He had the unconscious Lieutenant out of there half a minute before the plane sank, and in another minute a helicopter snatched them both out of the water and headed for the *Guadalcanal*.

As soon as they touched down on deck, Lieutenant Potter was hustled down to sick bay, where he came to before long. "Creeping concussive cranial thrombosis" was the doctor's diagnosis of what had happened, meaning delayed reaction from that bump on the head. He would be O.K. again in a couple of days.

Meanwhile, Joe was escorted up to the bridge, where a large delegation of officers, including the Admiral, was waiting for him. As he came on the bridge the Captain stuck out his hand to him and said, "Congratulations, my lad. That was a very brave thing you did this morning. I'm promoting you to radarman second class right here and now." So saying, he handed Joe a second-class rating badge and pumped his hand up and down while everyone on the bridge beamed approval. "I consider," continued the Captain, "that your conduct was in accordance with the best traditions of the U.S. Navy."

"Aye aye, sir," said Joe, "that is . . . I mean . . . aw, heck, sir. It wasn't nothing much."

"The hell it wasn't," said the Captain. "How in the world did you do it, anyway?"

"Well, sir, you see, sir, I done it the same way I fouled up the volume at the movies the other night, sir."

"Wh-wh-what did you say?" gasped the Captain as the jaws of all the spectators popped open.

So then the whole story came bubbling out; that is, all of it except Ensign Wigglesworth's part in it. Joe explained how he had leveled out that plane using the whip antenna with a piece of gum on the end of it the same as he had fiddled with the volume control at the movies. He made a clean breast of the whole awful business including the cigarette under the thermostat. He stated that, although he still thought he had a right to get even with the movie operator for taking his place in the chow line, he couldn't just keep quiet and let him go to jail for it.

By the time he had finished, faces which had assumed a grim set when the Deluge was first mentioned had softened tolerantly. It was obviously unthinkable to just sweep that flood under the rug and forget it. But the expression on all faces, even of those who were suffering from cracked ribs, indicated that in this case justice could be tempered with mercy. All eyes now turned to the Captain, curious as to how the Old Man would handle this unheard-of curve ball.

The Captain deliberated for a decent interval, doing his best to screw his face up into a stern expression, then cleared his throat, and said, "Bluberry, for what you did the other night you ought to be flogged, keelhauled, and hung at the yardarm."

"Yessir," said Joe.

"But I'm going to let you off with a warning," said the Captain. "You might call it a 'suspended' sentence. If you ever monkey with a thermostat again on this ship *you* will be suspended, by the neck, from the yardarm."

"Aye aye, sir," said Joe.

"And now getting back to that business this morning. The promotion to second class still stands; and I'm recommending you for an Air Medal."

Later that morning Ensign Wigglesworth met the squadron executive officer on deck. "Mr. Wigglesworth," said the exec, "what did you do about that Bluberry case that I mentioned to you yesterday?"

"It's all taken care of, sir," said Willy, "and the charges against him have been dropped."

"Good work, Wigglesworth," said the exec; "I'm glad to see a young officer take hold the way you have."

CHAPTER SEVEN

Very Deep Stuff

WHEN THE *Guadalcanal* sailed out the Golden Gate, it left Admiral Bates muttering in his beer about the way he had been sucked in on the intercept exercise. The Admiral naturally had to devote some of his attention to plans for defending the United States against foreign aggression and stuff like that there, but his main interest in life at this time was squaring accounts with Admiral Day.

While Bates was still sizzling, the new Polaris submarine USS *Lafayette* came into San Francisco on her shakedown cruise. When her skipper, Commander Hanks, called to pay his respects on Admiral Bates, he invited the Admiral to take a short cruise at sea in the *Lafayette*. Bates gladly accepted this chance to make a trip at sea, get a little salt air in his lungs, and have a look at this latest addition to the modern Navy. Next day the *Lafayette* put to sea with the Admiral to show him what she could do.

As the skipper showed the Admiral around, the old sea dog was completely flabbergasted. A new Navy had been born since he had last set foot on a sub twenty years before. The old-time pig boats were small craft of about 1500 tons, jammed with machinery so that there was barely room enough left for the crew. They were run by diesel engines, but had electric motors driven from a huge storage battery to enable them to run submerged. They were really surface vessels that had the ability to submerge to a depth of a few hundred feet and operate there at slow speed as long as the charge in the battery lasted. They could make twenty knots on the surface, but only five or six submerged, and they couldn't stay submerged more than about twenty-four hours.

The *Lafayette* was as different from the old pig boats as the *Missouri* was from John Paul Jones' *Bonhomme Richard*. She displaced 8000 tons, more than the light cruisers of the Admiral's younger days. The inside was like that of the Super Chief with air conditioning throughout, indirect lighting, pastel-colored bulkheads, and overstuffed furniture. She had all the comforts of home except wall-to-wall carpeting and female companionship. The old-time submariners never had it so good.

Her atomic power plant used no oil or air, so she could stay submerged for months, and was designed to operate that way rather than on the surface. She was perfectly comfortable at 1000 feet depth, and could go faster down there than she could on the surface. Her endurance was limited only by her food supply, and even with the crew eating high on the hog it was good for ninety days.

Her armament was sixteen huge Polaris rockets with a range of around 2000 miles, which could be fired while she was still submerged and wreak greater havoc than all the bombs dropped by both sides in World War II.

As Commander Hanks showed the Admiral around explaining all this, the Admiral's most frequent comment was "Well, I'll be damned."

The control room, corresponding to the bridge of a surface ship, was of particular interest to the Admiral. This is more like the switchboard of a big powerhouse than the bridge of a ship. The compartment is packed with an array of gauges, dials, instruments, warning lights, switches, valves, interlocks, and circuit breakers. Armored cables and insulated pipes run everywhere. About the only instrument the Admiral could recognize was the clock.

The Captain put his hand on the shoulder of a young sailor in a bucket seat with his feet on a pair of rudder pedals, holding a control stick between his knees. "This is the helmsman, Admiral," he said. "Actually, he flies this ship through the water with that stick the same way a pilot flies an airplane. He steers with the rudder pedals. Although you can't see it when we are submerged, he banks when he makes a turn, the same way an airplane does. That instrument right in front of him is an airplane's turn and bank indicator. He can make small corrections in depth with his control stick, and this other lad on the hand wheels over here moves the big diving planes, which correspond roughly to the horizontal stabilizer on an airplane. The chief over there watches the trim and balance of the boat and shifts ballast if necessary to keep her in trim if a large number of men move forward or aft—and also when we fire rockets. That control board of his shows him just how much water he has in all tanks and whether the boat is in positive or negative buoyancy."

"Uh huh," observed the Admiral.

"The officer of the deck stands his watch here and everything going on inside the boat is right at his fingertips on this panel. There's the gyrocompass—the speed indicator—depth gauge—condition of ballast tanks—the Christmas tree. . . . Now over on the other side we have the display of what is going on around us on the outside."

Taking the Admiral by the arm, he led him over to an array of electronic tubes. "This one is the fathometer that tells us how far we are from the bottom. This one is the search sonar that shows us what's on the surface all around us. And over here is a special ahead-looking sonar that shows us what's ahead of us on our same level. This is very important, because a lot of mountain peaks on the sea bottom don't show on the present-day charts that were made for surface vessels. Every now and then when we're running deep we find one of these peaks with that sonar set . . . which is a much better way of finding it than running into it!"

"Um," agreed the Admiral.

Indicating another scope, the Captain continued: "This is a special set we use for navigating under the ice. This is what the *Nautilus* used when she went to the North Pole. It bounces echoes off the bottom of the ice sheet and tells us how far below it the top of our scope is. When you're running deep and there's no ice around, this one gives you a clear picture of any ships directly above you for about a mile around. . . . And over here we have our passive listening arrays. We run very quietly ourselves and our underwater microphones can often pick up the noises from ships' propellers long before our sonar can get an echo from the ship it self. We pick up lots of other noises, too: the ocean is full of strange sounds from fish, waves, and other sources we don't understand yet." Tapping the operator on the shoulder, he said, "Ya hearing anything now, son?"

"Yessir," said the lad, "a school of propoises just discovered us."

"Put it on the loudspeaker," said the Captain.

The lad threw a switch, and the control room immediately sounded like feeding time in the bird house at the zoo. Porpoises are very curious and gabby animals. They were whistling and yelling at each other in great excitement. You could easily translate some squeals as "Hey, come over here and look what I found" and others as saying, "Holy cow, what a big son of a bitch" and others as "Hey, ma, what's that?"

The Admiral's eyes and mouth popped open in pleased amazement. "Can we see anything through the periscope now?" he asked.

The captain glanced at the depth gauge and said, "Nossir. Too deep now. Almost 700 feet. We hardly ever use the periscope on these kinds of boats anyway, because we usually run deep . . . and with all this sonar and listening gear we get just as good a picture of what's going on on the surface as we would through the scope. . . . We can even come pretty close to telling, after a little practice, whether a blip on the scope is a tanker, a tramp, a liner, or a warship, just from the size of the blip and the sound of her screws."

"Don't you have to come up every now and then and surface, or at least stick your scope up to have a look at the stars and check your position?" asked the Admiral.

"No, sir," said the skipper. "Our inertial navigation system over here takes care of that for us. It has inputs from the gyrocompass and propeller shafts, and it has delicate accelerometers which measure the accelerations on three sets of axes which are gyro-stabilized with respect to astral space and aren't even affected by the revolution of the earth. It integrates these accelerations twice, feeds the result into a computer. The computer gives you your latitude and longitude corrected for all such things as unknown currents, erratic steering, variable engine speed, and so forth. It's accurate to within a few hundred yards . . . has to be so we can shoot our missiles accurately."

"Well, I'll be gahdam," observed the Admiral. "But you have to come up every now and then to use your radio, don't you?"

"Nossir. We send and receive completely submerged. We couldn't keep our subs on station in the Arctic off Murmansk if they had to surface. They stay down all the time."

"We have a ship ten miles ahead on opposite course, sir," reported the OOD. "Think she's a single-screw merchant vessel."

"Very well," said the skipper. "Lemme show you what you can do with this submarine, Admiral. I'm going to take station on that ship and stay right under her for a while." Turning to the OOD, he said, "I've got her, son; give me a running plot of that ship so I can slide in under her."

"Aye aye, sir," said the Lieutenant, seating himself at one of the sonarscopes and picking up a grease pencil. "Bearing 015, distance five miles . . . I'll give you her course and speed in a minute."

A sailor took the seat next to him at the ice sonar, adjusted the headphones, and flipped the switches to warm up the set that would give them the overhead picture.

Watching the scope over the OOD's shoulder while the Lieutenant plotted the track of the approaching ship on the scope with his grease pencil, the skipper swerved out a little to give himself room for a 180° turn. He let the range close until the target was about two miles away and broad off his bow. Then, "Right full rudder," he said, and the helmsman shoved his rudder pedal and banked with his control stick into a tight turn. The only way you could tell that everybody was now standing at a 30° angle to the vertical instead of straight up was by looking at the turn and bank indicator.

Soon the lad on the ice-scope sang out, "Target on scope, sir," and the skipper shifted his attention to the overhead scope.

"Rudder amidships," said the skipper, "steady on course 270."

"Rudder amidships. Steady on course 270," repeated the helmsman.

A few more orders to the helm and a couple to the engines brought the blip in the ice-scope to the center and held it there. "There she is, Admiral," said the skipper; "directly above us and on same course. . . . Cut the hydrophones in on the loud-speaker," he added.

The man on the hydrophones flipped a switch and the loudspeakers picked up the "thrum thum thum" of a three-bladed propeller directly overhead.

"She's making 120 rpm, Admiral," said the Captain, glancing at his wristwatch. "Probably a 5000-ton tramp coming in from Hono-lulu. Wouldn't he be surprised if *he* knew what was sitting right under him now."

"Could you do this to one of our big carriers?" asked the Ad-miral, beginning to get a strange gleam in his eye.

"Sure," said the skipper. "No trouble at all."

"A carrier can make a lot more speed than that tramp steamer," observed the Admiral.

"So can we, sir," said the skipper. "We can keep up with any carrier. And if she runs at high speed, she'll soon have to refuel. We don't."

"Could you stay under her if she was squirming around trying to shake you off?"

"No strain," said the skipper. "We can turn much sharper than she can. You saw how easy it was to slip in under that tramp when she was on opposite course."

By this time the gleam in the Admiral's eye was getting incan-descent. "Let's go up to your cabin, son; I want to discuss some-thing with you."

"Aye, aye, sir!" said the skipper. "Mr. Bailey," he said to the OOD. "She's all yours. Head south and hold this course and speed till further orders."

Up in the cabin the Admiral said, "Captain, I believe you are scheduled to go to Honolulu next week."

"Yessir. We sail next Monday."

"Hmmmm . . ." said the Admiral. "Admiral Day is at sea now

but he's coming back in for the weekend and he is sailing Tuesday for Honolulu in the *Guadalcanal* with a task group of four cruisers and ten destroyers."

"Yessir."

"What are you supposed to do on the way to Honolulu?"

"Nothing has been prescribed for us, sir. This is our shake-down cruise and I can more or less write my own ticket."

"Will you be running surfaced or submerged?"

"Submerged. These boats normally run that way. We're more at home below than on the surface."

"Hah! That's fine," said the Admiral. "How would you like to join Admiral Day's task group unbeknownst to anybody in it, escort them all the way to Honolulu, keeping me informed as to what they are doing?"

Now it was the Captain's turn to get a gleam in his eyes. "You mean sneak in under them like we just did with that tramp and stay there?" he asked.

"That's exactly what I mean," said Admiral Bates.

"Sure. We can do that. No strain at all," said the skipper.

"They will be conducting flight operations, turning into the wind every now and then to launch and land, and changing speed. You sure you will be able to stay with them?"

"We'll stay with him like a barnacle," said Commander Hanks confidently. "It's no more difficult than it will be for his destroyers to keep station on him up on the surface."

"And I'd want you to send me a position report on him twice a day and report whenever he changed course or speed."

"No problem," said the skipper.

"There's just one trouble about this thing," said the Admiral. "I don't want him to know you are down there. How are you going to sneak under him without one of those destroyers in his screen spotting you?"

"Hmmmm," said the skipper. "That *is* a problem. Those tin cans have got almost as good sonar as we have these days. If we were lucky enough to find a thermal layer around 200 feet we could hide under that and fox them . . . but you can't depend on that. . . . hmmmmm. How much water does he draw, Admiral?"

"Thirty-five feet."

"Well, that's too deep for the main ship channel across the bar. That means he will leave Frisco by the Bonita Channel, doesn't it? So-o-o- . . . Lemme see something." The skipper consulted the chart lying on his desk. "Hmmmm," he said, putting his finger on the chart a few miles off the end of the channel. "Here's the hundred-fathom curve with sandy, level bottom. He'll go right over this spot getting his formation squared away for a great circle course to Honolulu. We could lie on the bottom here till he comes along, then lift off and stay under him. Nobody will have any idea we are there."

"Young man," said the Admiral, "I consider you to be one of the best naval tacticians since John Paul Jones."

"Thank you, sir," said Commander Hanks.

That Saturday night when the task group was in port for the weekend, Admirals Bates and Day sat at a table in the officers' club at Treasure Island, bringing each other up to date on the current scandals in Washington. All angles of the Billy Sol Estes and Bobby Baker cases, the TFX contract, and Mr. McNamara's refusal to authorize atomic power for the new carrier were duly examined and disapproved of.

Came a lull in the conversation, and the Bugler said, "Windy old boy . . . I must admit you really pulled the wool over my eyes on that last exercise. If it had happened to anyone else I would have thought it was funny."

"Well, that's the way it goes," said Admiral Day philosophically. "Sometimes a shenanigan works and sometimes it blows up in your face. I thought that one *was* pretty good though."

"My boys feel pretty bad about it," said the Bugler, "and they want to show CINCPAC they're not as bad as they looked on that exercise."

"Well, after all," said Windy smugly, "you can't blame them for that. How are they going to do it?"

"I've told CINCPAC I'm going to track you all the way out to Honolulu next week and keep him accurately informed of everything you do."

"Well now, that's fine," said Windy. "Your boys need the practice and it will give my controller's pilots some good intercept training, too. How far out do you want to keep the exercise going?"

"All the way to Honolulu."

"Hmmmm. That's 2500 miles." Admiral Day did a little mental arithmetic on the endurance of a patrol plane and said, "That will take a lot of planes to do the job. You gonna have 'em land in Hawaii to refuel?"

"None of my planes will land in Hawaii."

"Hunh. You gonna call in SAC to help you?"

"I wouldn't think of such a thing," said Bates indignantly.

"Well," said Day, "it will be a big operation before you get through with it. But of course it isn't much of a job to track us in a peacetime exercise. In wartime we would shoot your boys down before they ever saw our ships."

"My pilots will all be instructed to return to base if they are intercepted and I'll ground the plane for the rest of the exercise as if it had been shot down."

"Say, what kind of whisky have you been drinking?" demanded Day. "There aren't enough planes in the whole Navy to keep that kind of a show going."

"That's what *you* think," said the Bugler. "Your interceptors may not be as good as you think they are. There's a lot of air space to search up there for snoopers."

"Don't be ridiculous," said Day. "With the search radars on our cans and cruisers and our AEW planes, we can spot anything that comes within a couple of hundred miles of us. My Banshees can intercept it and knock it down within ten minutes of the time we get it on our radars, night or day. In wartime your patrol planes would be clay pigeons."

"Wanna bet we can't do it?" asked Bates.

"I'd be ashamed to take your money."

"You *wouldn't* take it, so don't lose any sleep over that. But I'll bet you my Army-Navy game tickets on it."

"Let's get this straight so there won't be any argument about it afterwards. You say you're going to track me all the way from here to Hawaii, reporting my position twice a day to CINCPAC."

"That's right."

"And any time my fighters intercept one of your planes it will turn around, go home, and take no further part in the exercise?"

"Yup."

"I suppose your gunners will just claim they are shooting *my* boys down and will keep boring in after we intercept them?"

"Don't worry about that. Any plane you intercept will turn around immediately. There will be no funny business about it."

"And how accurate are these position reports going to be? If you're intercepted by fighters, you know there's a carrier somewhere in the same ocean but you got to pinpoint us better than that."

"I'll report your position as accurately as you'll know it yourself," said the Bugler.

"Now I know you're balmy," said Day. "Your patrol planes can't navigate that well."

"I'm offering to bet you four Army game tickets on the fifty-yard line I can do this."

"It's a bet," said Day, shoving his hand across the table.

"Bet," said the Bugler, grabbing the hand.

On the way back to the ship that night Admiral Day shook his head sadly over the way his lifelong friend and rival was beginning to lose his grip. "Of course, he never was a John Paul Jones or a Horatio Nelson," he mused to himself; "but he used to be reasonably smart on routine things. . . . Oh, well . . . I guess we're all getting a little old and senile now."

At a staff conference in the Admiral's cabin next day, the chief of staff outlined the work he had planned for the task group on the way to Honolulu. "We have set up a program that will keep everybody busy," he said. "There will be flight operations day and night. The squadrons will shoot at towed sleeves, work with camera guns, and drop live bombs on raft targets. We will also tow sleeves for the Antiaircraft Batteries and let the cruisers have a crack at the rafts after the planes get through. There will be intercept exercises for the planes at night, and we'll make believe submarines are attacking the task group to give the destroyers a chance to drill on their antisubmarine tactics. It's all set up in the op order; we should get a lot of good training out of it, and everybody will be pretty busy."

When the COS had finished, Admiral Day said, "I've got a minor addition to make to your op order. Admiral Bates wants to exercise his planes in finding and tracking us. In fact, he has laid out a rather ambitious program for them to track us and report our position all the way to Honolulu. He has instructed his planes that they must turn around and go back to base whenever they are intercepted, and I want to be sure we spot their snoopers and intercept them before they get close enough to see any of our ships. I want all ships to keep their search radars alert, I want to keep early warning planes aloft, and I want four fighters fired up and ready on deck for intercept missions at all times. It should be fairly simple to intercept his patrol planes before they can plot our position accurately, and this job shouldn't interfere with the other drills you have laid out."

While this conference was in progress on the *Guadalcanal*, the *Lafayette* got underway and stood out through the Golden Gate, Hawaii bound, with a huge bone in her teeth. Her blunt nose, copied from the whale's, pushed up a great bow wave on the surface, but when submerged it gave her a streamlined shape that let her slip through the water much faster than she could on the surface. As she plowed out the channel, most of her 500-foot hull was awash, except for the big black "sail" amidships. Crowded into the little area in the top of the sail were the captain, navigator, and the lookouts. The ship being designed primarily to run submerged, the "bridge" area for surface cruising was little bigger than an oversized crow's-nest.

As they passed the entrance buoy at the end of the channel abeam the Captain yelled down the voice tube, "Stand by to dive." Warning howlers throughout the boat blared, everyone on the bridge plunged down the conning tower hatch, and the Captain took a last quick look around the horizon. Then he too went down the ladder, pulling the hatch shut behind him.

Before he got to the control room at the bottom, all diving stations were manned and reports were coming in from all through the ship: "Forward torpedo room ready," "Midship section ready," "Reactor room ready," and so on throughout the boat. The chief of the boat scanned the control board which showed the condition of all valves, hatches, and tanks, and watched the lights on the Christmas tree change from red to green as the hatches closed. When the tree was all green he reported to the exec, "Ready for diving, sir." The exec, who had been double-checking him, relayed the report to the skipper and the skipper said, "Take her down."

Except for the dials and gauges on the control board there was no way you could tell anything unusual was happening: she sank on an even keel, and you could hardly hear the tons of water pouring into the ballast tanks outside the pressure hull.

A sailor watching the depth gauge called out every 50-foot increase in depth, the boys on the trimming planes moved their wheels back and forth to hold the trim level, and the diving officer watched his board carefully. "Close all valves and vents," he said as they passed 100 feet.

"Steady her at 200," said the skipper.

"Steady at 200," repeated the diving officer.

It was all very businesslike and matter-of-fact, with no unnecessary chatter. But it would have been apparent to even the greenest observer that it was precisely done according to an exact routine, and that if any one man had started to make a booboo there were at least two others watching him like hawks who would have pounced on him and stopped it.

The skipper turned to the diving officer and said, "We're going to sit on the bottom here overnight, so I want slight negative buoyancy."

"Aye aye, sir," came the reply.

"Let's slow down now and scan the bottom carefully with our sonar and fathometer. I want to set her down on a level spot in about ninety fathoms."

The speed dropped down to bare steerageway. The ship sank slowly toward the bottom past 300, 400, 500 feet until the fathometer indicated only five fathoms below the keel.

"Let's keep her about this far off the bottom now and keep on going out till we get to the ninety-fathom curve. Then stop and ease her down on the bottom."

"Aye aye, sir," said the diving officer. The helmsman held his course, the lads on the diving planes kept the boat in trim, and she crept along gradually approaching the bottom, as the diving officer fiddled with his interior ballast tank, now letting in a little water, now blowing some out to bring her down slowly. When the depth gauge read 85 and the fathometer said 5 under the keel, he ordered, "All engines stop," and in a few minutes the *Lafayette* settled gently on the sandy bottom off the entrance of Bonita Channel.

"Okay," said the skipper. "We will sit here until tomorrow morning when the fleet sorties for Honolulu. I want to let the destroyers go over us and then to lift off when the carrier comes along. We're going to take station directly under her at 100 fathoms and stay there all the way to Honolulu."

Next morning bright and early a flotilla of minesweepers gave the Bonita Channel a thorough combing over, as they would have done in wartime, before any important task group would sortie from San Francisco. Of course their interest in what was on or anchored to the bottom only extended out to about the 30-fathom curve, so they turned back before they got to the *Lafayette*, with pennants flying from all their yardarms indicating "Channel clear, bon voyage."

Halfway back they met the ten destroyers coming out in column. The destroyers were also making believe this was a wartime sortie. At the end of the channel they fanned out and swept through a semicircular sector of twenty-mile radius pinging away with their sonars searching for any submarines that might be lurking out there waiting to torpedo the big ships. They would have found any that had been behaving the way submarines usually do behave—but, of course, not one that was lying doggo on the bottom in ninety fathoms!

Down on the bottom the *Lafayette* followed all this on their hydrophones and sonarscopes. The sweep wires towed by the minesweepers sang an unmistakable song as they cut through the water searching for mine mooring cables. The little craft were clearly visible on the *Lafayette*'s ice-scope as they passed overhead. When the destroyers came out, the thrashing of their four-bladed screws was audible on the hydrophones as soon as they cleared the Golden Gate, and the "ping-ping-ping" of their sonars filled the ocean with noise. They too passed in review overhead on the ice-scope. Next came the unmistakable screw noises of the heavy ships, and *Lafayette* lifted gradually off the bottom and began creeping ahead. The three cruisers appeared first in the scope and then came the big blip from the carrier. Watching the scope carefully, the skipper jockeyed his engine to keep the blip directly overhead and soon he was making fifteen knots on course west, 500 feet under *Guadalcanal*'s keel. The ice-scope showed a neat geometric pattern with the carrier in the center, the three cruisers in a V around her, and the destroyers in a bent semicircular screen ahead.

"Looks mighty pretty, doesn't it, Cap'n?" observed the exec.

"Yep," said the skipper; "I'll bet the Admiral gave 'em a 'well done' signal on that sortie."

That evening the *Lafayette*'s navigator consulted the dials on his computer and read the Latitude and Longitude as the ship's clock tolled eight bells. Then he wrote out a dispatch for the Captain to release: "From *Lafayette* to Com West Sea Frontier . . . 2000 position . . . Lat 39° 0 0 . . . Long 123° 10′ course 275, speed 17." The Captain scribbled his initials on it, gave it to the communications officer and said, "Squirt it out."

Ordinarily, to send a radio message of this kind would require transmitting for at least a few minutes. There are six bits of information in it, seventeen words, and to put it in Morse code takes about 500 dots and dashes. But on a squirt transmission you tape those dots and dashes and run the tape through a high-speed transmitter that spits the whole thing out in less than a second. To any snoopers listening in with a direction finder, the transmission is nothing but chirp that sounds more like static than a formal message, and is over too quickly to get a bearing even if you recognized it. The chirp goes on a high-speed tape at the receiving end, then the tape is slowed down and out comes the message in ordinary Morse code.

An hour later on the *Guadalcanal* the chief of staff handed Admiral Day Bugler Bates' dispatch to CINCPAC reporting the task group's position at 8 P.M. The dispatch had been sent in plain English on a circuit which the task group guarded and was addressed to them for "information." "They have our position pretty close, sir," said the COS, "and our course and speed, too."

"Humph," observed Admiral Day. "Knowing our time of departure and our destination, anybody could make an educated guess as to where we would be twelve hours later. Has he got any snoopers over us now?"

"Nossir," said the COS, "I just came from CIC. All the search radars in the task group have got clear scopes."

"Just to throw his estimates off a little," said the Admiral, "let's change course to the north by ninety degrees and hold it that way until sunrise."

"Aye aye, sir," said the COS. Soon a blinker signal went out from the flagship, lights winked all around the horizon as the task group acknowledged they understood, and then on the execute signal they all swung around to course north and readjusted the screen. The *Lafayette* didn't get the blinker signal, of course, but the change of course showed up right away on the ice-scope and she had no trouble keeping her "station."

Just before sunrise the next day, *Lafayette* squirted her next position report to Admiral Bates, he relayed it to CINCPAC, and at six that morning the COS handed it to Admiral Day. "They've still got us pegged," he said. "Position is accurate, and so are the course and speed. I've checked carefully with all our people and they say we've had clear radar screens all night. There have been no snoopers at any time."

"What the hell," said Admiral Day. "There's obviously a snooper up there somewhere. Build a fire under the task group skippers. Make 'em get out of their bunks and wake up their radar people. Send up some early warning planes and search around the task group to a range of 300 miles."

"Aye aye, sir," said the COS.

A sharp message went out to all captains telling them, in effect, to sound reveille in their Combat Information Centers and get the dopey radar operators on the job. Four early warning planes with huge radar dishes roared off from the *Guadalcanal* and climbed to 20,000 feet.

Half an hour later the squawk box in flag plot where Admiral Day was studying the chart announced, "AEW plane has bogey bearing east, 200 miles from task group, headed this way."

"Just like I thought," observed the Admiral; "there were snoopers up there all the time."

A moment later a great "WHOOM" on the flight deck indicated jet engines being lighted off, and the squawk box said, "Destroyers now have bogey on radar—altitude 30,000, coming this way."

"You see," said the Admiral to his COS. "You gotta ride herd on these skippers all the time. Otherwise they sit up in their sea cabins working crossword puzzles and everybody else on the ship goes to sleep."

Soon a group of six Banshee interceptors, led by LCDR Curly Cue, was flung off the catapults, joined up quickly in V formation, and disappeared to the east climbing with jets wide open.

"They're going up like homesick angels," observed the chief of staff as they faded from sight.

"Umph," observed Admiral Day. "Cut the controller circuit in on the squawk box so I can listen in on the intercept."

"Vector 090," said the squawk box. "Bogey is at 30,000 closing at 400 knots."

"Rajah," said Cue's voice. "Banshees climbing through 20,000, course 090."

A moment later a jubilant "Tallyho, Tallyho" came out of the squawk box, indicating that Cue had sighted the snooper. "We are deploying now for a split attack. Two sections whipsaw him from each side. I'll come in high out of the sun."

"Now we'll see," observed the Admiral, "whether Bugler's

planes turn around and go home when they're intercepted like he told me they would."

After a brief pause, Cue's voice came in again. "Hold it! Hold it! Lay off, you guys. Cancel attack and rendezvous on me headed west." Then, "Fighter section to *Guadalcanal*. Bogey is Pan American airliner bound for Tokyo. Am returning to base."

The chief of staff looked at the Admiral and shrugged his shoulders apologetically.

There is no point in recording the Admiral's terse comment in this family journal.

For the next twenty-four hours the radar dishes on the masts went round and round, operators in the CIC's fiddled with their gain and brightness controls and strained their eyes at every little snowflake that appeared on their scopes, the AEW planes orbited at 30,000 feet where their horizon was over 200 miles away and probed the wild blue yonder with their scopes. Nobody saw anything.

At four o'clock that afternoon the COS handed the Admiral another accurate report of position, course, and speed. The Admiral studied it for some time silently, and the COS knew better than to stick his neck out with any comment. Finally the Admiral said, "Get our radar experts and communicators up in staff plot. I want to have a conference with them."

When the experts were assembled with long faces, the Admiral asked, "Anybody got any ideas on what's going on here?"

Nobody did, or at least they weren't going to air any half-baked guesses at this point.

"We've had our radars going ever since we left Frisco," said the Admiral. "We've been talking back and forth to our planes in the air by radio and we've sent several dispatches to CINCPAC and Washington. We've been putting a lot of magnetic energy into the air. Isn't it barely possible he has been getting some kind of direction finder fixes on us? The Pacific Missile Range is in his bailiwick and they've got all sorts of fancy stuff that can track things clear to the moon. Couldn't they be tracking us and getting fixes on us?"

The experts batted that idea back and forth gravely, and their verdict was "improbable, but *possible*."

"Well, he's tracking us somehow," said the Admiral, "and it isn't by snooper planes. So we've got to start exploring improbable things. I want to shut down every piece of electronic equipment and every radio set in this task group for twenty-four hours. I'll change course and speed again as soon as we do, and then let's see what happens."

So for the next twenty-four hours the task group sailed westward using the same kind of search equipment that John Paul Jones used—the Mark I Eyeball of its lookouts. There wasn't an electron stirred anywhere in the group.

Next afternoon another astonishingly accurate position report was sent from San Francisco to CINCPAC.

Again the experts assembled with even longer faces in flag plot. "Gentlemen," said Admiral Day, "you all look like you're going to bust into tears any minute. I don't like this any better than you do, but . . . it's just an exercise, after all. I've known Admiral Bates man and boy since we were at the Academy together. I'll bet this is the most fun he's had with his clothes on in thirty years. . . . But how in the hell is he doing it?"

One of the communicators stuck up his hand, and said, "Sir, there is about one chance in a million that he has an agent planted in the task group with a short-wave ham radio set."

"Hah!" said Admiral Day, "I wouldn't put it past him. In fact that's just the kind of a lowdown under-handed sneaky stunt he *would* pull. He never bets on anything except a sure thing, so that's exactly how he is doing it. I should of thought of this myself."

"Of course," continued the expert, "this would be a serious breach of Navy regulations and is also a federal offense punishable by fine and imprisonment."

"Neither one of those facts would carry any weight whatever with the Bug- . . . I mean, with Admiral Bates in a case of this kind," said Admiral Day. "Would you be aware of it if any short-wave transmissions went out from the task group?"

"Up to now we wouldn't," admitted the expert, "because we haven't been watching for them. But I'll put special watches on right away. If that's what's happening, we'll spot his next transmission, DF it, and have the culprit up here in flag plot 5 minutes after he goes on the air."

"Okay, I wish you luck," said the Admiral. "If you catch him he'll wish he'd been born before radio was invented by the time I'm through with him."

But they didn't have any luck. When they met next day they were only one day's steaming out of Honolulu, Admiral Bates was still pinpointing them in his report, and they had no idea how.

LCDR Cue attended this meeting, and when the communicators admitted failure to spot any short-wave transmissions, he said, "Admiral, I think it's the *Lafayette* that's trailing us. You remember she sailed the day before we did. She can keep up with us without any trouble. She could be out there ten miles or so ahead of us, running at periscope depth, and only sticking a scope up occasionally. She has inertial navigators and squirt transmission for her position reports. I'll bet if we quit looking up in the air and put out our antisubmarine planes we'll find him."

"Hmmmmm . . . maybe you got something there, Curly," said the Admiral. "But, after all, our destroyers have been pinging away on sonar ever since we left. Wouldn't they have picked him up by this time?"

"Not necessarily," said Curly. "We've been running at high speed, which cuts down on the range of the sonars. Our destroyer screen is two miles ahead of us. I doubt if their sonar is good for any more than five miles at this speed. You can see our masts and superstructures through a periscope at ten. So I'll bet he's out there peeking at us about nine or ten miles away."

"Could be. Could be," said the Admiral. "Let's explore that possibility. Get all our ASW planes ready. When we launch them, I'll tell the destroyers to move the screen out another five miles and then we will slow down to creeping speed where their sonars will work best. In the next twelve hours we can comb the ocean around us so that we'll know where every fish bigger than a sardine is. Let's get going."

To make a long story a little bit longer, the destroyers and planes did everything to the ocean around the *Guadalcanal* except scoop it up in a bucket and strain it. But they didn't find anything.

Naturally, they didn't look *under* the carrier. Who the hell would think of such a crazy thing as that? Well, one screwball finally thought of it—Willy Wigglesworth—and he suggested it to LCDR Cue. Curly saw merit in it right away and went up to see the Admiral.

"Admiral," said Curly, "there's one possibility we haven't explored."

"What's that?" demanded the Admiral.

"Maybe he's under us."

"What do you mean, under us?"

Curly pointed to the deck and said, "I mean right smack below us a couple of hundred feet and keeping station on us down there."

The Admiral banged his fist on the chart table and snorted, "Well, now that somebody has finally thought of it, that's obviously the only answer to this thing, outside of black magic. . . . Could he stay there with all this maneuvering we been doing?"

"Sure. For a nuclear sub—no strain."

"But if he was down there he would have showed up on our fathometer, wouldn't he?"

"Yes. But out in deep water like this they usually don't pay much attention to the fathometer. He could have been there all the time without anybody noticing it."

"Get the navigator down here right away," said the Admiral.

A minute later the navigator popped into flag plot, saluted, and said, "You sent for me, sir."

"Yes," said the Admiral. "How deep is the water around here?"

"Plenty deep, sir," said the navigator. "We got 3000 fathoms for miles around."

"I want you to get me a fathometer reading right away," said the Admiral.

"I'm sorry, sir," said the navigator. "Our fathometer is out of commission."

"What's the matter with it?"

"We don't know, sir. It was working fine when we left San Francisco. But it went haywire when we crossed the 100-fathom curve coming out."

"What do you mean?"

"It just got stuck at 100 fathoms and has been there ever since. We can't seem to find out what's wrong with it."

"Well, I'll be a double-acting left-handed rubber swab handle," said the Admiral. "Do you mean to stand there and tell me your fathometer has read 100 fathoms ever since we left the Bonita Channel?"

"Yessir. Our technicians have been—"

"I'll tell you what's wrong with your cotton-picking fathometer," interrupted the Admiral. "It's the people who are reading the dials."

"How do you mean, sir?"

"For three days," said the Admiral, "your people have been bouncing echoes off a goddam submarine 600 feet under us."

This caught the navigator with his main sheet belayed. "I don't know what you mean, sir," he said.

"I mean just what I said. There's nothing wrong with your fathometer. The USS *Lafayette* is right underneath us at 100 fathoms. Been there ever since we cleared the Bonita Channel."

"I . . . I never thought of that, sir," stammered the navigator.

"Well," said the Admiral, "we didn't either until a few minutes ago . . . and it's a damned good thing for you we didn't; otherwise you might be looking around for a farm to settle down on as soon as we got into port. . . . Get the Captain down here," he said to the COS.

Soon the Captain strode in and saluted. "Good morning, sir. Nice weather we're having," he said briskly.

"Don't look now, Captain," said the Admiral, "but somebody is looking right at your bellybutton."

"How do you mean, sir?" asked the Captain, hastily checking to see if his pants were unzipped.

The Admiral explained.

"Well, I'll be gahdammed," said the Captain.

"You took the words right out of my mouth," said the Admiral.

"That's just the way I feel too. . . . Call one of those destroyers in from the screen and have him probe underneath us with his sonar."

Soon a destroyer was reporting, "Solid sonar target at 600 feet directly under *Guadalcanal*. Target evaluated as sub."

"How the hell do we flush him out of there now?" asked the Admiral. "Even in wartime we couldn't drop depth charges on him without blowing ourselves up. This is a hell of a situation."

"Why not have the destroyer call him on the underwater telephone and just tell him to come on up—all is forgiven," suggested Curly.

"Good idea," said the Admiral. "Let's try it."

Meantime, down at 600 the *Lafayette* had been enjoying life immensely.

All the task group's changes of formation showed up on her scopes and it was easy enough for the alert submariners to figure out what was going on above them and why. As soon as the destroyer screen fanned out to double distance and the task group slowed down, the skipper said, "I think they've finally begun to suspect that we are shadowing them, but they still don't know they're right on top of us."

However, when a destroyer fell back from the screen and took station astern of the *Guadalcanal*, it soon became obvious from its deliberate pinging that the cat was out of the bag . . . had its paw in the goldfish bowl, for that matter. The hydrophone man said, "He's holding his sonar beam right on us, sir; I think they spotted us."

"Well, it's about time," said the skipper. "It was fun while it lasted, anyway."

Then the red light on the underwater phone lit up and word came out of the squawk box, "Destroyer calling *Lafayette*. Over."

"Don't answer the phone. Let it ring," said the skipper. "We'll keep 'em wondering a little longer."

Back in flag plot on the *Guadalcanal*, the word came in from the destroyer: "They won't answer us. But we have a good solid echo on our scope now, and we're sure it's *Lafayette*. She's at 600 feet."

"I know how we can get her out of there, sir," said Willy Wigglesworth.

"How?" demanded the Admiral.

"Let go our anchor," said Willy.

"Well, now, I must admit that *would* get rid of her all right," said the Admiral. "But Polaris submarines cost the taxpayer a lot of money. Some nosy congressman might object if we dropped our anchor on one. This young man believes in direct action, doesn't he?" said the Admiral to Curly.

"Indeed he does," said Curly, thinking of the Twentieth Century Limited.

"I don't mean drop it all the way, sir," said Willy; "but let him *think* you are going to. You could tell him on the underwater phone we're going to let it go—but then only drop about twenty fathom of chain. That will make an awful racket in the water and with all his sensitive listening gear, it may make him nervous enough to get out from under us."

"No harm in trying," said the Admiral. "Call the bridge and tell them to drop the anchor to thirty fathoms. Have the destroyer tell him we're letting go 120 fathom of chain."

Down below in the *Lafayette* when the word came in on the underwater phone, "We're going to let go an anchor," everyone did a double-take and looked at the skipper. "Hah," he snorted, "it's a bluff. They wouldn't dare."

A minute later a din reverberated through the hull of the sub that sounded like a ton of bricks showering down on a tin roof. "The crazy son of a bitch—he did!" yelled the skipper. "Right full rudder. Let's get the hell out of here."

The *Lafayette* banked into a tight turn and slid out from under the *Guadalcanal*. "Send up a parachute flare," barked the skipper. "I'm not going to fool around with these silly bastards any more. Stand by to surface."

A minute later the long black hull of the *Lafayette* broke surface half a mile abeam of the carrier, white water pouring off her sides.

The conning tower hatch popped open and the skipper appeared. Admiral Day, watching through his binoculars, said to his flag lieutenant:

"Send an official message:

> From Commander Task Group
> To USS *Lafayette*
> Well done, you sneaky bastard."

Captain Hanks read this message to his crew on the loudspeakers, and had it published in the next Plan of the Day. The ship's carpenter made a fancy frame for it and it has hung in the wardroom of the *Lafayette* ever since.

That night Admiral Day stuck his Army-Navy game tickets in an air-mail envelope and dropped them in the box addressed to the Bugler with a note saying, "I'm praying for freezing rain that day so you'll catch pneumonia."

CHAPTER EIGHT

More Deep Stuff

THE DAY AFTER the *Guadalcanal* arrived in Pearl Harbor, Commander Hanks of the *Lafayette* came aboard to pay his respects to Admiral Day.

"Pleased to meetcha," said the Admiral as Hanks was ushered into the cabin. "Siddown, young man. I sort of feel as if we already know each other."

"Would it be proper to say I served under, or at least operated under, your command for the past four days, sir?" asked the Commander.

"Hah!" snorted the Admiral. "It would be improper, flippant, and disrespectful to say it . . . but I know damned well you're going to say it in every officers' club around here whether I like it or not."

"Yessir," said the Commander. "We learned a great deal working with your fine task group last week."

"Hunh," grunted the Admiral, "You're not the only ones who learned something. I *meant* that *well done* signal I sent you. Every word of it."

"Aw, you probably say that to everybody, sir," said Commander Hanks modestly, who knew very well that this wasn't true. The Admiral was notorious throughout the fleet for deflating eager beaver young skippers who tried too obviously to make an impression on him—by simply sending them a public signal saying

"*Fairly* well done."

"You should know better than that," declared the Admiral.

"Yessir," said Hanks, thinking of several classmates who were still trying to live down the Admiral's damning faint praise.

"Now," said the Admiral, "tell me about these Polaris subs. From what I hear they're quite different from the ones I chased all through the war during the Battle of the Atlantic. I'm damned glad the Germans didn't have them or maybe I wouldn't be here."

"That's right, sir. First of all, these new boats are true submarines. The old ones weren't. They could submerge for a while, to make an attack or to hide, but they were really surface ships. They could go much faster and much farther on the surface than they could submerged. It's the other way around with us. We are designed to operate more efficiently under water than we can on the surface. On the surface our blunt bow pushes up such a big bow wave it cuts down our speed. Submerged, our streamlined shape enables us to go just as fast as you can."

"Yes, I found that out," said the Admiral.

"Even our sonars and listening gear work better submerged than on the surface. The deeper we go the farther out they reach. And as you know, we can often find cold layers in the water and by getting under them we, in effect, put a tin roof over our heads that the surface sonars can't penetrate. Then, of course, there's the matter of firing our rockets. If we had to surface to do it we might get clobbered by an alert enemy. But we don't have to surface. We fire our whole battery of sixteen Polaris missiles without ever sticking up a periscope."

"Tell me more about that," said the Admiral. "How the hell do you know how to aim them down there?"

"Our inertial navigation system keeps track of our position very accurately. It's an array of fantastically sensitive gyros and accelerometers tied in to a mechanical brain that grinds out our latitude and longitude continuously. . . . It has sensors that can detect even a slight crosscurrent in the water that we don't even know about ourselves, and make allowances for it. I won't try to explain it to you because I don't really understand all I know about it myself."

"I know what you mean," said the Admiral. "Don't you ever have to correct this thing?"

"Not really. We *do* like to check on it now and then by sticking up a periscope for a few seconds at night and getting some star sights or by a loran fix, but whenever we do get outside fixes they agree so closely that we just assume the computer is more accurate than the stars or loran. Actually, we never have to surface with these boats. We can stay submerged for months at a time."

"I can believe that for missile subs that just patrol back and forth waiting for the word to fire at fixed targets on land. But how about commerce raiders? We're still building subs to attack ships."

"Yessir, we are. But they are true submarines too, and with their atomic power plants they never have to surface. They can go out from New London, submerge at the 100-fathom curve, patrol the North Atlantic, and find a convoy either by listening or by sonar. They can sink all the ships in it and return to New London without ever sticking a periscope up."

"I don't believe it," said Admiral Day.

"It's true, Admiral, they've got inertial navigation, hydrophones, sonar . . ."

"Yeah, I know. You told me about all that. But I still say they can't stay submerged all the time for a number of reasons. The first one is the thing that killed the cat—curiosity. Curiosity is one of the strongest human emotions, and no matter what all your hydrophones and sonarscopes tell you, you're going to want to stick a scope up and take a little peek now and then."

"Well . . . maybe you've got something there, Admiral."

"And you're going to *have* to do it whether you want to or not, because when you come back in claiming you sank a whole convoy CNO won't believe it unless you can tell him you *saw* the ships sink."

"That's right too," admitted Commander Hanks.

"And finally, SecDef's public relations flicks are going to demand photographs that they can put on the cover of *Life*."

"Okay, Admiral," said the skipper. "I can't argue with you on that one. But *theoretically* anyway a sub never has to come up these days except to get more chow for her crew."

"Now, getting back to the Polaris sub," said the Admiral; "those sixteen rockets you've got poised and ready there pack a bigger wallop than all the stuff used by both sides in World War II."

"Yessir."

"That's a hell of a responsibility you're carrying around."

"Yessir."

"What's to prevent you from going berserk and blowing the world apart?" asked the Admiral.

"One man can't do it, sir. The physical setup is such that my exec must cooperate with me to fire the rockets. He has a key to one lock. I have a key to another. We both have to know the order to fire is legitimate and both must turn our keys before anything can happen."

"Only two of you?" asked the Admiral. "Civilization, if you can call it that, is betting pretty heavily on you two."

"Theoretically, I suppose you *could* say that the two of us, acting in collusion, could fire an unauthorized shot. But, actually, I doubt if it could happen. Some others on the boat would know about it and stop it. The communications officer certainly would know if an order to fire had been received or not. I would say at least three, and probably more, officers would have to go berserk before you could fire an unauthorized shot."

"How about a phony message telling you to fire?"

"Impossible, sir. Unless the people who sent it had access to that briefcase that goes wherever the President goes and has the up-to-date code words in it."

"Suppose a sneak attack blasted Washington off the face of the earth. What happens then?"

"There is a definite chain of responsibility set up for giving the order to retaliate if Washington is wiped out. There will always be someone left to do it, no matter how hard they hit us. . . . And the whole system is set up on a 'fail safe' basis all the way from the President right on down to me."

"How do you mean, 'fail safe'?" demanded the Admiral.

"It means that if something goes wrong anywhere along the line, whether it's a mechanical accident or a human error, it automatically stops everything and makes any further action impossible. The system is absolutely foolproof."

"After you've lived as long as I have, son," observed the Admiral, "and met more of the high-powered fools who run this world and seen what kind of incompiffflery they are capable of, you may not be so sure of that. But, of course, in case of a sneak attack it really doesn't make a hell of a lot of difference, does it? The order to fire is like Gabriel blowing his horn. What's the use of coming home after you've done it when you know your homeland has been laid waste too? The only way Polaris can accomplish its mission and justify its existence is by never being used!"

"That's right, sir," agreed the skipper. "The way the world is run now, we have to keep it ready for instant use, the Russians have to know it is ready, and we must never use it. It's a pretty delicate knife edge for the fate of civilization to be balanced on."

"Well, there isn't much you and I can do about it," said the Admiral. "May the good Lord guide you, son. . . . Where do you go from here?"

"Back to San Francisco, sir. We're leaving two days from now."

"We go back a few days later. I may see you there. I'd like to take a short cruise with you there if we can arrange it."

"Be pleased to do it any time, sir."

Next day the Admiral paid his respects to CIC Pacific Fleet, Admiral Jones.

"Come in—come in, Windy," said Admiral Jones. "I've been looking forward to seeing you again. I followed your progress out here with great interest. Kept close track of you all the way, in fact."

"Harrumph," observed Admiral Day. "That young submarine skipper is a sharp character. I was very much impressed with him."

"So am I," said the CIC. "And he *should* be sharp. They're getting the pick of the whole Navy now for those Polaris submarine skippers, and they're entitled to it. Those young men with their three stripes carry a bigger load in some ways than I do with my four stars. You know, I've got a dozen of those subs in my fleet, but if they ever decide to shoot I'm not even in the chain of command. The word goes from the White House to the captain of the ship and I just get an information copy of the dispatch."

"It's a different Navy from the one we grew up in. . . . In the old days, before radio, the skipper of a ship often had to act on his own initiative and could commit the United States on fairly important matters of national policy. Now he can't do anything on his own, but he can blow the whole world apart when they tell him to push the button! . . . Well, what have you got scheduled for me on the way back to Frisco?"

"An air defense exercise like the last one where you pulled that shenanigan on old Bugler. Your group is supposed to attack San Francisco, and he—with help from Continental Air Defense and SAC—is supposed to defend against you. My operations people are briefing your staff on the details of it now. It's a pretty straightforward operation and the Bugler is just itching for another crack at you. I doubt if you'll get away with anything on him this time."

"Maybe not. But I've got some pretty shrewd characters working for me. We shall see."

"Oh, yes, one other thing," added the CIC. "There will be six submarines working with the Air Defense people this time. They're going to be on a picket line about 1500 miles out from S.F. to see if they can intercept you as you cross it. It's just a scouting exercise for them. They're not supposed to attack."

"Okay, we'll see if we can slip through them. Will my friend in the *Lafayette* be one of them?"

"Yes. He leaves for his station tomorrow. And he has to go there and try to find you when you cross the line. No monkey business of lying on the bottom here this time."

On the *Guadalcanal* next morning Admiral Day met with what he called his "Dirty Trick" board to discuss the forthcoming operation on the return trip. Lieutenant Commander Curly Cue was a charter member of this board, and to this meeting he brought along Ensign Willy Wigglesworth.

"Admiral, I want you to meet a newcomer in our squadron. This is Ensign Wigglesworth, sir."

"Please to meetcha, Mr. Wigglewaggle," said the Admiral.

"Mr. Wigglesworth occasionally has some . . . er . . . original ideas. He's the one who thought of looking under the ship for the *Lafayette*," added Curly.

"That's fine," said the Admiral. "Always glad to see young officers who are thinking about something besides the next boat to the beach. . . . Now, gentlemen, how are we going to outsmart these people this time?"

"Admiral," said the chief of staff, "this is a pretty straightforward operation, and it's laid out primarily as an exercise for the Air Defense people in finding the task group. They've got a big area to cover and will have quite a job doing it. But there isn't much we can do except make a high-speed run straight in, intercept their snoopers, and try to reach the launching point before they get their SAC helpers out to klobber us. I suggest we detour up to the north and curve down from the direction of Alaska. We may find some foggy weather to hide in coming that way. Outside of that I haven't much to offer."

"That's okay," said the Admiral. "Lay it out on that basis. There is one little joker I'd like to try on them, though. Their long-range scouts and snoopers will be relying mostly on radar. They know that we've got a carrier, three cruisers, and ten destroyers, and they know that a group of that sort always cruises with a bent screen of destroyers ahead and the heavy ships in the center in a nice geometrical formation that can't be mistaken for anything else on a radarscope. They will be flying quite high where they can't actually see the ships too clearly, and some of the scouts will be Air Force characters who don't know an aircraft carrier from a Staten Island ferryboat anyway. So . . . right after we leave here I'm going to pull the carrier out of the formation and run in all alone with her several hundred miles away from the rest of you. Their scouts will find the formation, all right, but observing from high altitude mostly by radar, I don't think they'll notice that the carrier isn't in it. And if any of them happen to run across the lone carrier, especially if it's at night, they won't think one little blip all by itself is a carrier. . . . What do you think of that, boys?"

"I don't think it will fool 'em," said the COS. "For one thing, our formation will only have the three cruisers in the center. I think they would spot that on their radarscopes."

"Put a destroyer in where the carrier belongs," said the Admiral. "That will cut the screen down to nine ships instead of ten, but I don't think they'll be sharp enough to catch that."

"A destroyer won't make anywhere near as big a blip on the radar screen as the *Guadalcanal* does," objected the COS. "The cruisers will show up much bigger than the can. If their scouts are on the job they will get suspicious and come down low for a good look."

"I know how we can lick that, sir," said Ensign Wigglesworth.

"Good, Mr. Wigglesbotham," said the Admiral. "Let's have it."

"We just diddle with the search radar on the destroyer that is posing as the carrier. Our radars will spot any snoopers coming over us. Have the destroyer point one of his search antennas at the snooper and have it rigged to amplify and repeat back the blips it gets from the search radar of the snooper. It would be the same thing as magnifying an echo ashore. If you yell at a cliff half a mile away your voice is pretty weak by the time it gets there and even weaker by the time the echo gets back; but if there's a mike at the cliff that feeds your voice into a loudspeaker, the echo can blast your ears off."

The Admiral nodded approvingly, and said, "I predict a bright future for you in the Navy, Mr. Woggle—"

"Wigglesworth, sir," said Willy.

Turning to his electronics people, the Admiral said, "What do you technical experts say? Since you didn't think of it first, no doubt you have dozens of reasons why this won't work."

"Nossir. It will work all right. Sorry we didn't think of it ourselves. We can just modulate the incoming signal into the high-frequency oscillator of the heterodyne condensers and—"

"That's exactly what I had in mind," said the Admiral. "You gentlemen work out the details. That should take care of their aerial scouts and snoopers. Now, don't forget they're going to have a scouting line of subs. What can we do about them?"

"I don't think we have to worry too much about them, sir," said the COS. "They rely mostly on their hydrophones on a search mission. They can usually hear propellers much farther away than they could see the ship on their radar even if they were surfaced.

A big formation of ships making twenty knots stirs up a hell of a commotion in the water. They will hear us forty or fifty miles away and there won't be any doubt about what they are hearing once they pick us up."

"That's right," said the Admiral. "And if any of them should happen to hear the carrier they will know it's just one ship all by itself. I don't think they'll even suspect it's us. And to help them conclude it isn't, I'm going to approach S.F. on the great-circle course from Honolulu, the way the tourist ships do."

"There's a couple of more angles we can work on that, sir," said Ensign Wigglesworth.

"Okay, Mr. Whiffleworth, let's have them."

"Wigglesworth," said Willy. "The *Guadalcanal* has got four screws. Most tourist ships are twin-screws. The subs can tell when they're listening to a four-screw ship very easily. I suggest we make the run in using only two screws."

"Fine idea, young man," said the Admiral. "If you'll pardon the pun, that oughta screw 'em up."

"One more thing," said Willy: "there's an outside chance that a sub might come up near the surface to stick up a periscope and take a look."

"There's a lot more than an outside chance, if you ask me," observed the Admiral.

"If he does it in daytime, the jig will be up. But if he does it at night, I think we can still fox him."

"How will we do that?"

"Those tourist ships are lit up like a saloon on Saturday night. We can rig a couple of rows of lights along the side that will look like portholes at night. We can paint false stacks with the Matson Line colors and insignia on them on that big stack of ours and shine lights on them so they'll be quite conspicuous. Unless he comes up real close aboard, nobody would think we were anything but a tourist ship."

"Wonderful," said the Admiral. "Tell the Captain of the *Guadalcanal* to do it right after we are out of sight of land. . . . What's your name again, young man?"

"Wigglesworth, sir. William Wigglesworth."

"Okay," said the Admiral. "I'm just going to call you Bill if you don't mind."

"Aye aye, sir," said Willy.

As the *Lafayette* sailed out of Pearl Harbor next day, the Admiral sent her the following message: "Don't believe all the idle rumors you hear down there at 100 fathoms. Come up and take a look now and then. Good luck. Day."

Two days later the task group stood out, formed up off the entrance, and took a northerly course from Diamond Head as if bound for Alaska. During the night the *Guadalcanal* broke off from the group and headed southwest to pick up the Hawaii-San Francisco shipping lane, one of the destroyers taking her place in the center of the formation.

The *Guadalcanal* jogged south about a hundred miles below the great-circle course to San Francisco, where she wouldn't be likely to encounter any shipping, and by sunset the next day she had three lines of exterior lights rigged on each side of her hangar deck and two phony smokestacks painted on her own big single stack. The sailors who rigged the lights and painted these phonies figured the officers were a little bit nuts, and maybe they were right. The Captain had the chief engineer shut down the two inboard main shafts and jack up the speed on the outboard ones so that anybody listening on a hydrophone would hear only two screws. That evening, after dark, Lieutenant Commander Cue flew around the ship several times and reported that from a mile or so away she looked more like a floating amusement park than an aircraft carrier.

While this was going on at sea, preparations for the exercise were also in progress on the West Coast. This was to be a joint Navy-Air Force show with SAC and Continental Air Defense participating. The DEW line of Continental Air Defense would be alert to spot any air-attack group coming in from seaward and to intercept and knock them down with Air Force fighters. It was up to the naval forces under Admiral Bates to scout for and find the task group before they got to launching position. SAC had several wings of bombers with fighter escorts poised and ready to swoop out and klobber the ships as soon as Admiral Bates found them.

To find the ships, Admiral Bates' staff laid on a big search operation for the patrol planes covering an arc from Kodiak clear down to the Gulf of Lower California, extending out to a range of 2000 miles. It takes a lot of planes to keep a sector this big covered, so all the patrol squadrons on the West Coast got into the act. To take care of the unlikely event that the task group eluded the aerial scouts, six fleet subs, including the *Lafayette*, were stationed on a scouting line 1200 miles out from San Francisco. The dice were heavily loaded against the incoming task group, and it seemed unlikely they could launch their planes before the defenders would find them and blow them out of the water. Admiral Bates was smugly confident there would be no snafu this time.

Two thousand miles from San Francisco the first snooper found the task group up to the northwest near Alaska. There was a lot of haze and fog up that way, so they never did get a good look at it, except on the radarscope. But that was enough. The scope showed the ships in the standard task group formation with the four big ships in the center and the bent antisub screen of destroyers ahead. Nobody bothered to count the destroyers in the screen and it probably wouldn't have made any difference if they had. The four big blips in the center accounted for the carrier and the three cruisers, and nobody would have been interested in why one destroyer was missing. The snooper stayed up at 40,000 feet and after cracking off his contact report to San Francisco began shadowing from a range of ten miles, expecting to be intercepted and "shot down" very soon.

The contact report to Admiral Bates' HQ triggered a far-reaching chain of events. Messages went out over the hot lines to Continental Air Defense HQ and SAC, and squadrons of bombers roared down the runways at Navy and SAC bases throughout the Northwest.

Fighter groups rendezvoused with the bombers at 60,000 feet and away they went out over the North Pacific toward Alaska. Following the constant stream of position reports from Admiral Bates' snoopers, they had no trouble finding the task group about

1800 miles northwest of San Francisco. Unhampered by any fighter opposition, the SAC planes swarmed over the task group making deliberate bombing runs that would certainly have put the whole group on the bottom had they been playing for keeps. The lead bombers all came back with photos taken through the bombsight lenses to prove it. The escort fighters were a bit put out that nobody came up from the task group to dogfight with them, but far out at sea they didn't have enough fuel reserve to go down and strafe the ships trying to stir up a fight.

As the bombers and fighters headed back to base, several photo-reconnaisance planes flew over taking high-altitude pictures of the ships, which were presumably sinking by then. The leader of the bomber wing cracked off a message to SAC: "Navy task group sunk. No opposition."

While the task group up north was being klobbered, the *Lafayette* was patrolling across the great-circle course from Honolulu to San Francisco. She was down at 500 feet with her delicate electronic ears cocked for the unmistakable symphony of propeller beats produced by a large formation of naval ships.

On a patrol of this kind a nuclear sub settles down to a routine in which there are only three days in the week: Yesterday, Today, and Tomorrow. Since you never see the sun, you have to look at the clock to figure out what time of day it is. You stand your watch, eat your meals, read books, watch movies, play acey-deucey, hit the sack, and go on watch again. You never have to worry about what you're going to do tomorrow because it's the same as what you are doing today.

After dinner one night in the crew's lounge, the "chief of the boat" was regaling some of the younger members of the crew with what might be rather loosely described as "reminiscences." In the submarine service the chief of the boat is the senior enlisted man in the crew and is the No. 2 man on board next to the Captain despite the fact that officially the regulations say the executive officer is. On the *Lafayette*, the chief was a veteran of a dozen war cruises in the Pacific and, like all old-timers, he didn't let a narrow regard for the facts cramp his style when telling a tale.

"This Navy ain't what it used to be," he announced judicially to the circle of young atomic technicians gathered around him.

"No, and I'll bet it never was either," muttered one of the young lads to the guy sitting next to him.

"I made three cruises in the *Squark* during the war," continued the chief. "You could pretty near hoist her aboard this craft, but we really gave the Japs hell with mustard and horseradish on it. Sank 150,000 tons of ships, including a brand-new aircraft carrier. Red Ramage was our skipper. He's a vice admiral now. Got the Congressional Medal of Honor. There was never a dull moment when you went to war with Red. He wasn't scared of *nothin'*. He took us right into Tokyo Harbor once and we sat on the bottom, stuck up the periscope, and watched the horse races going on ashore."

"Gee," said a couple of his listeners.

"And on the other side of Tokyo Bay from the race track there was a big navy yard where they had just finished building a new aircraft carrier, a big son of a bitch of about 50,000 tons. There was a whole crowd of Japs in silk hats and dress uniforms around the building ways, they had the guard and band lined up, flags were flying all over the place, and tugboats were standing by at the end of the building ways. Then while we were sitting there on the bottom watching them they fired a 21-gun salute, the whistles started blowing and the band playing and I'll be damned if the carrier didn't come sliding down the ways right out into the bay."

"Could you hear the band playing through the periscope?" asked one of his skeptical listeners.

"Naw," said the chief, "but you could see the steam coming out of the whistles, so we knew the band musta been playing, too. Anyway, just as the Japs' brand-new carrier coasted out into the middle of Tokyo Bay, Red Ramage put four torpedoes into her and blew her up.

"I wish you could of seen all them Jap naval officers, jumping up and down waving their arms and screaming when she capsized and sank . . . made 'em madder than hell, and they heaved depth charges and bombs around all over Tokyo Harbor. I didn't think we'd ever get out of there alive. But Red pulled us out. He always did."

"Even if that was *so* I wouldn't believe it," announced a doubting Thomas among the listeners.

"Why not?" demanded the chief.

"We got a book in the ship's library about the Congressional Medal winners and I was reading Admiral Ramage's citation in it the other night. He got it for barging into a convoy on the surface at night and shooting it up with his deck gun. There's nothing in the book about blowing up a carrier coming off the building ways."

"Yeah. That night battle on the surface was later on," said the Chief. "We didn't even report that business in Tokyo Bay because we figured nobody would believe it anyway."

One of the other listeners poked the skeptic in the ribs and said, "Listen, kid, don't you know that after a story like that has been told often enough it becomes naval history, and it's unpatriotic to argue about it?"

On that philosophical note the bull session adjourned.

Around midnight the hydrophone operator picked up screw noises approaching from the west. After listening a few minutes he reported to Captain Hanks, "She's a twin-screw ship with three-bladed propellers making 150 rpm. They sound like fairly big wheels."

"Okay," said the skipper. "See what she looks like on sonar."

The sonarman beamed his set in the direction of the incoming propeller beats, sent out a few pings, and reported: "Bearing 275°, range 4 miles, speed 18, course 080. I get a big blip and a good solid echo—she's a pretty good-sized ship."

The navigator laid this dope down on the chart and the Captain said, "Right on the great-circle course from Honolulu. Probably some passenger liner. Can you estimate her size yet?" he asked of sonar.

Pretty soon the sonarman said, "She's a big one, sir. I estimate five or six hundred feet long."

"Let's go up to periscope depth and take a peek at her," said the skipper.

"Aye aye, sir. Take her up to forty feet," said the exec to the helmsman.

As the depth gauge slowly eased up to forty, the quartermaster swung the scope around to the bearing indicated by the hydrophones and the skipper took his station at the eyepiece. At forty feet he gave the order "up scope," electric motors shoved the slender tube up ten feet above the surface, and the skipper took a quick swing around the horizon, as all prudent submarine skippers do when coming up, before settling down on his target. It was a clear, dark night, but a black one. The horizon was empty except for a brilliant array of lights four miles to the west.

The skipper studied the two illuminated funnels with red and white bands around the top, the three long rows of lighted "portholes," and the bright green starboard light, and then announced, "Yep. She's a tourist ship, all right. Let's surface and surprise her by saying hello."

"Stand by to surface," sang out the exec, and warning howlers sounded throughout the boat. A few minutes later the *Lafayette* broke surface, the conning tower hatch popped open, and the skipper climbed out into the top of the sail, followed by a signalman with a blinker light.

"She looks like a waterfront saloon on a Saturday night," observed the skipper. "Give her a call with your light."

The signalman began blinking his searchlight with the "AA" Morse code call for an unknown ship.

On the signal bridge of the *Guadalcanal* the chief quartermaster yelled down at the signal men, "Hop to it, you dopes. Answer that guy calling us out there."

From the flag bridge below, Admiral Day, who was on hand to watch the forthcoming launch of the air group, yelled, "Take it easy up there. Let 'em call a couple of times more before you answer 'em. We're supposed to be a cruise ship with a bunch of dopey signal floozies, not a man-o'-war."

"Aye aye, sir," said the chief.

A minute later, the *Guadalcanal* answered, using merchant ship procedure, and the *Lafayette* asked, "What ship?"

"Grace Liner *Oahu*. Who you?" came back the reply.

"Tell her USS *Lafayette*. I'm submerging. Good-bye and good luck," said the skipper.

As the signalman finished blinking, Captain Hanks yelled down the voice tube, "Stand by to submerge," and followed the signalman down the hatch. At the bottom of the ladder in the control room, the exec handed him a priority dispatch from Western Sea Frontier: "Enemy Task Group located 1800 miles NW of San Francisco. Patrol planes tracking continuously. Attack groups are en route to target."

"Well, that's the end of that tea party," observed the skipper. "Take her down."

On the flag bridge of the *Guadalcanal*, the Admiral observed, "Just like I said. No matter how much fancy electronic gear they put on those buckets, the skippers will always want to come up and have a look now and then.

"I want a copy of that exchange of signals," he added to his chief of staff. "You can launch our attack group now whenever you're ready."

Just before sunrise the *Guadalcanal* swung into the wind and launched her whole air group to attack San Francisco. Continental Air Defense had already written off the task group as sunk by SAC and were not looking very hard for any attack coming in from seaward. Besides, the air group came in at wave-top level until it sighted land and so was too low for the search radars to see in time to do anything about it. The planes were on their way back to the carrier, and San Francisco was theoretically as flat as the day they had that "big fire" back in 1906, by the time the interceptors got to them.

Bugler Bates was about to crack off a hot dispatch to Day protesting this attack after he had "sunk" the whole task group when his COS laid the just-developed films of the photoreconnaissance planes in front of him and the skunk was out of the refrigerator. There was the task group, in pretty parade formation—but with a destroyer occupying the *Guadalcanal*'s spot.

Admiral Bates' comments at this point shocked and embarrassed even his Marine orderly, who was a veteran of twenty-four years' service with four rows of campaign ribbons.

By the time the *Guadalcanal* arrived in San Francisco the lights had been unrigged and the phony smokestacks painted out. However, Admiral Day had colored photographs taken before the stacks were painted out, and the first boat ashore took a set of them to Commander Western Sea Frontier.

When the *Lafayette* anchored next day the Admiral's flag lieutenant took an envelope over to her with another set of pictures, copies of the exchange of blinker signals on the night of the attack, and the following note from Admiral Day:

Dear Hanks—
Suggest you back up your computers, accelerometers, and atom smashers with a fail safe attachment on the periscope.
                                                    Day

CHAPTER NINE

Willy Wigglesworth and the Press

IN SAN FRANCISCO Commander Cue sent for Ensign Wigglesworth and said, "Willy, we're going to have a reporter from *Time* magazine aboard next time we go out."

"That's too bad," said Willy. "I don't like *Time*."

"Neither do I," said Curly, "but it's just one of those evils we have to learn to live with until enough people get mad enough about it."

"You mean like they did in Boston that time they threw the tea overboard?" asked Willy.

"Yeah," said Curly. "Anyway, I'm appointing you public relations officer and I want you to take this guy in tow when he gets aboard."

"Cap'n, this might turn out to be a disastrophy," said Willy. "I don't like *any* newspapermen, let alone a *Time* reporter."

"Why not?" asked Curly.

"I don't know. Some people don't like strawberries. I think maybe my mother was frightened by one just before I was born. Anyway, I'm allergic to politicians, Hollywood press agents, TV commercials, snakes, and newspaper reporters."

"Well, you've got the job now," said Curly. "Do the best you can with it."

"Aye aye, sir," said Willy.

Just before the *Guadalcanal* sailed next day an alert character bustled up the gangway, shot a few piercing glances around the quarterdeck, and announced, "Parker, *Time* magazine."

Parker, known to his associates as Ace, was a brash young news-hawk on the make. He had made a couple of minor scoops in his budding career and came aboard the *Guadalcanal* determined that if the Navy was trying to cover up anything on this ship he was going to unearth and expose it.

"Yes, sir, Mr. Parker," said the officer of the deck, "we've been expecting you. Ensign Wigglesworth has been detailed to show you around. He'll be up in a minute."

A few minutes later, as Willy was showing Parker to his state-room, he asked, "Ever been aboard an aircraft carrier before, Mr. Parker?"

"Yes, indeed," said Parker, who had covered the commissioning ceremony of the *Coral Sea* when the ship was alongside a dock.

"Anything in particular you are interested in?" asked Willy.

"I just want to look around at first and see what goes on," said the newshawk, lifting an eyebrow to show he suspected that plenty of sinister things went on. "I'll have to interview the Admiral and the Captain, of course, and maybe even some sailors, too, depend-ing on what leads I uncover." He peered intently around the hangar deck as though he might uncover a lead or two then and there.

"I've got quite a program laid out for you," said Willy. "By the time we get to San Diego you ought to have enough for several good stories."

"Uh-huh," said Parker. "How do I get my stuff ashore while it's still news?"

"By radio," said Willy. "Just give it to me and I'll see that it's properly cleared and filed with the outgoing traffic."

"Whadaya mean, *cleared?*—censored?" demanded the scribe.

"Call it that if you want to," said Willy. "I call it 'checked for security.' But that won't be any problem because I won't show you anything you can't write about—like the atom bomb magazine."

"They told me my Pentagon press card would let me go anywhere on board," said Parker.

"With your press card, plus a background check by the FBI, security investigation by CIA, and a Q clearance from the Atomic Energy Commission, they *might* let you peek in the magazine door for a few seconds," said Willy. "Otherwise, no dice."

"What's so secret about an atom bomb these days?" asked Parker. "The Russians have got 'em."

"I know," said Willy. "But we've got a new kind that can knock the whole world flat on its ass. We're trying to keep it to ourselves."

"I'll take that up with the Admiral," said Parker, "and maybe I'll write about some things besides those you show me. How do I know they won't mangle my stuff before sending it out?"

"They will always discuss anything with you that ought to be changed," explained Willy, "and you'll get an exact copy of what the radio room sends out."

"Humph," observed Parker, scowling ominously to show it had *better* be exact.

The next day Willy began his program of showing Parker what makes the wheels go round on the *Guadalcanal*. There are many wheels on a big aircraft carrier and explaining them is no small job.

He dressed Parker up in a G suit, took him up to the ready room, and had him sit in on a pilot briefing. There he rubbed elbows with pilots ranging from eager new kids fresh out of Pensacola to tough old pros from the Korean War and even Admiral Halsey's Third Fleet. When word came over the squawk box, "Pilots man your planes," he shepherded him across the flight deck through the whirling props, snorting jet intakes, and hot exhausts, and buckled him into the rear seat of an A8J.

Ace was rubbering around when they got fired off the catapult and the sudden G forces slammed his head back against the rest where it should have been after the "ready to go" signal. His hard helmet absorbed most of the jolt. They rendezvoused with the rest of the air group and ran through half an hour of tactical maneuvers with Willy explaining everything over the interphone as he expertly tootled the plane through the drill in the middle of the formation.

On the landing Willy came up the groove with a "Roger" all the way from the landing signal officer, snagged the No. 1 wire just as the plane ahead pulled out of the landing area, and boiled out of it himself just in time for the plane behind him to take his "cut" and get aboard. Not a bad morning's work, if I do say so myself, thought Willy as he climbed out on the wing to help Parker get loose from his harness.

Ace had unbuckled his harness in the air, so he got his head banged up against the instrument board from the reverse G forces on landing.

"Howdya like it?" asked Willy.

"All right," said Parker. "Seems like a kind of slam-bang, hit-or-miss operation though."

They spent the afternoon in the Combat Information Center. CIC is the brain center of the task group. Everything that happens is channeled there by radio, radar, sonar, a voice tube, then evaluated and acted on by the controllers or passed up to the Admiral or the Captain if it's too big for them to handle.

In the old days the bridge was the place on a ship where all top-level decisions were made. Now on most ships, when things start popping, you'll find the Captain and maybe even the Admiral in CIC. There they can "see" everything for miles around at night or even in fog on the big vertical glass plotting board on which sailors with grease pencils plot the dope as fast as it comes in.

"These guys all write backwards," observed Parker as he stood next to one of the plotters behind the big board.

"You're on the wrong side of the display board," explained Willy. "It reads right on the other side."

Willy got Parker a set of earphones and let him listen in while the controllers were running an intercept.

"It sounds like a bunch of comic strip characters with all this 'Roger,' 'over,' and 'Wilco' stuff," observed Parker.

"This is where Buck Rogers got that lingo from," explained Willy. "There's a reason for all of it too. You've got to follow an exact drill or the air would be jammed when things get hot and all those funny words are picked so they can't be mistaken for any other words."

Next they went aft to the landing signal officer's platform on the port end of the flight deck. "Paddles," as the LSO is called, is a cross between a one-armed paperhanger with the itch and a cat with fleas on a hot stove when he is waving the boys in. He has a sharp-eyed sailor helper who checks to see that the incoming pilots don't forget to lower their wheels and hook as they turn into the groove. If they do, Paddles waves them off and debits their account in the geedunk shop with fifteen gallons of ice cream for the flight deck crew.

Sometimes pilots crowd the port side too close coming up the groove and Paddles and his helpers have to go overboard from the platform. A net sticks out over the side to catch them. The webbing of the net is badly scorched from the language they use when they land in it.

Willy explained the new mirror landing system which brings pilots aboard by guiding them in with a narrow beam of light. The LSO listening to the explanation spat contemptuously. He had just given a lad a frantic wave-off after an erratic zigzag approach up the groove. "If that guy had been coming in on that beam thing they would of found blood all over but no brains when they swept up the wreck," he said.

They spent the rest of the afternoon with the flight deck crew. Willy explained how the white, yellow, red, and green T shirts indicated the fire fighters, traffic directors, ordnance men, and arresting-gear operators. They watched a grizzled chief respot the deck for the next flight, using miniature scale models on the "ouija board" in his office at the base of the island. Then they saw the plane captains and tractor drivers translate his plans into action, squeezing planes into spots with inches to spare on either wing just as the ouija board said they could. The tractor drivers all think they are cut out to be jet pilots, and except when they have planes in tow, they go roaring around the deck in a way that would paralyze the wildest hot rodders with fright.

At the end of the busy day Willy asked, "Ya getting any stuff ya can use, Mr. Parker?"

"Maybe," said the newshawk.

The next day Willy gave him the $10 rubberneck tour of the

ship from the anchor windlass room on the fo'c'sle to the rudder room just over the screws. The bower anchors weigh twenty tons, about a pound for each ton of ship, and their cables are forged from steel bars as big around as the fat end of a baseball bat.

The Bosun who showed them around the fo'c'sle was a grizzled, salty character with so many years of sea duty he was reputed to have served as an apprentice boy with Noah in the Ark. He handled those big anchor cables as if they were watch chains, could make a flying moor with one hand tied behind him, and could slap a cross cringle gosset on both chains while he was putting the mooring swivel on without getting more than half a fathom of slack in either chain. He explained the workings of the fo'c'sle, the anchor windlass, and the chain lockers to Parker in words that were encrusted with barnacles and would have warmed the heart of Father Neptune. Parker didn't dig him at all.

They were shown around the engine room and fire rooms by a relaxed character called Scuttlebutt Grogan. Scuttlebutt, a first-class petty officer and veteran of World War II, had made chief several times but had never been able to hold it because MPs and shore patrol officers are so narrow-minded. He was the fresh-water king of the ship and explained how he distilled all the fresh water used on board out of sea water, and how it took about half a gallon of fuel oil to distill one gallon of fresh water. He had unprintable opinions about the landlubbers who come out of boot camp these days wearing sailors' clothes and who think, for gawdsake, that all you have to do to get water aboard ship is to open a valve in the bottom and let it in. "I've actually seen 'em try to use fresh water to swab the deck," he said in awed tones as if he had caught them trying to burn trash in the magazines. "I'm getting out on thirty at the end of this cruise," he observed as he showed them through the engine rooms. "They don't need practical monkey-wrench engineers like me any more. Everything is getting automated now. Pretty soon all it will take to run this bucket is a guy wearing glasses who needs a haircut sitting in a control booth punching buttons."

Next the Chief Master-at-Arms took them through the crew's quarters and messes. The Chief, with six gold hash-marks on his sleeve, obviously figured that, no matter what the Captain and the Admiral might think, this was *his* ship. "I have a hell of a time trying to run this ship with the juvenile delinquents we're getting in the Navy these days," he observed.

"You don't think much of present-day sailors, do you, Chief?" asked Willy.

The Chief spat contemptuously. "We got a new bunch of twenty fugitives from the draft board just before we sailed. Fresh out of boot camp. You oughta see 'em. I'd swap the whole bunch for a bucket of oily rags."

"Do you have any trouble maintaining discipline with the new type of sailors?" asked Parker.

The Chief looked at him in amazement. "Discipline?" he snorted. "There's no such thing in the Navy as discipline any more. The biggest mistake this Navy ever made was when it abolished flogging. You can't look cross-eyed at a sailor any more or he writes to his congressman about brutality."

They had just arrived in a bunkroom where a group of sailors were loafing and horsing around. "Get out of here, you rubber swab handles," roared the Chief. "Get the hell up on deck where you belong."

The sailors fled like leaves before an autumn gale.

"Every man has his own bunk and locker now," observed Willy. "Before the war they used to sleep in hammocks and keep their clothes in a sea bag."

"Used to wash in a bucket, too," said the Chief. "Now we got individual wash bowls, showers with curtains on them, deluxe plumbing in the heads, movies on the hangar deck every night, and two chaplains to tell your troubles to. The Navy ain't what it used to be," he added sadly.

"How many sailors have you got in the brig now, Chief?" asked Willy. ("That's the ship's prison," he explained to Parker.)

"None," said the Chief. "I never put nobody in the brig on none of *my* ships. But if they get out of line they wish they *were* in the brig before I get through with them."

Next the chief commissary steward proudly showed them around the galley, bakeshop, butchershop, and mess halls. "We feed on the cafeteria system," he explained. "That's the only way you can feed on a big carrier where you have continuous air operations and people are always eating at odd times. The chow lines are open twenty-four hours around the clock."

"There's the menu for dinner tonight," said Willy, pointing to a blackboard in the galley. "They have a choice of steak or roast chicken today."

"You can take all you want in the chow line," said the CMAA, "but you gotta eat all you take. When I catch 'em trying to throw food away I give 'em a bad time."

"How many men do you have on KP duty?" asked Parker.

"Hardly any now," replied the chief. "We got mechanical spud peelers, dishwashers, and garbage disposal. About all the mess cooks have to do now is wipe off the tables and swab the decks."

"You mean to say the *cooks* do that?" asked Parker.

"Not the rated cooks," said Willy, "It's the KPs that you're talking about. We call 'em mess cooks in the Navy. The regular galley personnel used to be called ship's cooks but under the new rating system they call themselves food preparation technicians."

"They're still belly robbers in my book," growled the CMAA.

"It's quite a job feeding 3000 sailors," observed the commissary steward, "but we serve three good meals a day, fair weather or foul, whether we're in the tropics or North Atlantic. It's all the same to us."

"That's the one big thing about the Navy," said the CMAA. "That's why I shipped in it instead of the Army. You always take your bunk and your mess table into battle with you."

The bakeshop was presided over by a fat sailor in an immaculate apron and a chef's hat who looked as though he had just stepped out of the galley in the Waldorf.

"How many loaves did you bake today, Frenchy?" asked the chief.

"Two thousan'," replied Frenchy, "an' now I gotta make eight hondred goddam lemon cream pies . . . *pies* I don't mind . . . but when the order sheet says make whip cream on top, that'sa too much."

"He's always beefin' about something," said the chief. "If we didn't specify whip cream, he probably would put it on anyway."

On a shelf near the door there were six big cakes with fancy frosting and "Happy Birthday" on top in big red letters. "Who are they for?" asked Parker.

"Everybody gets a cake on his birthday," explained the chief. "The exec's office gives us a list of the birthdays every week. It makes the kids feel better when they're away from home on their birthdays. It was the chief master at arms' idea," he added.

"Yeah," growled the CMAA, looking embarrassed. "You gotta wet-nurse these kids all the time or they're apt to bust out crying in their roast beef and mashed potatoes."

Next stop on the tour was the ship's store, owned and operated by one Satchel Aft Jones, veteran of many battles in Admiral Halsey's Third Fleet and many more with the police along the waterfronts of the world.

"What kind of stuff do you sell here?" asked Parker.

"Everything a sailor needs," said Satchel Aft proudly. "Toothpaste, shaving soap, razor blades, stationery, comic books, and poogie bait."

"Poogie bait?? What's that?"

"Jewelry," said Satchel Aft. "Necklaces, earrings, wristwatches, brooches, fancy lipsticks, compacts, engagement rings—even wedding rings if you've got to get one."

"Why should the government sell that kind of stuff to sailors?" demanded Parker.

"That's what the shysters along Canal Street are screaming all the time," said Satchel Aft. "Credit jewelry outfits—the junk industry, I call 'em. They got pretty near as big a lobby in Congress as the oil industry. They sell you a lot of phony stuff on credit, charge you too much in the first place, and give you easy terms so you'll be paying for it the rest of your life. All my stuff is legitimate. If you pay for diamonds or gold, that's what you get. You pay cash on the line and that's the end of it. Four percent profit for Uncle Sugar and no overhead for bill collectors or lawyers. But there's plenty of trade left for the junk dealers—you'll see dozens of them on the dock when we get into San Diego. Sailors are leery of stuff they buy from the government. Instead of getting their money's worth in my shop, a lot of them would rather buy junk ashore and get screwed."

Next door to Satchel Aft's emporium was the geedunk shop. "What in the world do they sell?" asked Parker.

"Gook," replied the CMAA. "Ice cream, candy, pop, Coca-Cola, Seven-Up, and all that kind of bellywash. These guys lap it up," he said, shaking his head sadly at the idea that two-fisted sailormen could fall to such depths.

"Where do you get your ice cream from?" asked Parker.

"Make it out of powder," explained the chief. "We can turn it out by the barrelful. Whenever we refuel a destroyer at sea, we always give them about twenty gallons. During the war we used to swap movies during fueling, and when a destroyer came alongside with a hot Betty Grable film they often demanded fifty gallons before they would give it to us."

On the way back to the hangar deck they passed a dogged-down watertight door with a sign on it, "KEEP OUT . . . YOU TOO." Alongside it was a big trash bin. "That's the incinerator compartment," said Willy. "You can't throw trash overboard because we don't want to leave a trail of stuff behind us that the enemy might find and follow in wartime, so we burn it all up in a big trash furnace in there. Would you like to see it?"

"Oh . . . I don't think that would be of any interest," said Parker.

"The guy who runs it is a real character," said Willy, "Fatso Gioninni. You might get a couple of good stories out of him. Somebody ought to write a book about him."

The chief master at arms frowned apprehensively at the idea of anybody's interviewing Fatso and led the way farther on.

"No," said Parker, "let's go on and see something else."

Their next stop was the main radio where half a dozen radiomen sat in front of typewriters with phones clamped on their heads listening for the ship's call letters among the dots and dashes chattering constantly on the circuits they were guarding. As one began pounding his typewriter, Willy explained: "This ship's call letters wake them up like an alarm bell. They claim that they can copy traffic automatically after a while. They say the dots and

dashes come in their ears, bypass their brains, and make the right
fingers move on the keyboard. They don't even know what they're
copying. One of them told me he can read a comic book and copy
traffic at the same time."

"Yeah," said the supervisor, "I've heard 'em claim that, too. But
I let one try it one time and the dispatch he was copying from
CNO came out full of zots, whams, and zowies. You can't bypass
a radioman's brains, because he hasn't got any."

"The coding machine is in that room over there," said Willy,
pointing to a door with RESTRICTED AREA painted on it in big red
letters. "Only communications watch officers are allowed in there.
They take an incoming secret dispatch, run it through the machine and break it, and give you the clear. They code the outgoing
stuff on the machine and on short messages they sometimes stick
meaningless padding on the end to make it harder for snoopers to
just guess what the message is about. During the Battle of Leyte
Gulf, when Admiral Halsey got sucked in by those Jap decoys and
left San Bernardino Strait unguarded, Nimitz sent him a message;
'Where are your battleships?' Some crazy CWO stuck padding
on the end: 'All the world wants to know.' When Bull Halsey
read it he didn't recognize it as padding, and he yanked off his hat,
threw it on the deck, and jumped on it."

"Here's some new gear we just installed," said the supervisor.
"Side-band radiophone. Ham operators have been using it for
years to talk to friends on the other side of the world. The military
services have just got wise to it. We can talk to any Navy radio
shore stations with it and they can hook us in to the Bell Telephone System. So now the Admiral can sit up in his cabin, dial us
on the ship's phone, and we can put him through to the Pentagon
or the White House."

"Can't ham operators or anyone else listen in?" asked Parker.

"Wouldn't do 'em any good," said the supervisor. "We put it
through a scrambler and all they'd hear would be a squeal. They
unscramble at the other end and it comes out plain English
again."

"Could I call my office on that?" asked Parker.

"Sure, if you got permission from the Captain. We get emergency calls from ashore every now and then too. Last cruise a sailor's house burned down when we were halfway to Honolulu. His wife phoned in and we flew him back to San Diego."

Next they went down to the armory to meet the Marine Top Sergeant who had six rows of ribbons on his chest, including a purple heart with four stars in it. When they came in the top kick and the chief bandmaster were discussing how the band should sound off while a VIP visitor inspects the guard. "Ten shun!" barked the Marine, snapping to attention as if Ensign Wigglesworth were a four-starred Admiral.

"Carry on," said Willy. "This is our Marine Top Sergeant, Mr. Parker, and this is our bandmaster. . . . There's an old saying in the Navy that you've got to have three things to make a happy ship—good chow, a good laundry, and a good band. We've got 'em all on this ship."

The bandmaster beamed in agreement, while the top kick frowned dubiously.

"Have you ever been in any actual landings, Corporal?" asked Parker of the grizzled Marine.

"Only at Guadalcanal, Tarawa, Iwo Jima, and Inchon," said the Marine, regarding Parker as if he were something the cat had done but neglected to cover up.

"What kind of a ship is this?" asked Parker. "I mean as a combatant unit."

"Don't know," said the Marine. "Never seen 'em in a fight. It's a happy enough ship. But that doesn't prove anything. I've seen outfits that was just a big happy mutual admiration society but they didn't know how to pour piss out of a boot. Holler 'boo' at 'em and they'd run for home. I've been in other outfits where nobody ever opened his mouth except to curse somebody out. But when the enemy showed up we beat the living hell out of him."

When they got back to the wardroom that afternoon and sat down for a cup of coffee, Willy and Parker had seen more of the ship that day than many sailors see in a whole enlistment.

"I've just about run out of ideas now," said Willy. "I hope you've got enough stuff for a story."

"Frankly, Wigglesworth," said Parker, "all we've seen has been routine stuff that has been pretty well hashed over before. I haven't found anything that's newsworthy yet."

"Oh," said Willy. "Well . . . uh . . . just what kind of stuff are you looking for anyway?"

"Things with an exclusive angle to them. Unusual things that our readers ought to know about."

"You mean like an atom bomb being missing from the magazines—or the Admiral smuggling dope aboard and selling it to the sailors?" asked Willy.

"Nuts," said Parker. "But I haven't interviewed the Admiral and Captain yet. I suppose I might get something out of them."

"Yeah," said Willy. "You might as well see them as long as you're out here anyway. What time would be convenient for you to see the Admiral tomorrow?"

"Any time at all," said Parker.

"Okay. I'll have him stand by," said Willy.

That evening Commander Cue asked Willy, "How are you making out with your *Time* man?"

"Not so good," said Willy. "I've been busting a gut to get a story for him. I've had him in places on this ship that I didn't even know there were. I've let him talk to everybody from the Jack of the Dust and Captain of the Head to the Chief Master-at-Arms and Marine Top Sergeant. But he isn't impressed. He wants an exclusive angle."

"These *Time* reporters are hard to please," observed Curly. "They want to get the *Time* slant on everything. If they were covering the burning of Rome they would want to peg the story on the piece of music that Nero was playing on his fiddle instead of on the fire."

"I'm arranging interviews with the Admiral and the Captain for him tomorrow," said Willy. "If he doesn't get an angle from them, I may have to take drastic action with him."

"Oh, oh!" said Curly, thinking of the president of the Pennsylvania Railroad. "Don't drop him down the forward elevator shaft or get him sucked into a jet intake. The Pentagon public relations people might not like it."

"I won't," promised Willy. "But I think I know how to fix him good—in a way he won't even be able to squawk about after I do it."

Later that evening Willy got a pad of the legal paper used for the records of courts-martial and boards of investigation, sat down at a typewriter in his stateroom, and concocted the record of an imaginary investigation on the *Guadalcanal*. It was a stem-winding, breech-loading dilly that might have won him an Oscar if he had been writing a TV script. It told how two floozies had been smuggled aboard in San Francisco just before sailing for Honolulu, had set up shop in the paint locker, way up in the bow, and had made themselves over two thousand bucks before being discovered and locked up in the isolation ward of the sick bay. It gave the stowaways' names and addresses and the names and rates of the sailors who had sponsored this enterprise, smuggled food up to the gals, and shared in the profits until apprehended.

There were legal papers signed by all principals saying that they stood on their constitutional rights and refused to say anything until they were properly represented by lawyers. There was a paper purporting to come from the ship's legal officer recommending that the sailors be tried by general court-martial and the women be indicted in the federal courts. There was a recommendation by the Captain to the Admiral disapproving of this and recommending no official action because it might generate undesirable publicity for the Navy. Finally there was an endorsement by the Admiral approving the Captain's recommendation and directing that the gals be turned over to the FBI in Honolulu for shipment back to the mainland on a slow boat and the sailors were to be put aboard the next transport plane that took off for Antarctica. No official papers about this were to leave the ship and the Admiral would inform CNO of it by personal letter.

When Willy got through manufacturing these documents he stuffed them all in a big manila envelope, stamped SECRET on it in big red letters and wrote "Admiral's eyes only" under the stamp. Then he put it in his bottom drawer, turned in, and slept soundly till morning.

Parker's interview with the Admiral next day was not a howling success from the point of view of either party. The Admiral gave Parker a good solid rundown on the importance of sea power in the atomic age. He explained how the great industrial plant of the United States depends on strategic imports to keep going and would come to a grinding halt if our seaborne trade were cut off. He pointed out that the airplane could never replace the ship for hauling bulk cargo and that to bring a shipload of cargo from Australia to the United States in airplanes, you had to send three tanker loads of gas to Australia to fuel the airplanes.

Parker did not seem to be impressed, so the Admiral took another tack and held forth on the newly blossoming field of ocean-ography. He pointed out that three quarters of the earth's surface is salt water but what lies under that surface is almost unknown. He said we know a great deal more about outer space, the moon, and Mars than we do about the 75 percent of our own planet that is covered by the oceans.

He told how scientists were just beginning to realize that the oceans were vast reservoirs of untapped resources: oil reserves that could carry us for years; vast mineral deposits just waiting for us to find out how to get at them; and plenty of food to take care of the exploding populations. He explained how the Navy was getting into oceanography with both feet, had just set up a new office in the Pentagon to deal with it, and was asking for several hundred million in the next budget for research in this field. But when he got through it was obvious to the Admiral that he had been wasting his time.

Parker then undertook to see if he couldn't pry something worthwhile out of the Admiral with a few shrewd questions. He asked for his opinion on current U.S. foreign policy. The Admiral said that all he had to do with foreign policy was to help carry it out by doing what he was told. The reporter gave the Admiral a chance to air his feelings on the issues of the coming presidential election but he passed on that one too. Parker then took another tack and tried to quiz the old salt about the new type of A bomb they had on board. The Admiral professed to know nothing about any *new* type. When Parker persisted along this line, the Admiral informed him rather frostily that even if they had a brand-new type he certainly couldn't be expected to spill all the minor details of it just to make a feature story. At the end of the interview it was obvious to Parker that he had wasted his time, too.

When they parted, Parker was of the opinion that the Admiral was a stuffed shirt. The Admiral's opinion of Parker could not have been printed in any reputable journal.

Parker's interview with the Captain was equally unsatisfactory. The Captain gave him a good pitch on the educational opportunities that a naval career offers to young sailors and on the number of men on board who were taking special courses that would fit them for jobs in the Navy or out of it. He discussed the ship's athletic programs designed to build up growing boys physically and occupy their spare time. He spoke proudly of the fine conduct of the boys ashore and of the generally high morale of the crew.

Parker stated that in his experience he had often seen happy outfits that broke and ran when the shooting started, and asked the Captain when the *Guadalcanal* had last been in action against an enemy. The Captain admitted that this had been several years back, during the Korean War, before he took command. Parker pointed out to him that he therefore really did not know how well his happy, studious sailors who behaved so well ashore might act in battle.

The Captain seemed to clam up after this interchange, and when Parker tried to quiz him on atom bombs, he got no further than he had with the Admiral.

That afternoon Curly met Willy in the wardroom coffee lounge and said, "I've just been talking to the Admiral and the Captain about your reporter friend."

"Oh," said Willy, "I arranged interviews for him this morning. How did they get along with him?"

"They didn't," said Curly. "They both would like to keelhaul him."

"As long as they feel that way about it, perhaps something along that line can be arranged," observed Willy.

"Don't do anything that his heirs can sue the government for," advised Curly. "We gotta be reasonable, you know."

"I won't do a thing, Cap'n," said Willy. "I'll just fix it so he can do things himself that he may not want to brag about when they backfire on him."

"If I knew what you had in mind, I'm pretty sure I'd probably have to forbid it," said Curly.

"Matter of fact," observed Willy, "if this turns out the way I think it will, we may wind up with a nice story in the next issue of his magazine."

The next morning Willy made a date with Parker to meet him in the wardroom coffee lounge ten minutes after flight quarters was sounded. All hands go to their stations when flight quarters sounds, so the lounge was empty when Willy peeked in there a minute after the bugles had blown. Willy popped in, laid a big unsealed manila envelope marked SECRET on the table and beat it up to the ready room where his squadron mustered.

Willy hung around the ready room half an hour to give Parker plenty of time to get to the coffee lounge, spot the secret envelope, and get curious about its contents. By the time he came bustling into the lounge apologizing for being late, Parker was scribbling in his notebook and his eyes were as big as golf balls.

"Sorry I'm late," said Willy.

"That's all right," said Parker. "Think nothing of it. I've been checking over some of my notes on the things you showed me," he added, stuffing the book in his pocket. "What's the program today?"

"Chart house, signal bridge, and navigation bridge," said Willy. "We'll get going as soon as I have a cup of coffee."

When Willy was halfway through his coffee, one of his pals burst into the coffee lounge with a worried look on his face, grabbed the manila envelope, muttered "Boy-oh-boy!" and scurried out with it.

"I want to send a message to my magazine," said Parker. "How do I do it?"

"Just write it out, give it to me, and I'll file it for you," said Willy.

Parker tore a page out of his notebook and scribbled on it "Aboard atomic carrier *Guadalcanal*. Have big story for you when I get in. Hold space for it. Parker." On the way up to the bridge,

Willy handed the message in to the Communications Office for clearance and processing.

Parker seemed preoccupied while the Chief Quartermaster was explaining to him all about the fathometer, loran, chronometers, and sextants. He didn't seem much interested, either, when the Chief Signalman put on a special signal drill with a nearby destroyer and filled the yardarms with bright-colored flags. On the navigating bridge, he politely declined Willy's offer to let him steer the ship for a while and took only casual interest in the landing operations which they watched over the air officer's shoulder in Fly One, just aft of the Captain's easy chair on the port side of the bridge.

While they were watching the landings, a messenger came up from Communications with a note suggesting that the words "atomic carrier" be deleted from Parker's message and be replaced by the "USS."

"Why?" demanded Parker.

"I should have caught that myself," said Willy. "This isn't an atomic carrier."

"It's got A bombs, hasn't it?" demanded Parker.

"Yes. But all the big carriers have. The *Enterprise* is the only carrier with atomic propulsion that Mr. McNamara has let us build so far."

"Your censors go over things with a fine-tooth comb, don't they?" observed Parker as he okayed the change.

When they went below after flight operations, Parker found a note on the desk in his stateroom, "Call Main Radio. Dial 347." This note had been put there by one of Willy's confederates and 347 was not the number of main radio. It was the number of Willy's stateroom.

After leaving the wardroom, Willy hurried down to his room, where several of his pals were assembled and they settled down to await developments. Soon the phone rang and things began to develop.

"Parker. *Time* Magazine," said the voice on Willy's phone. "I have a note here to call you."

"Yes, Mr. Parker," said one of Willy's pals. "Navy Radio, San Francisco, is trying to get you on the side-band voice radio circuit. Hold on and I'll put you through. . . . NSSQ calling NSXY . . . NSSQ calling NSXY . . . come in please. Over."

"NSXQ to NSXY. We have Mr. Parker on the phone now. Over."

"NSXY to NSSQ. Roger. The New York long-distance operator has been trying to get him. Have him hold and we'll put New York through, over."

"NSSQ to NSXY. Roger. Mr. Parker is holding."

As Parker listened, there followed a make-believe conversation back and forth between long-distance operators and some buzzing and clicking on the line as Willy's pals went through the rigmarole of putting a call through to New York and then to the switchboard in the Time-Life Building. One of the boys was an expert at imitating female voices and put on quite a convincing act.

While this was going on, Parker asked the *Guadalcanal* "operator" if this call would be scrambled and was assured that it would be. He asked would it be monitored, and was told no.

Finally a man's voice came on the line and said, "Parker, this is the New York office. Can you hear me all right?"

"Hear you loud and clear," said Parker. "Go ahead, New York."

"Look, Parker. *Newsweek* is breaking a big story about the *Guadalcanal* date-lined Honolulu. Evidently it's a hot one, but we can't find out much about it, except that it's something that happened on their cruise to Honolulu last month and was hushed up. Have you any idea what it could be? Over."

"I know all about it, New York," came Parker's confident reply. "That's the story I told you to hold space for. Put a stenographer on the line and I'll give it to you now."

In the next ten minutes Parker dictated the tale he had got from the secret folder. He was a sharp reporter and remembered what he had read almost verbatim. When he had finished dictating, he said, "I haven't been able to get the Admiral and the Captain's comments on this yet, but I'll see them this afternoon. They may not want to talk, but now that the story has been broken they'll have to. Over."

"Okay, Parker," said Willy's pal. "Thanks a lot. Good work, Ace. Over and out."

When Parker hung up, Willy observed to his pals, "Hook, line, and sinker. Now the fun begins."

At lunch Parker told Willy, "I gotta see the Admiral this afternoon."

"You just saw him yesterday," said Willy.

"I know. But I gotta see him again. This is urgent."

"Okay," said Willy. "I'll make an appointment for you."

Parker came right to the point with the Admiral. "Sir, I would like to get a statement from you about that business on the cruise to San Francisco."

"Hunh?" said the Admiral, taken unawares. "What do you mean? That foolishness with the *Lafayette?*"

"No, sir. I mean the stowaway incident."

"Stowaways? I don't know what you're talking about."

"I mean the two prostitutes that stowed away in San Francisco and weren't discovered till you were almost in Honolulu."

"Good God!" said the Admiral. "This is news to me." He buzzed for his orderly and said, "Tell the Captain I want to see him right away."

"I thought you knew all about this, sir," said Parker. "Didn't you direct that these women be turned over to the FBI in Honolulu?"

"This is the first I've heard about it," said the Admiral. "This is outrageous. Where did you get this story from?"

"I can't tell you, sir," said Parker. "I have an obligation to protect my sources, you know."

When the Captain came in, the Admiral said, "What's this about women stowaways on this ship on the trip to Honolulu?"

The Captain was just as amazed as the Admiral had been.

"Young man," said the Admiral to Parker, "I think your 'source' has taken you for a sleigh ride."

"I think my source was pretty reliable," said Parker. "I have reason to believe this thing is being hushed up."

"Do you mean to stand there and accuse me of lying?" demanded the Admiral.

"Sometimes denying a bad story isn't considered lying," said Parker. "The State Department does it all the time . . . sometimes even the President does, like in the U-2 incident."

"Well, Parker," said the Admiral, "I'm telling you that there isn't a shred of truth in this story and you're going to look pretty silly if you send it out."

"It has already gone out," said Parker, "so there's no use trying to cover it up any longer."

"That's your tough luck then," said the Admiral. "And now, Mr. Parker, get the hell out of my cabin before I lose my temper."

Outside the cabin the Captain said, "Parker, you've just been *had*, that's all, and I can't really say that I'm sorry for you. A story like that couldn't possibly be hushed up. Everybody on the ship would know about it five minutes after the gals were found—hell, five minutes after they came aboard, for that matter. If you won't take my word for it, I suggest you inquire around among the sailors. And you had better kill that story you sent your magazine about it."

Parker asked the next five or six sailors he met if they knew anything about the floozie stowaways. None did, and their eager inquiries for further details convinced him that he had indeed been hoaxed. However, his inquiries started a rumor going which was all over the ship in five minutes that there were a couple of floozies up in the paint locker and the painter had to call the CMAA to break up the curious crowd that collected there.

Now Parker hit the panic button. That story he had dictated would call for a big play in the magazine and would make them look very foolish indeed. It would certainly get him fired and would make him the laughingstock of the Press Club. He had to kill it right away.

He hurried down to his room and dialed the number he had called that morning to get main radio. No answer. He beat it down to main radio and told the CWO he had to talk to his New York office on side-band radio. The CWO said he would have to get permission from the staff to use side-band. The staff communications officer informed him that the side-band channel was held clear for emergency traffic from the Pentagon, but he could send his message via regular radio in the normal manner.

"But I talked to my office on side-band this morning," protested Parker. "They called me from New York."

"Sometimes shore stations on the circuit will let a call to the ship come through," explained the communicator, "because if the Pentagon wants the circuit they can always cut in. But *we* have to keep the circuit open. Send your message regular radio. It ought to be delivered in five or six hours at the most."

Parker could visualize the presses beginning to roll with the phony story while he struggled with Navy red tape trying to kill it. He scribbled a message: "To Time N.Y. Kill stowaway story I phoned in this morning. Parker."

Then he hastened down to the wardroom coffee lounge to steady his nerves with a cup of black coffee.

Among those gathered around the urn was Willy. "What's the matter, Parker?" he asked. "You look worried."

"Humph," replied Parker, filling his cup.

"Have you got your story written yet?" asked Willy. "We got a lot more things I can show you if you want me to."

"I've seen a lot more than I want of this bucket already," observed Parker.

After about ten minutes a messenger from the radio room handed Willy a copy of Parker's outgoing message to *Time* with a note from the CWO saying, "We are holding this for verification. There is no record of any outgoing side-band traffic today. Please check with Parker."

Willy pushed the note across the table and Parker blew up when he read it. "Good God," he said, "hasn't my message gone out yet?"

"No. You see what they say. They just want to make sure it's correct before sending it."

"I wrote it myself," stormed Parker. "There's no reason for them to doubt it. I gave it to them half an hour ago and here they are diddling around trying to make up their minds whether I mean it or not."

"Keep your shirt on," said Willy. "There's no hurry."

"No hurry, hell, the magazine goes to print tonight," roared Parker. "That message has got to get out right now or there will be all hell to pay."

"But they say they don't know anything about any story you sent," said Willy. "They would have to clear anything you sent for security so there must be some mistake."

"God damn it, I sent it by side-band radio," said Parker. "What if I didn't clear it. I'm killing it now."

"Come down to my room for a minute," said Willy. "Maybe we can straighten this out."

"Please, Wigglesworth," pleaded Parker, "get that message out, will you? I'll be ruined if you don't."

"Sure. In a few minutes. Come along with me."

In his stateroom Willy said, "My friend, you have been had so many ways I can hardly count them."

"Whadaya mean?" asked Parker.

"First of all, you fell for the phony stowaway story."

"Anybody might have made that mistake," said Parker. "It all looked pretty official."

Willy reached into a drawer, hauled out the big manila envelope, and tossed it on his desk. "It was in an official envelope marked SECRET. Do you always sneak a look inside envelopes you find lying around that aren't addressed to you?"

"Never mind preaching to me now," said Parker. "I've got to get this message off to New York before it's too late. Time's awasting."

"Before coming aboard you signed an agreement to clear your stuff, but you tried to sneak this one out anyway."

"All right, I did. We can argue about that later on. But I've *got* to kill that story I sent off—right *now!*"

"Relax, Parker," said Willy. "No story went out."

"Whadaya mean? I phoned it to New York myself this morning."

"No, you didn't," said Willy. "You phoned it to this room right here and some friends and I canned it for you in case you have any use for it," he added, tossing a small can of tape from a recorder on the desk. "A couple of guys put on an act about long-distance operators. But nothing ever went off the ship."

"Well, I'll be gah-dam," said Parker. "It didn't go out! Whew!"

"But you're not all the way off the hook yet, you know," said Willy.

"How come?"

"You sent your editor a message this morning saying you had a big story for him. Remember? That one did go out."

"Yeah, that's right, I did send one," said Parker.

"Do you want to cancel that now and tell them that you went off half-cocked?" asked Willy. "That you've been out here a week and can't find a story?"

"No," said Parker. "I don't. . . . I'll tell you, Wigglesworth, you showed me some good stuff around the ship; the Captain and the Admiral gave me some too. I got enough for a good story right now. If I get busy on it right away I can get it off in time to beat the deadline tonight. . . . I'll see ya later, kid."

That afternoon Parker filed a long story to *Time* about life in the *Guadalcanal*. It was full of colorful human interest angles about what goes on on the lower decks and had a lot of good solid stuff about the importance of sea power in the atomic age and on the fascinating new field of oceanography which the Navy was pioneering. It was cleared without changing a word, got a nice play in the next issue of *Time*, was condensed in the *Reader's Digest*, and the Navy League got reprints and mailed them to all its members.

That evening after Commander Cue had seen a copy of Parker's outgoing story, he sent for Willy and said, "Wigglesworth, as a PRO you are a genius. You are hereby appointed permanent press relations officer for this ship."

"I wouldn't do that if I were you, Cap'n," said Willy. "It's dangerous. I'm not cut out for the job and it scares me to think of what might happen."

CHAPTER TEN

Much Ado About Nothing

THE TIME story was quite a feather in Willy's bed as a public relations officer and pundit on naval strategy and tactics. He began to feel he might be a budding Samuel Eliot Morison or even Alfred Taylor Mahan. He also felt somewhat under obligation to Ace Parker, in a way. After all, you couldn't really blame Ace for the fast one *he* had tried to pull. The only reason Willy had been able to booby-trap him was that their minds both worked in the same devious channels when they felt that red tape was infringing their constitutional rights. So Willy felt that he ought to dig up some sort of lead for Parker to repay him for the sympathetic and penetrating piece he had produced, under Willy's guidance, about sea power.

Willy had shown Parker everything he could on the ship. So he turned his mind to the wonders of the sea and sky around them. There was plenty of good stuff there, if you just had the wit to recognize it. No spot-news stories but *Time*'s big brother, *Life*, might find a good picture story somewhere in the wind and wave. Suddenly an idea hit Willy—the Green Flash!

The Green Flash is a scientific fact that few people know about, and many of those who have heard of it don't believe it. When the sun sets behind a sharp sea horizon and there is no haze whatever, its upper limb changes from flaming orange to brilliant green a second or so before it disappears. It is a spectacular and astonishing thing when it occurs, but it isn't always predictable. Often atmospheric conditions aren't right and nothing happens.

Aboard ship is a good place to see it. But seafaring men are a skeptical lot and after someone in the know has assembled them a couple of times at sunset to see it and nothing happens, they are convinced from then on that the guy is a liar. It can also be seen from the western shore of tropical isles. But in the tropics most observers are half crocked by sunset so those who have not seen it attribute stories about it to the rum.

But it *does* happen. When it does, you are well repaid for the times when you looked for it expectantly but didn't see it.

Willy was one of the initiated, having seen the flash several times in the Mediterranean. He hunted up Parker and said, "Mr. Parker, I've got an idea that might make a story for *Life*. There would be some good colored pictures in it and *you* could write the story on it. Do you want to hear about it?

"I'll listen to anything you say, Wigglesworth," said Parker warily; "but whether I will believe it or not is a horse from another kettle of fish."

That afternoon Parker, Willy, and a number of his aviator pals assembled on the signal bridge near sunset to observe this phenomenon of the green flash. While the sun was still several diameters above the horizon, Willy explained the scientific facts of life about it.

"You see," said Willy, "the earth's atmosphere acts like a prism and refracts the sun's light. When you put a narrow beam of light through a prism, it splits up into all the colors of the rainbow. The same thing happens when the sun's rays shine through the atmosphere. But the sun's disc is half a degree wide, so you don't get just one narrow beam from it. You get a lot of beams and, although they split up, they get scrambled back together and come out white sunlight again while the sun is high. But when the sun is setting, the bundle of beams is getting narrower, and when just a sliver of the sun is left you see the green part of the spectrum. Actually, the last sliver turns ultraviolet, but you don't see that because it blends in with the blue of the sky."

"Why don't we see it every day, Dr. Einstein?" asked one of his listeners.

"Lots of times there's a little haze in the air that you can't see," said Willy. "Unless the air is perfectly clear, the sun just gets redder and redder as it goes down and you don't see the flash."

"How does it look for today, professor?" asked another skeptic.

"Good," said Willy. "We got a clear sharp horizon and no haze. At least I don't *think* there's any. The sun is only about a diameter above the horizon now and it's still too bright to look at it. That's a good sign."

As the bright disc touched the horizon and began fading to orange, all hands watched expectantly. When it was half gone and was flaming red, Willy said, "It will stay this color until there is just a little sliver left peeping over the horizon. Then, maybe, two seconds before it is gone, BOOM! It turns just as green as the starboard light."

All hands concentrated their gaze on the sinking sun. An expectant hush fell over the crowd. Curious signalmen joined the group and looked west too. The sun got smaller and smaller and redder and redder and then disappeared.

All eyes swung around and glared indignantly at Willy, whose face got almost as red as the sun. After a moment of silence, a lieutenant said, "I think you're full of crap."

All heads nodded grave agreement and the crowd drifted away, leaving only Parker with Willy.

"But it *does* turn green—sometimes," said Willy. "Today the air must not—"

"*I* believe you, Willy," interrupted Parker.

"Thanks, pal," said Willy. "I am touched by your faith in me."

"I looked it up in the encyclopedia," said Parker.

"Humph," grunted Willy. "Well, anyway, when it happens, you could get a series of real good color pictures out of it and I know a couple of nice gimmicks you could use too, if *Life* goes for the idea."

"Go ahead. I'm listening," said Parker; "I think there's a *Life* story here, all right."

"You can freeze the flash," said Willy, "and make it last for an hour or so if you want to."

"How do you do that?"

"Photograph it from a high-speed plane. There are plenty of planes these days that can fly around the world faster than the sun goes around it. So you put your cameras in a fast plane and loaf around till you get the flash just as the sun is going down. Then you head west and fly just fast enough to keep the sun peeking over the horizon at you. It will stay green. Then you can speed up a little, bring some more of the sun back up over the horizon, and it will go red. You can fiddle with your throttle and make it go red and green whenever you want to."

"That's a whale of a gimmick," said Parker. "You tinker with the sun like it was a traffic light. Damnedest thing I ever heard of."

"You can see the flash at sunrise too," continued Willy. "It's harder to see it in the morning because you have to be looking at exactly the right place to catch it. At sunset you've got your eye on the sun as it goes down, so that's no problem. And, besides, at sunrise the kind of people who are interested in such things as the flash usually have too bad a hangover to concentrate."

"I think *Life* will grab at this," said Parker.

This was to be the *Guadalcanal's* last day at sea. Next morning at the crack of dawn she would launch her air group to fly in to North Island and land about sunrise. Later the ships would come in and tie up to piers lined with happy wives, kids, sweethearts, jewelry salesmen, and bill collectors.

While dinner was being served in the wardroom that evening, word boomed over the loudspeakers: "Now hear this! All personal messages must be in the radio room by twenty hundred."

"What's that all about, Willy?" asked Parker.

"Everybody is allowed to send personal messages to their families the last night at sea, telling them when they'll get in."

"Hmmm," said Parker. "Might be some good human-interest stuff in them. Could I see them?"

"No," said Willy; "they're supposed to be private, you know. And most of 'em just say 'home by six-thirty in the morning. Don't get up.'"

Later that evening a group gathered around the TV in the wardroom listening to the news . . .

"Washington, D.C.—The flying saucers which have been seen all over the country this week appeared over Washington last night. They were seen both visually and on radar over the National Airport and also in the restricted air space over the White House. Fighter planes were scrambled from Andrews Air Force Base to intercept them but were unable to make contact. A continuous air patrol is being flown over the Washington area to intercept all unidentified incoming traffic. The NACA and Air Force refuse to comment on the objects seen last night."

"Holy cow," said a listener. "Little men from Mars!"

"Aw, it's prob'ly just another gag like the one Orson Welles pulled when they scared the pants off everybody in New Jersey," said another.

"This is no gag," said a believer. "The man said the Air Force scrambled fighters from Andrews. They must of thought *something* was up there."

"People have been seeing them all over the country for a couple of months now," said another; "and all the reports aren't by screwballs, either. Weather observers, college professors, and even airline pilots have seen them. They can't all be wrong. The Pentagon thinks there's something to it because they just set up a special task force called UFO, Unidentified Flying Objects. They're going to collect all the reports, feed the data on them into a computer, and find out what the hell is really happening."

"They better allow for the GIGO factor," said Willy.

"What's that?"

"Garbage In—Garbage Out."

"It's all very well for you to sit there and wisecrack," said the believer, "but it's no joking matter. I think those things are real and we'd better by a damn sight take them seriously."

"You guys are funny," observed Willy, "I tell you about a known scientific fact like the green flash and none of you will believe it. But you hear a fairy story on the radio about little men from Mars and you swallow it whole."

"The newspapers have been full of stuff about saucers, too," said the believer. "Newspapers don't go for every wild rumor they hear on the radio. Most editors are skeptics and they check pretty carefully before they print anything."

Ace Parker frowned and shifted uncomfortably.

"Nuts," said Willy. "Most of them will print anything that will make headlines and sell newspapers."

"You're exaggerating now, Willy," said Parker. "Some of the tabloids do that, but the responsible press are pretty careful about what they print."

"Oh, yeah?" said Willy. "How about the AP stories on the Loch Ness monster, and the Abominable Snowman. Editors are supposed to be real sharp characters, but some of them remind me of the Marine recruiter who shipped a midget in the corps."

"All right. Come on. How could a midget get in the Marines?" demanded Parker.

"That's what the general raised hell about when he saw the guy," said Willy.

"Okay. How did he get in?"

"The little son of a gun lied about his height," said Willy. "And some editors will believe anything you tell them if you just whisper it to 'em in a dark corner."

"Come off it, Willy," said Parker. "You booby-trapped me once, but that was a special case where you could stack the deck on me. You couldn't do it again. Most editors *are* shrewd cookies who can spot phony stories. They have to be."

"Matter of fact," said Willy, "they'll sometimes blow up nothing into a big story if you give them half a chance. They can take a routine story that you give them in which everything you say is plain fact, hang a slanted headline on it, and make a spectacular bum out of you."

"I'm beginning to think you've got a grudge against the press," said Parker. "They won't usually do that to you unless you've got it coming to you. I will admit, though, that the headline you put on a story can make a lot of difference. Like the time the goofball got loose in the bug house, raped one of the nurses, and escaped. That was just a routine story til some genius of a headline writer got hold of it.'

"What then?" asked Willy.

"He headlined it 'NUT SCREWS AND BOLTS,' " said Parker. "A half a dozen old ladies cancelled their subscriptions but hundreds of new subscribers signed up."

"Well, anyway," said Willy, "you guys watch the headlines in tomorrow afternoon's San Diego papers, and you'll see what I mean."

"What the hell are you cooking up now, Willy?" demanded Commander Cue. "Whatever it is, I probably ought to issue strict orders against it."

"I'm not cooking up anything, Cap'n," said Willy. "But I may turn a burner up a little bit under something they've already got cooking."

"Are you holding out another scoop on me, pal?" asked Parker.

"No," said Willy. "It hasn't happened yet. But it will. Tomorrow morning. Look in the afternoon papers."

Next morning Willy was assigned to fly one of the early warning radar planes ashore. As the air crews manned the planes just before sunrise, Willy said to his radarman, "Bluberry, I want you to pay careful attention to everything I say on the interphone while we're flying in, and to put it all down in your logbook. I'll want you to take some radar bearings for me, so get your set warmed up."

"Aye aye, sir," said Bluberry, fiddling around helping Willy adjust his shoulder harness before retiring to the after cockpit.

Soon the flight deck bull horns boomed "Stand by-y-y to start engines." Starters whined, the flight deck burst into thunderous song, and the ship started swinging into the wind.

Usually on a deck load launch there will be one or two aborts when pilots turn a plane down because she drops off a few revs on the right mag or the oil pressure is a little low. But not on the morning when they are flying back to the beach! Crocks that have been hangar deck lilies for the whole cruise are hauled up to the flight deck, and expert mechanics manage to get them coughing and wheezing. Cautious pilots who ordinarily can detect one plug missing in a double-banked engine will nod their heads as if she was snorting like a wild bull on the open range during the warm-up. When Fly One gives the "are you ready?" sign they shove their fist out thumb up, and go staggering down the deck practically flapping their wings to nurse the old crate into the air and head for the barn.

Willy went off the catapult that morning, which is much easier than flying off. When you fly off you've got to hold her straight along the center line of the deck, ease her off at the bow, and go into a climbing right turn, watching out for the slipstream of the guy ahead just as you go over the bow. But from the catapult, it's just WHAM and there you are . . . a little groggy from the G forces, but in the air and on your way.

The air group rendezvoused over the ship 200 miles offshore and headed for the beach just as the sun was peeping over the horizon. Since the guppy plane is a lot slower than the fighters and bombers, Willy headed in by himself.

Soon after they got squared away on the course to North Island, Willy picked up the interphone and said, "Bluberry, make a note. I see a brilliant saucer-shaped object about five degrees on the starboard bow."

"Aye aye, sir," said Bluberry, scribbling in his book.

"It seems to be a little smaller than a full moon," said Willy, "and it's too bright for me to look right at it; take a look yourself, Bluberry, and see if you agree."

Bluberry stuck his head up into the plastic canopy over his cubbyhole, looked out ahead, and said, "I don't see anything but the sun out there, sir."

"I'm not asking you for any opinions about what the thing *is*," said Willy. "All I want to know is, do you see a brilliant saucer-shaped object out there a little smaller than a full moon?"

"Well . . . uh—sure," came the reply.

"Now take note, Bluberry," said Willy. "We're headed almost right toward that thing. I'm going to give her the gun and see if we can catch up with it." So saying, Willy shoved his throttle against the stop and the air speed meter wound up to 350 knots.

"Are you sure you feel all right, Mr. Wigglesworth?" asked Bluberry.

"Sure, I feel fine," replied Willy. A couple of minutes later he said, "We're not gaining an inch on it. Now I'm going to see if we can climb up as high as it is," and he hauled back on the stick and started climbing.

"I think you're nuts, *sir!*" said Bluberry.

"You're entitled to your own opinion about that, Bluberry," replied Willy. "But you can get in trouble if you go around saying things like that about your superior officers in this Navy."

Pretty soon Willy said, "Take another look now, Bluberry, and see if you think we're any closer."

Bluberry looked, said, "Nossir, not a bit," and tightened up his shoulder harness, checked his Mae West, and mentally reviewed the bail-out and ditching procedures.

Next Willy said, "Beam your radar out there five degrees on the starboard bow and see if you can get an echo off it."

Bluberry cranked his radar screen around and probed the sky for a minute, muttering some remarkable observations about the feeblemindedness of present-day naval pilots. "No return from out there," he reported on the interphone.

Willy throttled back to normal cruise and said, "Make a note in your book that for the past ten minutes, this thing has been ducking in and out behind the clouds and that now it has disappeared in that big cumulus to the east."

"Aye aye, sir," said Bluberry.

As they neared the coast they flew under a solid deck of cumulus cloud about a thousand feet above them. Willy called on the interphone and said, "Stick your head up again, Bluberry, and see if you can find that thing anywhere."

Bluberry poked his head up, looked all around, and said, "Nossir. I don't see it any more."

"Neither do I," said Willy.

When they landed and taxied up to the line, Bluberry scrambled out on the wing to help Willy out of his shoulder harness and asked, "How do you feel now, Mr. Wigglesworth?"

"I'm fine," said Willy. "Now I want you to come into the office with me, listen, and make a tape recording while I phone a story in to the paper. They may ask you to verify some of the facts I give 'em, but don't go popping off with any opinions. Just stick to the facts."

In the office Willy started a tape recorder going, dialed the San

Diego *Union,* and got the city editor on the line. "This is Ensign William Wigglesworth, U.S. Navy, sir," he said. "I am attached to VF Squadron 103 on the USS *Guadalcanal.* I just flew in from the ship and on the way I observed a phenomenon that may be of interest to you."

"Uh huh . . . what was that?" asked ye ed.

"I observed a brilliant saucer-shaped object in the sky. I tried to—"

"What's that again? A flying saucer, you said?"

"It was the *shape* of a saucer," said Willy. "I tried to catch up with it, but I—"

"Wait a minute," said ye ed, "I want to get another man on this line and take this down—get on that other phone," he barked at a rewrite man, "and get this story. . . . All right, Mr. Wigglesworth, start over again. What were you saying about a flying saucer?"

"I was flying in from the *Guadalcanal* this morning about 150 miles out from San Diego at 5000 feet and I saw this brilliant saucer-shaped object a little on my starboard bow—"

"How big was it?" asked ye ed.

"Not quite as big as a full moon," said Willy.

"What was it doing?"

"It ducked in and out among the clouds for about ten minutes and then it went into a big cloud and stayed there."

"Okay. What were you doing at this time?"

"I flew wide open for about five minutes after I sighted it, making 350 knots, but I couldn't catch up with it. I climbed from 5000 to 20,000 feet, but didn't seem to get any closer."

"I'll be damned," said ye ed. "How clearly did you see this thing?"

"Perfectly," said Willy. "It was good clear air and I could see it just as plain as day except when it ducked into the clouds."

"Did it seem to be taking evasive action?" asked the ed.

"Well, I don't know if you could call it that, sir," said Willy, "but I couldn't catch up with it no matter what I did."

"Could you see any windows or anything in it?"

"No," said Willy; "it was too bright and too far away. I tried to get closer, but I couldn't. Couldn't get any radar return off of it, either."

"Holy catfish!" said ye ed. "Tell the composing room to hold the front page," he said in an aside to one of his helpers. . . . "Lemme get your name and unit right."

"Ensign William Wigglesworth, U.S. Navy. Attached to fighter squadron 103 on the USS *Guadalcanal*."

"That's fine, Ensign Wigglesworth. Did anyone else see this thing?"

"Yessir. My radar operator saw it too. I'll let you speak to him," and he handed the phone to Bluberry.

"Hello," said Bluberry. "Yeah. I was in the rear seat of Mr. Wigglesworth's plane this morning and I seen everything he did. It was just like he told you."

"Give us your name and home town," asked the editor.

"J. Bluberry, radarman 1/C, from Fremont, Nebraska."

"What do you think it was?" asked the editor.

"You'd better ask the pilot about that," said Bluberry. "I'm just the radarman."

"The pilot said you couldn't get this thing on radar. Is that right?"

"It sure is," said Bluberry. "I pointed the radar beam right at it and turned the power way up. No radar return at all."

Willy took back the phone. "That's about all I can tell you, sir," he said. "I thought you might be interested."

"We sure as hell are," said the editor. "This is a big story. Stick around where you are for a while, will you? I want to send a photographer down to get pictures of you and your radarman. He'll be there in ten minutes."

"Okay," said Willy. "We'll wait."

As the editor hung up, he yelled at his rewrite man, "Fix that story up right away." Then to his helpers, "Banner headline. Right-hand column, front page"; and to another, "Put this story on the ticker to AP. Tell our radio and TV stations. They'll probably want to get exclusives on this while it's still hot."

Ten minutes later, the *Union*'s photographer showed up at the hangar all out of breath and got pictures of Willy and Bluberry standing alongside their plane. "What's this all about?" he asked. "The office said something about you guys seeing flying saucers."

"No comment," said Willy.

"Oh. Playing it cozy and clamming up to put the bite on the radio and TV people, are you? Well, all I got to do is get pictures."

Meantime things were happening in the newspaper office. The front page for the afternoon edition was pulled and reset with the saucer story in the right-hand column under a banner headline. Associated Press came back on the teletype from New York and asked for comment by the Admiral on the saucers seen in his bailiwick. Both the TV and radio stations wanted immediate interviews with Willy and Bluberry. The editor got Naval District Headquarters on the phone, and after some argument they put him through by side-band to Admiral Day on the *Guadalcanal*. Admiral Day stated that he knew nothing about this alleged saucer sighting, but agreed to have a press conference as soon as his ship got in around noon. A dispatch went in from the Admiral to the air station to have Wigglesworth and the CO of his squadron report to the Admiral as soon as the carrier tied up. Meantime, AP in New York had queried the Pentagon about this saucer sighting in the Pacific Fleet and CNO shot a dispatch to the *Guadalcanal* asking the Admiral what was coming off here. By the time the *Guadalcanal* tied up, the afternoon paper was on the street with a headline, LOCAL NAVY PILOT CHASES FLYING SAUCER, a delegation of reporters and radio and press men was pacing impatiently up and down the dock, and quite a head of steam had been generated.

When Willy trooped up the gangway with the press delegation, he had the afternoon paper in one hand and his tape-recording machine in the other. When he was shown into the Admiral's cabin, Commander Cue was already there. So was Ace Parker. The reporters and TV men had to wait outside.

"What's all this uproar you've stirred up about flying saucers," demanded the Admiral, "and why wasn't I informed by dispatch about this when it happened?"

"Admiral," said Willy, "a lot of people have jumped to some farfetched conclusions. There was no reason for telling you anything about this. In fact there was nothing to tell about at all until they blew it up into something."

"What do you mean? Didn't you give them this story?" demanded the Admiral, holding up the paper.

"Yessir. I gave it to them all right. And it's all true, every word of what I told them. And everybody who flew in this morning saw the same thing I saw; I gave them the story, but I didn't write the headline on it."

"Hah!" snorted Commander Cue. "I'll be gormswoggled with a rubber swab handle. May I see that paper again, Admiral?"

The Admiral handed him the paper. Commander Cue skimmed through the story hastily, with Parker looking over his shoulder. Then he said, "I'm sorry, Admiral. We've all just been had by this character."

"How do you mean?" asked the Admiral.

"All he saw was the sun. Matter of fact that's all it *says* he saw in the story here," said Curly.

"Yessir. That's right, sir," said Willy, "just the little old sun is all I saw. And I've got a tape recording here of exactly what I told the newspapers. Do you want to hear it, sir?"

"Yes. Lemme listen to it," said the Admiral.

Willy played it through. The Admiral looked at Curly and Parker and raised his eyebrows.

Curly said, "He's right, sir. It was a deliberate booby trap, but actually every word he said was the gospel truth."

"I agree," said Parker.

"So . . . what do we do now about that mob that's waiting outside for a press conference?"

"I'll handle 'em, sir," said Willy.

"And just how do you propose to do it?" asked the Admiral, who was beginning to get a bit leery of giving Ensign William Wigglesworth carte blanche to handle anything.

"Just tell them the whole truth," said Willy. "There isn't a thing they can do about it except get mad and kill the story. They won't even print a retraction because it would make them look too silly if they did. They'll just drop the story from the rest of the editions today and in a day or so it will go away."

"I think he's exactly right," said Parker. "They can't do anything else."

"All right," said the Admiral. "Let the lions and tigers come in."

The conferees crowded into the cabin and waited respectfully for the Admiral to start things going.

"Gentlemen," said the Admiral, "I won't beat around the bush with you. There has been a mistake and this whole business is much ado about nothing."

"What do you mean, sir?" asked several newsmen who had their pencils poised.

"I'll let Ensign Wigglesworth do his own explaining," said the Admiral.

"Gentlemen," said Willy, "all I saw on the way in was the sun."

There was a stunned silence for a moment, and then a reporter said, "Then why in the hell did you give us this story about flying saucers?"

"I didn't say a word about flying saucers," said Willy. "And even in your own story in the paper, the only mention of flying saucers is in the headline. I said I saw a saucer-shaped object. That's all I said and I got a tape recording of my phone call to your editor if you want to hear it."

"Holy cow," said the *Union* reporter, "lemme out of here. I gotta get on the phone and kill this thing right away." He hustled out headed for the nearest phone booth on the dock.

"Anybody wanta hear a playback?" asked Willy.

Nobody did.

Finally the AP man said, "Well, why the hell didn't you *say* you thought this thing was the sun?"

"Nobody asked me what I thought it was."

"You're a smart little bastard, aren't you?" asked the reporter.

"I think the same about you," replied Willy, "except you're not very smart."

"Gentlemen," said the Admiral, "I suggest that if you wish to continue this conference any further, you adjourn to the alley behind the warehouse on the dock."

As the reporters filed out, Commander Cue said to Willy, "Wait for me outside, Ensign Wigglesworth."

A few minutes later, Curly emerged from the cabin and said, "Mr. Wigglesworth, I believe I told you yesterday evening you had a permanent job as PRO for this command?"

"Yessir," said Willy.

"Well, that was a slight exaggeration," said Curly. "You're fired."

"Aye aye, sir," said Willy.

At the San Diego airport that afternoon, Willy and Parker were having a drink at the bar as Parker waited for his plane back to New York.

"That saucer deal was a lowdown trick," said Parker, "but I must admit you were pretty cute about it."

"It couldn't miss," said Willy; "it was like swiping gin from your grandmother's medicine chest."

"I've read in some of the history books," said Parker, "about how Admiral Halsey had a 'dirty trick' department on his staff. Now that I've seen how you Navy guys work, I feel sorry for those poor Jap admirals. I don't blame them a bit for tearing up the Geneva Convention."

CHAPTER ELEVEN

Wired for Sound

SOON AFTER this Curly shoved off for Annapolis on two weeks' leave. The Commander had been a star football player in his Academy days and was planning to visit his classmate, Jumping Joe Sifton, Navy's great all-American quarterback, who was currently on duty at the trade school as backfield coach. Joe and Curly had been shipmates in the *Enterprise* during the war, as fighter pilots in VF Squadron 6.

On the plane going east Curly scanned the football scores in the Sunday paper and shook his head sadly. William & Mary 47—Navy 3; Army 55—Notre Dame 0. The Army-Navy game was only a month away, and it seemed that a naval disaster was impending that would rival the blowing up of the *Maine*. Army was well on its way to its second undefeated season in a row and was the unanimous choice of all the experts for the mythical national championship title. Navy's only claim to fame was that they had showed up on time for every game.

"I don't think Army's that good or Navy that bad," said Curly, showing the paper to the Lieutenant sitting next to him.

"Maybe not," said the Lieutenant; "but on the basis of comparative scores, I'd say that Army figures to have a slight edge in the odds at Philadelphia next month."

"You an Academy man?" demanded Curly.

"No, sir. But I often root for Navy anyway," said the Lieutenant.

"Of course, comparative scores don't mean a thing in an Army-Navy game," observed Curly. "The student bodies at both Academies get so hopped up that the teams don't play according to form, and it's never a pushover no matter what the past records show."

"Uh-huh," observed the Lieutenant.

"My first class year," said Curly, "we were national champs and had Sifton at quarterback. You've heard of him, haven't you?"

"Jumpin' Joe? Sure. Everybody's heard of *him*. All-American three years in a row."

"That's right," said Curly. "And Army was just an also-ran that year. But they gave us a hell of a scare and we were lucky to nose them out 17 to 14."

"Uh-huh," said the Lieutenant. "But Army has won 25 in a row so far, and I can hardly remember when Navy won its last one."

"Well, all right, young fella. I'm telling you there's always a chance in an Army-Navy game. And don't you forget it."

"Uh-huh," said the Lieutenant.

"You don't sound very convinced," said Curly.

"I'm not . . . and I don't think you are either, for that matter."

"Yeah. I guess you're right about that," admitted Curly. "But, like I say, you never can tell in an Army-Navy game."

In the bar of the officers' club at Annapolis next evening Curly, Jumpin' Joe, and one of the civilian coaches were hoisting a few when who should come strolling in but old Hawsepipe Smith. Hawsepipe had been a fighter director in Combat Information Center on the *Enterprise*, and whenever three old *Enterprise* sailors get together, there is always a lot of serious reminiscing to be done.

Fighter pilots are not allowed to reminisce in the bar of the officers' club at the Naval Academy because it wakes up the retired admirals in the library at the other end of the building, and also because bystanders are apt to be jostled and get elbows poked in their eyes when the boys start gesturing to show how they accomplished their feats of derring-do.

So Curly, Jumpin' Joe, Hawsepipe, and the line coach adjourned to Joe's room on the next deck and hauled the planes out of the hangar. Pretty soon the air was full of weaving arms the way it always is when aviators are lying about their exploits. All the old battles had to be refought and explained, presumably for the benefit of the line coach. But even if he had gradually evaporated nobody would have noticed.

For the next couple of hours Curly, Hawsepipe, and Jumpin' Joe dived and zoomed all over the place, dogfighting with Japs that outnumbered them 10 to 1. They had been a great fighting team on the *Enterprise,* a hot-shot outfit of sharp flyers and good gunners backed up by fighter directors who knew their stuff. Whenever they got their sights on a Jap, he came down in flames. And the *Enterprise* fighter directors down in Combat Information Center had been experts at putting the finger on the Japs for the pilots.

Old Hawsepipe would sit down there with a big cigar in his face and call the plays for them just as a quarterback does. He could spot a Jap when he was just a suspicion of a tiny blip on a radarscope and coach the boys in the air into position for a kill. They had all learned to depend on Hawsepipe and do exactly as he told them.

"I remember the first Zero I ever knocked down," said Curly. "I came at him out of the sun," he explained with his elbows cocked up and his palms extended one behind the other. "He never knew what hit him. He was just sitting there, fat, dumb, and happy, when I let him have it with all six fifty-calibers. Blew up right in my face, he did. . . . I thought for a while I was going in the drink with him."

"I remember a Betty I shot down," said Jumpin' Joe. "Made three passes at him and riddled him every time. I'll never forget the little Jap tail gunner looking up at me the last time I bored in. His plane was just a big ball of flames, but he wasn't scared—just disillusioned. He couldn't believe it. His mouth was wide open, and his eyes were as big as horse apples."

"You remember the day of the Turkey Shoot?" asked Jumpin'

Joe. (This was one of the major turning points of the war, known to naval historians as the First Battle of the Philippine Sea, but to all aviators as the Mariana Turkey Shoot.)

"I'll never forget it," said Curly. "Our squadron commander was Dave McDonald, and he was always rising hell with us about radio discipline and making reports in proper official language. If you didn't follow the book he would chew you out like a Marine sergeant. When we ran into the Jap air groups that day all he could say was 'Gawd Almighty, look at all the Japs.' CIC kept yelling at him asking how many? Where? What kind? What altitude? and he just kept saying, 'Gawd Almighty! There are a million of them!' And then finally, when asked to report on the progress of the battle, he said, 'They're falling like autumn leaves.' And that's the way it was, too. Wherever you looked, the air was full of Zekes and Zeros and Bettys. We knocked 'em down like clay pigeons, but more kept coming. Toward the last I was only shooting one gun at a time to save ammunition. By the time it was over there was blood, guts, and feathers all over the Pacific Ocean."

"Yeah," said Hawespipe, "that's the way it was, all right. We knocked down over 450 Japs that day. The best pilots they had, too. And how about the next day, when we found the Jap fleet late in the afternoon and you guys had to come aboard after dark?"

"That was the goddamdest rat race of the whole war," observed Curly. "We all knew by the time we found the Japs that we couldn't get back till long after dark, and some of us were too low on gas to make it all the way back anyway. But nobody was turning back that day! After the attack nobody bothered about trying to rendezvous with his own outfit—we all just headed east and joined up with anybody we could see. Squadrons and air groups were strung out in a long line, with everybody throttled way back to save gas. When the sun went down we still had 150 miles to go, and some of the boys were beginning to go in the drink. The air was full of Maydays and ditching reports from then on, with everybody giving a rough estimate of how far west of the fleet they were just before they went in."

"It got darker than all hell after sunset," continued Curly, "and nobody really knew where we were going. Nobody was trying to navigate. We all just headed east and followed each other, glad to be among friends. About a half hour after dark we spotted searchlights sweeping up in the sky beyond the horizon, after Admiral Mitscher gave the order to turn on the lights. Prettiest sight I ever saw. I thought of the Bible story about the Promised Land. I never could see why the headline writers made such a big thing out of turning on the lights, and old Pete Mitscher couldn't either. Only thing he could do."

"But after we got back, that's when the fun began," said Jumpin' Joe, taking over the narrative. "Hardly anybody had ever made a night landing before, and it wasn't long before half the decks were fouled up with crashes. They were waving 'em off from one ship and telling them to go to another, but some of the boys were so low on gas they weren't taking a wave-off. They'd land anyway, and pile one crash on top of another. Nobody cared a damn about airplanes that night. If you couldn't taxi out of the gear right away, they just made you get the hell out of the plane and shoved it overboard to make room for the next guy. Before long it was everybody for himself and some of the boys even tried to land on the battleships with their wheels up."

"CIC was a madhouse that night," observed Hawsepipe. "We had 130 planes in the water, but only 76 people were lost. . . . We sank three Jap carriers in those two days and they never recovered from it."

Then Curly spread his hands out and cocked up his elbows and said, "Remember the day when I hid in the clouds until those three Bettys came stooging along, and then I popped out and clobbered all three of them? Boy, was I on the beam that day!"

"Yeah," said Hawsepipe; "and who was it that put you in that cloud in the first place, kept you circling in there for ten minutes, and then told you just exactly how and when to bust out of it? I'll bet you've forgotten who that was—but I was there, too, that day, my intrepid friend. Try to remember that when you tell the story hereafter."

"That's right; so you were, pal. You were the quarterback of the team," conceded Curly.

"Now that we've shot all the Zeros down again," said Hawsepipe, "how about giving us the lowdown on this game we've got coming up with Army? How do our chances look, Joe?"

"There's only one word for it," replied Joe, "—grim. We've got good material for a change, this year—lads who can run, block, kick, and pass. But we've got nobody to run the team. I spend five days a week sweating it out with these kids, trying to teach them what I know about being a quarterback. But you can teach a lad only so much; the rest of it just has to be born in him."

"But golly, Joe," objected Hawsepipe, "I should think that this two-platoon system you could practically run the team from the bench. Why do we need quarterbacks on the field when we've got the best quarterback Navy ever produced sitting on the bench?"

"Sure, you can do a lot from the bench. But the big chances to bust a game wide open come and go too fast to do it from there. The boys on the field have to spot the break when it comes up, and cash in on it the next play, otherwise a smart coach on the other bench will be plugging that opening at the same time that you are sending word in to hit it. We've lost three games so far this year that we would have won if we could have checked signals on one play and called a new one from the bench. And our opponents have made touchdowns on plays that we had all figured out on the bench before the ball was snapped. It's the same as if you pilot characters on the *Enterprise* had no way to talk to us from the air unless Combat Information Center sent another plane up. It's too slow."

"How about Army?" asked Hawsepipe. "Are they as good as the sportswriters claim?"

"I can answer that in three words," said Joe, "yes and no. I've scouted every game they've played this fall. They've got a powerhouse of a team with some mighty fine backs, but they've also got some glaring weaknesses."

"Of course," observed Curly, "Army doesn't play the schedule we do. Half of their games are against girls' schools. You don't learn much from watching them, do you?"

"You'd be surprised how much you can learn. I know all their plays now just as well as I know our own, and most of the time I can tell where the ball is going and who will carry it the minute they start walking out of the huddle. I've spotted about a dozen dead giveaways by which their backs betray when they are going to carry the ball, and by which the passers and kickers tip off what they are going to do."

"No doubt you pass this dope on to the midshipmen when you think of it?" asked Hawsepipe.

"You bet your life I do. But there's a lot of things you just learn to size up as they happen, and you can't pass that kind of stuff on to anybody," said Jumpin' Joe. "If we are lucky and get the breaks we might make a ball game out of it in Philadelphia for one quarter. We've got some good lads on our club; man for man, they're almost as good as Army. But they are inexperienced; they blow up under pressure. If we only had a seasoned quarterback to keep them on the beam we might take the Kaydets. Boy, I wish I could run that team from the sideline, the way you guys in CIC used to run the air battles.'

"Maybe our boys are better than you think," said Hawsepipe. "We looked pretty good against Notre Dame."

"Notre Dame never makes a bum out of us. Don't forget Rip Miller has been assistant director of athletics at Navy for years. He was one of the seven mules on Notre Dame's Four Horsemen team, and those Irish stick together, you know. We've got a lot of good, hard-hitting kids, but there's no football brains in the club."

"Just like old Fighter Squadron Six on the *Enterprise,*" said Hawsepipe. "If you guys had been on your own instead of having a cool head like mine to tell you what to do, the Japs would have plastered the Pacific with blood all over, but no brains."

"Leave us not get involved in any arguments about that," said Curly. "Anyway, now we've got the lowdown on the Army game . . . By the way, where are you working these days, Hawsepipe?"

"I'm up at the new Naval Ordnance Laboratory just outside of Washington. I'm working on stuff that's going to put you stick-and-throttle boys out of business—guided missiles."

"It will put your old racket in the ash can too, won't it?" said Curly. "Those missiles won't need any Combat Information Center quarterback to tell them where to go. I hear they will steer themselves automatically with target-seeking devices."

"Yeah," said Hawsepipe. "You ought to see some of the stuff we are working on now. We are building miniature radar sets that will fit into the nose of a small rocket. The whole set isn't any bigger than a pack of cards, but it's got a transmitter and receiver in it, complete with batteries."

"A little thing like that must be very fragile," said Curly.

"Fragile, hell! We put them in antiaircraft projectiles now, in place of the old-time fuses, and shoot them out of a five-inch gun. I don't call that fragile. They've got vacuum tubes the size of a peanut in them—no wires in them at all. We just draw a wiring diagram, using metallic paint, and stick that in the missile."

As he made this last remark, Hawsepipe had picked up Jumpin' Joe's plastic gold flying helmet, which was lying on the sofa, and was turning it over in his hands. "Say," he said, looking inside it, "since when have they been putting earphones in football helmets?"

"That's not a football helmet," laughed Joe. "That's one of the new hard, flying helmets the jet jockeys wear now."

"So-o-o-o," said Hawsepipe, "a flying helmet, the man says. Well, it certainly looks exactly like the gold helmets the Navy team wears, and it feels just about as rugged."

"They're made out of the same stuff," said Joe. "As a matter of fact, they both serve the same purpose—to protect the brains, if any, from bumps."

A faraway look had come into Hawsepipe's eyes. It was the kind of look that means "Caution, Man at Work." You could almost see the wheels going around inside his head.

After a minute Hawsepipe said, sort of casually, "He sits right there and tells me that this thing here isn't a football helmet."

"That's right," said Joe.

"But it looks like one, it serves the same purpose, it could be used for one. And tucked away inside it's got a radio receiving set."

"Yeah!" said Joe. "All the blow-torch pilots have been wearing—" His jaw dropped open. A great light began to dawn on him, and finally he said in an awed voice, "Well, I'll be darned."

"You ought to be," said Hawsepipe. "Here you've got the answer to a football coach's prayer clamped right on top of your head every time you go out to put your flight time in, and all it means to you is a flying helmet. I've always said I could see how you aviators earn your flight pay, but what do you do to earn your base pay?"

"But those are just earphones in that thing," protested Joe. "You've got to plug them into a receiver in the plane."

"I can make receivers at the Naval Ordnance Lab that will fit in the same space as those phones," said Hawsepipe, with the air of a carpenter saying he can saw a piece of wood in two.

"But after the first scrimmage they would be junk," said Joe.

"Oh, yeah? I suppose you think the Kaydets tackle harder than a five-inch gun kicks."

"Blow me down," said Jumpin' Joe. "If each one of the players had one of these helmets, I could sit on the bench with a walkie-talkie and—"

"Excellent, Dr. Watson, excellent," said Hawsepipe.

"Look!" said Joe, all excitement by now. "I can get you fifty of these helmets from the Naval Air Station at Patuxent tomorrow. How long will it take your gun club at the Ordnance Lab to fix them up for us?"

"Well," said Hawsepipe, "as the Air Force general said when the bomb missed the pickle barrel, 'The difficult we do immediately, the impossible may take some time.' I can have fifty for you in two weeks."

"How about job orders and bureau approval, and all that stuff?"

"Nothing to it," said Hawsepipe. "We've got an all-weather-flying project up there I can hang it on. We've got more dough for guided missiles than we can spend anyway, and rather than turn some of that money back to the Treasury to be wasted we can just shift it to this improved type of flying helmet."

Next day the Navy set up task forces to implement this program in a gung-ho fashion. At the Naval Ordnance Laboratory a "Frantic" priority was placed on a project to equip fifty jet flying helmets with miniature radios for "top secret" missions. This was to be a crash program having right of way over even Atomic Energy Commission and CIA projects.

In midmorning an Athletic Association truck from Annapolis

screeched to a halt, delivered the helmets, and Hawsepipe rushed them into a high security area in the electronics lab that had been hastily cleared for them.

In Annapolis that afternoon the football squad met in the gym behind locked doors guarded by Marines for an hour's "skull practice." They came out of the session looking as smug and wise as a tree full of well fed owls.

The atmosphere around Annapolis took on a sudden change. Before long everybody knew that something big was cooking and that it smelled pretty good. All sorts of rumors got loose, most of them planted by the the coaches, but none of them near the truth. The Navy has had long experience in keeping snoopy outsiders—such as newspaper reporters, congressmen, and the Secretary of Defense—from finding out about things they shouldn't know. They guarded this secret more closely than the Manhattan Project. The Admiral was given a very vague and evasive briefing that something big was cooking, and had sense enough to just look wise and keep his nose out of it.

Of course during the month preceding the Army game everybody around Annapolis always gets hopped up on wishful thinking and common sense gets the deep six. Every year the whole Navy is able to convince itself that this time they've got a chance to upset the applecart and beat Army. Often they don't really believe this, but they are able to work up a lather of hysteria that makes them think they believe it.

Old sea dogs whose shrewd and seasoned judgment was battle-tested in the Pacific many times let their emotions run away with them as the end of November approaches. They can calculate the precise odds in any naval engagement except this annual clambake with West Point. They go up to Philadelphia with a faraway look in their bleary eyes, full of gin and hope.

Of course, the coaches always put out the usual malarkey in October no matter how grim and hopeless Navy's chances are. But this time you could tell they meant it.

After word got around, large sums of money were bet. Even Holy Joe, senior chaplain at the Academy, laid $20 on the game; and he never bets on a sports event unless it is fixed, unless he is in on the fix, and unless the fixers are honorable and trustworthy characters who are personal friends of his.

When Curly got back to San Diego and advised Admiral Day to bet all the money he could on Navy the Admiral at first considered grounding him and asking the Bureau of Personnel for a new squadron commander. Curly couldn't let even the Admiral in on the big secret. But admirals can always be persuaded that Navy *is* going to win. The old duffer finally bet a hundred bucks on the game with an Army general, thus starting a rumor going in service circles which got all the way back to the Pentagon that one of the top admirals in the Pacific Fleet had gone nuts.

The game itself now had assumed a permanent place in naval history alongside the exploits of John Paul Jones. It was about the biggest upset in sports history since the David and Goliath fight. It started off just about the way the experts expected, with Navy fumbling the opening kickoff away to Army on its own 20-yard line. It looked as if the rout was going to begin before the crowd even got settled in its seats.

At this point even the Army rooters were pulling for underdog Navy—not rooting for them to win, of course, but just hoping they could put on a decent show and play some sort of game worth watching. They hoped Navy might fight them off for a quarter or so and be able to hold the final score down to maybe 21 to 0.

But Navy stopped the next four plays by Army's powerhouse as if they had called the plays themselves and knew exactly where they were going. Those cadets got smacked into the dirt as if they hadn't even read their own press clippings.

It was a rout, all right, but it didn't go according to the previously prepared script. Army was rammed back on its heels and held there the rest of the game. Nobody would believe it at first, and even when Navy went into the last quarter with a 14-to-2 lead, some of the radio announcers were still talking as if this couldn't last and the roof would fall in on Navy any minute.

But Navy outgeneraled the Army all the way. When Navy had the ball, Army never knew what was coming up next. The Navy quarterback mixed up his off-tackle slants, fakes, reverses, and passes like a magician.

Whenever there was a time out during the game, two sailors

would rush out onto the field pushing a fancy-looking water cart and Navy players would gather around it with their heads down close to it. For a minute in the second period Jumpin' Joe thought Navy had been caught with its pants ajar. The referee got a hell of an electric shock trying to take a drink from this cart. But the fast-talking sailors explained to him that there was an electric ice machine inside the cart.

Those sailors weren't any ordinary swab jockeys. They were hot-shot electronic technicians. And that "water cart" was full of troubleshooting machinery to fix busted helmets in a hurry.

Some of the sportswriters said it reminded them of the kind of quarterbacking Navy used to get back in the days when Jumpin' Joe Sifton was making All-American. When Army had the ball, it seemed as if Navy knew more about each play they pulled off than Army did themselves. Any number of times, Cadet ball carriers were brought down by gang tackles of four or five Middies on plays that had been fooling the opposition all year.

The Navy defense shifted on almost every play. On some plays linesmen would pull out and head for the spot where the ball was going before it was snapped. When Army were trying to set up their passes, they would run a couple of plays into the line, with a decoy fading way out as if to get a pass. Navy's defenses would pay no attention to him. Then another play would start the same way, but wind up with a pass to the decoy, and the whole Navy backfield would be swarming around the receiver before the pass was halfway there.

When Navy was on the offensive they spent hardly any time in the huddle. They would just sort of bump their heads together in a bunch and then rush right back to the line of scrimmage. Their two touchdown plays came without any preliminary huddle at all, and without any signals being called. They just sort of exploded out of the debris of the previous play while Army was still picking themselves up and rubbing the dirt out of their eyes. It looked as if somebody was running the team by telepathy.

Out in San Diego that evening in the Officers' Club, Commander Cue was explaining to Admiral Day the secret of the great upset. At the end of his exposé, he said, "I can just see what all the headlines are going to say tomorrow: 'Fired-up Navy upsets favored Army.' But Navy wasn't *fired* up—it was just *wired* up."

"By the great horn spoon, I'm about ready to believe anything can happen these days," said the Admiral. "I wouldn't even be surprised if we have rockets in orbit around the world and men walking around out in space before long."

"Could be," agreed Curly. "Of course, Admiral," he continued, "this stuff I just told you is still top secret. If the Army ever finds out about it they'll blow the roof off the Pentagon. There will probably be a Congressional investigation and the Joint Chiefs will hold a special session and annul that game by a 3-to-1 vote."

"That's right," said the Admiral gravely. "They might even get so mad about it they would bring Louis Johnson back as Secretary of Defense; and God help the free world if that happens!"

CHAPTER TWELVE

Willy's Mission to Moscow

SOON AFTER the saucer episode, Ensign William Wigglesworth was promoted to the rank of Lieutenant Junior Grade, and Admiral Day drafted him for duty as his flag lieutenant. News of this appointment swept through naval circles in San Diego like a hurricane warning and left the community in a state of shock. Heads were shaken sadly, and opinions were given that the Admiral was growing barnacles on the brain.

A flag lieutenant is supposed to be a social secretary. He is the Admiral's personal aide, keeps track of all his official and unofficial commitments, screens incoming phone calls, opens the mail, and greets visitors. Aboard ship he must have at his fingertips the protocol section of the Navy Regulations Book. He must know how many side-boys to produce for visiting VIPs, ranging from junketing congressman to cannibal chiefs from the UN. He must know whether a maharajah gets thirteen or fifteen guns and how many ruffles and flourishes the bandmaster must give an air vice marshal.

Ashore he must be familiar with all the fine print of Emily Post's latest volume on etiquette. He must also know what uniform and medals the Admiral has to wear to a state dinner for the Poobah of Pakistan and must not pinch the hostess in the fanny at formal receptions or spit tobacco juice on the ballroom floor. He should always be immaculately dressed and must be a smooth operator who can say no in a way that takes ten minutes and leaves his victim with the impression that he has done him a big favor. He tags along wherever the Admiral goes, nudges the Admiral's elbow and raises an eyebrow whenever the old gentleman leaves his zipper open, and never takes any action whatever on his own initiative, except to whip out a cigarette lighter when the Admiral decides to have a smoke.*

There were many people in naval circles around San Diego who feared that Willy was not the right type for the job. They thought his philosophy of life was too carefree and frivolous, and that he lacked proper respect for long-established, traditional ways of doing things. They predicted that he would upset tea carts and bust balloons all over the place and turn top-level naval functions into Roman holidays.

But they were wrong. Willy took to the new job as if he had taught Perle Mesta all she knew. He abandoned his evil companions in the air group and was not seen any more hanging around the bar in the BOQ. Some of his old friends said that his promotion had gone to his head. But although junior grade lieutenant *is* a great leap forward from ensign, it is only a half-stripe, and that certainly isn't enough to change a man's whole way of life. At least, not of a man like Willy.

As is so often the case when dissolute young officers give up their wanton ways and become respectable citizens, a good woman was the cause of it. Willy had fallen in love.

It was not with any of the many Navy brats around Coronado whose mothers are alert to get rid of them with a military wedding in the Air Station Chapel. Nor was it one of the many local civilian gals who lurk behind the potted palms in the officers' club ready to pounce on young bachelors wearing wings and drawing flight pay. Willy evaded all these snares but fell for the Queen of the Ball, the top banana of the local 400, U.S. Senator Worthington's baby daughter, Mary.

Mary's coming-out party at the Hotel del Coronado had been

---

* In justice to a number of fine young officers who had the misfortune of serving as my flag lieutenant and who did a fine job under difficult circumstances, I must point out that this book is pure fiction. It is also pertinent to observe that old sailors are notorious liars and that retired ones are the worst of all.—D.V.G.

the highlight of the social season, but it was really just a sort of dry run for the one her mother figured on having in Washington when Congress met again.

The Senator and his wife were old friends of Admiral Day's and often had him in for dinner, which is how Willy got within hailing distance of Mary to begin with. At first her mother had taken a dim view of Mary's running around with a jg aviator. There were several young bachelor senators in Washington that Mama had her sights on. But Admiral Day assured the old gal that this boy had good stuff in him and was headed for the top. And Mary didn't always do what her mother said anyway.

Courting and winning Mary from the horde of drooling suitors who darkened her door in Coronado had been the damnedest rat race Willy had got into since Grandma left the gate open and the pigs got out. Eligible young bachelors swarmed around her place like students in a campus riot, and Mary's mother examined their credentials the way the CIA screens Q clearances. Nobody took Mary out on a date until Mama had verified the marriage license of his grandparents and got a Dun and Bradstreet on his Old Man. But Willy and Mary soon found that they were kindred spirits, love broke out between them, and they hauled off and announced their engagement.

To say that Mama squawked like a stuck pig over this would be a gross understatement, and of couse you don't use that kind of language anyway in speaking of Mrs. Worthington. But Mary was her mother's daughter, had a mind of her own too, so love overcame all, and the impending nuptials were announced.

Two weeks later, on a bright cold morning, Willy looped and swooped high in the sky over San Diego in a Banshee fighter leaving a long white fluffy trail behind him. Willy, making a test flight, had found that at 50,000 feet his plane made vapor trails that morning. Since the test required that he stay up there for a while, he occupied his time by writing MARY in the sky in huge, white letters for all the world to see, just as many a small boy writes his lady-love's name on a fence.

At this point in Willy's life there wasn't a cloud in his own sky except for the fluffy white ones he was trailing behind him that morning. Now that love had triumphed, he and Mary would soon be living happily ever after and the future looked like a straight in approach on the main runway with a gentle breeze.

. . . True, old lady Worthington was planning a wedding that would probably have to be held in the balloon hangar. It was shaping up as the biggest middle-aisle event since the Napoleon-Josephine nuptials. But for Mary's sake, Willy was prepared to bear this cross.

To top it all off, Willy's tour of sea duty would be up on the date set for the wedding and he had been promised a month's leave before reporting to his next assignment. This job was to be as a jet test pilot at the Naval Air Station, San Diego. So, any way you looked at it, Willy had the world by the tail with a downhill drag.

When he had finished putting the name of his love up over the world where it belonged, Willy throttled back on his jets, popped his dive brakes, nosed over, and whooshed straight down five miles closer to earth so he could have a look at it himself. Then, well pleased with his handiwork, he spiraled around the NAS, North Island, greased his Banshee in to an eggshell landing, and taxied up to the line.

In the locker room Willy shifted from his G suit to a spick-and-span, blue uniform with aiguillettes on the shoulder, and brand-new gold stripes glistening on the sleeves. Willy took a whisk broom and brushed the lint away from that extra half-stripe which made him feel a foot taller. Someday he might get to be an admiral and sport a broad gold band on his sleeve. But it wouldn't seem as big as this narrow one did now.

Looking at Willy as he emerged from the locker room, you could easily see why Admiral Day had picked him for flag lieutenant. Regardless of any other factors, he *looked* the part, and was obviously a sharp, alert young officer that any admiral would be proud to have on his staff.

When Willy strode into his office in the Administration Building a few minutes later, his feet now on the ground but his head still at 50,000 feet, the yeoman handed him the following priority dispatch:

From: BUREAU OF NAVAL PERSONNEL
    Lieutenant junior grade William Wigglesworth detached from present duty. Proceed and report to U.S. Embassy, Moscow, for duty involving flying as assistant naval attaché for air. Keep Navy Department advised of your movements.

Willy clung to the edge of the desk while the wreckage of his dreams came crashing down around him. Then he shook his head like a fighter pilot who has just pulled out of a dive too fast and tottered into the sanctum of his boss, Admiral Day.

When the Admiral read the dispatch he let out a low whistle and said, "Say, this is a surprise!" Thinking back on some of Willy's escapades that he knew of, he added, "Very ill-advised assignment, if you ask me. Could easily result in an all-out atomic war with Russia."

"They can't do this to me, sir. I never heard of a deal like this before. They didn't even consult *you* about it—did they, sir?" asked Willy.

Studying the dispatch, the Admiral began to bristle up. "They've got no right to shanghai somebody off my personal staff without even asking me about it. I won't stand for it. Who do those Office of Naval Intelligence guys think they are? I'll show those cloak-and-dagger monkeys they can't push me around that way. I'll phone the Chief of Naval Operations. I'll . . . I'll . . ."

The Admiral's head of steam fizzled out, and after some moments of ominous muttering, reason returned. He grinned sheepishly at Willy and said, "On second thought, Willy, this looks bad. I hate to say this, but there's no use kidding ourselves. It looks to me like you have *had* it."

"But, Admiral, this cannot be. They promised me that test pilot job at the air station here. You recommended me for it. . . . Couldn't *you* do something, sir?"

"Son," said the Admiral, "you know I'll go to bat for you any time I think it will do any good. In fact I've done it a couple of times, haven't I?"

"Yessir, I know that—but in both *those* cases the police were *wrong!*"

"So they were," said the Admiral, "but in this case I'm afraid I can't do a particle of good. This is high-level stuff, cooked up by the Office of Naval Intelligence. They wouldn't yank you out this way without consulting me unless it was urgent. These diplomatic jobs are special cases. Before orders to a job of this kind are issued, they are cleared through the State Department, FBI, CIA, the Soviet Embassy, and all the top offices in the Navy Department. The Department is committed to this thing now and I would be just batting my head against a stone wall trying to get it changed."

Willy realized this was all true. In desperation he said, "Admiral, I just can't take that job. I'd be lucky to get in four hours flying time a month out there, and by the time I come back, I'll be a chairborne desk pilot. It's just a cookie-pushing job anyway, and there are urgent personal reasons, too, which you know all about. . . . Maybe if I went to Washington myself and explained things, I could get it changed. Would there be anything wrong about that?"

"That's okay if you can swing it," said the Admiral, "but this deal has the earmarks of the Chief of Naval Intelligence on it, old Admiral 'Teacup' Twitters. I don't think you'll have much luck talking Teacup out of this assignment. Once he makes up his mind you have to blast to change it. Your personal plans won't cut any ice with him at all. The only way you could move him would be to convince him that you aren't suited for the job. And when you get right down to brass tacks, you are ideally suited for it, Willy. I'll admit it's a waste of good flying talent to send you there, but you are the attaché type, my boy."

That night Willy broke the news to Mary, who took it calmly like the thoroughbred she was, and said, "Okay, Willy, so we go to Moscow. We can get married next week. Worse things than that could happen to us."

"But what's your mother going to say about this?"

"We will have trouble with Mother. The second truckload of invitations went out today. But I wasn't looking forward to that Roman holiday Mother is planning any more than you were. We'll have a nice quiet family wedding . . . quiet, that is, except for the fuss that Mother raises about it. Come on, let's face the music and get it over with."

Mrs. Senator Worthington was a formidable character. If she had ever tangled with the battleship *Missouri* on a collision course, there is no doubt whatever the *Missouri* would be the one that eventually had to give way. She had been making her own rules of the road so long that she now took it for granted that she had the right of way over all others. Back in Washington, where it sometimes became necessary for her to lower the boom on famous ladies, they referred to her as "that belligerent old blister" but were careful not to plan parties that might conflict with hers. If the Navy Department thought they could upset her plans for a wedding merely by issuing a set of orders, they might find they had another think coming.

When Willy and Mary entered her sanctum, Mrs. Worthington was about to dictate a letter to her secretary. "Just a minute, children," she said, "I want to get this letter off tonight."

Then she said to her secretary, "This goes to the president of Atlas Oil Company. You've got his home address in your files. Send it there—not to his office.

George—

Some months ago your people sent me a letter saying your accounting department was being computerized and that this would improve the accuracy and promptness of your service. They enclosed a credit card for me to use at your service stations.

Since then, instead of a bill I have been receiving little cards each month with holes punched all over them and a number up in the corner which is supposed to tell me how much I owe you.

Evidently somebody punched the wrong hole some months back and got my fuel oil budget account crossed up with some tires I bought at one of your service stations and paid for in cash.

Ever since I have been writing letters back and forth to your people trying to straighten out this snafu but things just get more and more confused and they can't get their computer to say who did what to whom, and who ought to pay for it.

I think the only way for me to get my household account

in order again is to pay cash for everything from now on.

Will you please take the enclosed credit card and stuff it up your computer.

Sincerely,

Dolly

"Get that in the mail first thing in the morning," said Mrs. Worthington to her secretary. Then turning to Willy and Mary she said pleasantly, "Good evening, children, what's on your happy minds tonight?"

Willy simply handed her the telegram from the Navy Department and battened down for the expected storm. Mrs. Worthington wasn't the least bit perturbed. It took more than a silly telegram from the Navy Department to ruffle her hatch covers.

"That's ridiculous," she said. "Pay no attention to it."

"But, Mrs. Worthington," said Willy, "its orders—from the Navy Department."

"I can see where it's from as well as you can, young man," said Mrs. Worthington, like an admiral saying it isn't necessary to call his attention to a lubberly maneuver by a ship in his fleet, "and I think it's a sad state of affairs when the Navy wastes the taxpayers' money sending stupid telegrams like that one."

"But that stupid telegram is an official set of orders and it says I've got to be in Moscow next month."

"That's absurd," said Mrs. Worthington. "How can you be in Moscow next month?"

"Never mind *how*, Mother," said Mary. "He's *got* to be there."

"Mary, you've always been a scatterbrained child. Don't you realize the wedding is three months from now? Willy can't possibly go to Moscow before that."

"Mother, the Navy doesn't base its plans on wedding dates. When they say 'go,' you've got to go."

"Hunh!" sniffed Mrs. W., shaking out her topsails and bracing her yards. "That's what they think. All my invitations have gone out, I've got people coming from all over the country, and I've made all my arrangements. The Navy can just guess again."

"Mrs. Worthington," said Willy, "I hope I can get these orders changed. But if I can't do it, then I'll have to go, and there's nothing we can do about it."

"Well, maybe you can't do anything about it—but I can," said Mrs. W., her sails filling up in a way that indicated small craft should seek shelter. "The Senator is on the Armed Forces Committee and the Chief of Naval Operations, old Stinky Parker, is a good friend of ours. I'm going to phone the Senator long-distance right now, and I'll have those orders canceled by tomorrow morning."

"Please don't do that, Mrs. Worthington!" pleaded Willy.

"Why not?" snapped Mrs. W., the same way that the fleet flagship whips the "Interrogatory" flag to the starboard mainyard arm when the Admiral gets mad.

"Because you just can't do things that way in the Navy. They never forgive you."

"You don't have to do anything, young man. I'll take care of this whole business and you won't have to lift a finger."

"That won't make any difference, Mrs. Worthington," said Willy. "If you get the Senator to throw his weight around, he'll get the orders changed, all right. But the Navy resents political pressures to get duty assignments for junior officers. They will lay for me from now on and eventually they will nail me and send me to Siberia."

"They're sending you there *now*, aren't they?" demanded Mrs. W., unlimbering her main battery and securing loose gear about the decks. "I'm going to phone the Senator in Washington right now. You can't stop me, and they can't hold it against you."

"Mother," said Mary, slowly and deliberately, "don't you do that!" The young lady's decks were obviously cleared for action, too, and her battle ensigns were flying.

Mrs. Worthington, having lived with her baby daughter for twenty-one years, could recognize storm signals when she saw them. There was a tone in Mary's voice that warned all prudent seamen a hurricane might be making up.

"I'm the one who's marrying Willy. I'm marrying into the Navy and I'm going to abide by the Navy rules the same as he does. Wherever they send him, I'm going to go. I'm warning you right now that, unless Willy can get those orders changed *himself,* your plans for that three-ring-circus wedding are off. If you barge into this and get Daddy to interfere, Willy and I will elope and get married in Tijuana tomorrow."

Mrs. Worthington leveled a shrewd, calculating look at her daughter. She was enough of a tactician to know when she was licked and when strategic retreat was better than getting sunk with her colors nailed to the masthead. She knew that Mary had a mind of her own and could be a chip off the old battle-ax. The storm warnings were unmistakable now. So, while her rigging was still intact, she assumed an air of injured innocence, put her helm alee, came about, and sailed majestically out of the room.

"I meant every word of that, Willy," said Mary. "Where you go I go."

"I know that, Mary, and that's one of the reasons I love you so much. But I just can't drag you out to a place like Moscow—the Russians keep our people cooped up there like monkeys in the zoo."

"Wherever you go is good enough for me. But I can't understand why they should waste the best jet pilot in the Navy on a job like that!"

"I don't know what's behind it," said Willy. "I'm going to Washington to try and talk them out of it, but I haven't got any very good ideas yet on how to go about it. If I got publicly plastered and picked a fight in the lobby of the Army-Navy Club, that might do it. But there must be a better way than that."

"Sure. You could punch an old lady in the nose in front of the White House or you could join the Communist party. But we've got to use a little more finesse than that. We don't have to convince anybody except that coffee cup admiral in the Intelligence Office that you're not cut out to be a diplomat."

"That's right," said Willy. "Just Admiral Twitters; he's the man."

"Okay, then. Let's figure out a way of making him think you would be a Missouri mule in the Ballet Russe. If he is the *only* one who thinks so, that won't be so terrible. . . . Now look—I've got an idea—you can create an impression in one minute that you couldn't live down in a lifetime—but if it's only with one man that wouldn't be so bad. . . ."

When Mary finished outlining her idea, Willy said, "Mary, I always knew you were wonderful but I didn't know until now what a genius you are. You ought to be the Chief of Naval Operations."

"I'll settle for Mrs. William Wigglesworth and let you worry about being CNO."

"I'll be on my way to Washington bright and early in the morning, and I'll bet by the time I get back, those orders will be canceled."

Shortly before noon next day, Willy flew his Banshee into the rat race that is called a traffic pattern around Washington, D.C., and by skillful piloting managed to come out alive and land at the Naval Air Station, Anacostia. He checked in at the BOQ, phoned the Pentagon, and made half a dozen appointments to pay his respects that afternoon to various admirals he knew. He also made a date to see Admiral Twitters promptly at 3 P.M. Then he shifted to his best blue uniform, shined himself up for inspection, and went over to the officers' mess where he lunched on sauerkraut and Brussels sprouts.

Right after lunch Willy showed up at the Pentagon carrying a small handbag and began paying the series of calls he had mapped out. They were purely social calls—just dropping in and saying hello to old (and highly placed) friends. So half a dozen aviator admirals who knew and liked Willy had the pleasure of a five-minute chat with him, and the opportunity to observe that he was his usual fine-looking self, full of health, vigor, and good spirits— just the sort of young officer any of them would be glad to have on their staff.

At 2:30 Willy dropped in on Vice Admiral Cuddahy, Chief of Naval Personnel, who had known Willy in the Mediterranean and had given him glowing efficiency reports as an up-and-coming young officer who would make his mark in the Navy.

"Delighted to see you, Willy," said Admiral Cuddahy. "And I'm glad to have a chance to talk with you, because I want you to know I had nothing whatever to do with this Moscow assignment."

"Oh . . . ?" said Willy.

"As a matter of fact, I did my best too block it. I figured it was wasting high-powered flying talent to send you there. But old Twitters went over my head and high-pressured the Chief of Naval Operations into approving this thing as a special case. He had a long song and dance about the State Department, U.S. prestige in diplomatic circles, and about some gawdawful jam the present incumbent had got into. The ambassador himself demanded his immediate relief. The CNO swallowed the story, approved the deal, and there was nothing I could do about it."

"I certainly appreciate your going to bat for me, sir," said Willy. "I'm due for an interview with Admiral Twitters at three o'clock and I'm hoping I may still talk him out of this."

"I wish you luck, Willy, and I'm afraid you're going to need a lot of it. Drop in afterwards and let me know how you make out."

Willy left Vice Admiral Cuddahy's office at a quarter to three, lugged his bag into the gentlemen's room just across the hall from ONI and locked the door behind him. In the next few minutes a startling change was wrought in Willy's appearance. He whipped off his number one uniform blouse, and his immaculate white shirt and stiff collar. Out of the bag came a crummy white shirt with a badly soiled soft collar. Willy donned this garment and put on a black tie with egg spots all over it. Over this he put on a blue uniform coat that looked as though it had been slept in and had caught all the eggs that missed the tie. He mussed up his hair, doused it with cheap perfume, sprinkled something that looked like dandruff on his shoulders, and with a black grease pencil quickly fixed his finger nails as though he had just finished assembling a crankcase.

Promptly at three o'clock, Lieutenant jg Wigglesworth presented himself to Admiral Twitters' flag secretary, looking as if he had ridden the rods of a coal gondola all the way from San Diego. A look of astonishment spread across the flag secretary's face as he called Admiral Twitters on the squawk box and informed him dubiously that Lieutenant Wigglesworth was waiting.

"Send him in," came the brisk reply.

If the flag secretary was astonished, Admiral Twitters was flabbergasted by the apparition that barged into his office, with its blouse unbuttoned, its hand extended, and strode up to his desk and said "Hello, Admiral Twatters. I'm Lieutenant Wigglesworth, your new naval attaché for Moscow."

The Admiral couldn't have been more startled if Willy had announced that he was Christopher Columbus. He gaped and had a choking spell while Willy seated himself at the desk and immediately launched into his script.

"Admiral, I'm tickled to death to get this job. At first I didn't want it. But you can't always get what you want in this Navy, so I figured I would just make the best of it. Now that I've got used to the idea I kind of like it. Ain't that the right way to look at it, Admiral?"

Admiral Twitters coughed up an incoherent reply and frowned at Willy's unbuttoned blouse.

Willy buttoned the blouse, began scratching at a spot on it, and continued pleasantly, "I thought you'd like that attitude, Admiral. When things don't work out the way I want them to, I just say 'Neechevo!'—that's Russian, Admiral. I've got a good-looking babe teaching me the language," Willy explained with a knowing leer.

Admiral Twitters, beginning to suspect that Willy was drunk, pulled his chair over and leaned closer to get a whiff of his breath. Willy exploded that theory very quickly. He uncorked a resounding Brussels sprout burp and said, "Oops, pardon me, Admiral. Did I get any on you? Must have been something I et. —As I was saying, I'm looking forward to going to Moscow and meeting them foreign diplomats from all over the world. I just dropped in to see if you had any special dope to give me before leaving, sir."

"No! . . . No!" said the Admiral weakly, ". . . er . . . your name is Lieutenant William Wigglesworth?"

"Yessir. That's right, sir."

"Your present job is aide and flag secretary to Admiral Day out at San Diego?" inquired the Admiral incredulously.

Willy picked something out of his nose, examined it casually, and wiped his finger on the seat of his pants. "Nossir, flag lieutenant, sir, and Admiral Day is a very fine gent, sir. . . . Well, Admiral, I don't want to take up too much of your valuable time, so if you have no further instructions, I'll beat it now."

Admiral Twitters shook his head groggily, so Willy rose, about-faced, and got the hell out of there. The Admiral groped with a trembling hand for the button that summoned his chief of staff.

"What in heaven's name is the matter with this alleged Office of Naval Intelligence?" he demanded. "With all the sources of information in the Navy Department at your fingertips, all the records of the Bureau of Personnel at your disposal, you pick the worst misfit I've ever seen."

"Wh . . . what's wrong, sir?" stammered the COS, who hadn't seen Willy.

"*What's wrong?* This fellow you recommended for Moscow was just in here and he's—he's—well, he's just absolutely impossible! . . . Now I *am* in a jam. . . . But this *can't* be the same man Cuddahy was so hot about!"

So saying, Admiral Twitters flipped a switch in the interoffice squawk box and soon had Vice Admiral Cuddahy on the line. "This is Twitters. Didn't you tell me a few days ago that a Lieutenant Wigglesworth was a good man for that Moscow job?"

"Yes, I did," came the reply. "Matter of fact I said he was too good a man, and I still say so!"

"Do you know this fellow *personally?*" asked Admiral Twitters.

"Yes, indeed," replied Admiral Cuddahy, "I know him well. He was in to see me only twenty minutes ago. Nice lad. I like him."

"Good God!" said Admiral Twitters, and hung up.

Admiral Twitters shook his head sadly at the chief of staff and said, "I always knew these aviators were a ragtime outfit but I never would have believed that vice admiral aviators would tolerate a clown like that one!"

Meantime Willy had slipped into the gents' can across the corridor from the flag secretary's office and in five minutes emerged into the halls of the Pentagon again, his usual spick-and-span self. Back in the office of the Chief of Naval Personnel, he received an enthusiastic but puzzled welcome from Admiral Cuddahy.

"How in the world did you do it, Willy? I never heard of old

Twitters changing his mind that fast before, especially after committing himself as he did on this deal. You're a miracle man."

"He was noncommittal with me, sir," said Willy innocently. "He didn't say more than a half dozen words, and he didn't promise anything."

"Well, he phoned me a little while ago," said Admiral Cuddahy, "and seemed to be all worked up about you. He was sort of incoherent and blew up in the middle of our conversation. His chief of staff called right afterwards and said ONI wanted your orders canceled, right now, this afternoon."

"Oh," said Willy. "I wonder what happened." Butter would have melted in his mouth.

"The hell you do," grinned Admiral Cuddahy. "You know darned well what happened and someday I'm going to worm it out of you. Meantime we will go back to our previous program for you. Thirty days' leave in June and then the air station at San Diego."

"Thank you, sir, thank you very much, sir," said Willy, grabbing the Admiral's hand, "and now, Admiral, I won't take up any more of your valuable time—good-bye, sir, and thank you again."

Before the Admiral could change his mind, Willy took off out of there as if rocket-propelled, and was last seen disappearing toward Anacostia in a cloud of dust.

Next morning Admiral Cuddahy received a puzzling memorandum from the Office of Naval Intelligence. It stated that the reason for requesting cancellation of Lieutenant Wigglesworth's orders was "uncouth personal appearance and habits." Vice Admiral Cuddahy studied it incredulously. Usually a memorandum of that kind goes into an officer's record jacket in the Bureau of Personnel for the guidance of future promotion boards, and constitutes a serious black mark against him.

"Uncouth," muttered Vice Admiral Cuddahy. "Why, Willy is about the couthest officer I know . . . there's some kind of monkey business behind this, and next time I see that young scoundrel I'm going to take a rubber hose and beat it out of him. Meantime old Twitters must be in a foul mood this morning so I'm not going to stir him up by nosing any further into this affair."

So saying, Admiral Cuddahy tore up the memo, dropped it in the wastebasket, and thus terminated Willy's Mission to Moscow.

That evening Mrs. Senator Worthington was chatting with Mrs. Hardleigh Able, one of her cronies in Coronado. "Yes," said Mrs. W., "I just put my foot down, sent him to Washington, and got things changed. I think he went right to the top and saw the Chief of Naval Operations . . . just goes to show that you can get your rights, even in the Navy, provided you stand up for them in a firm but gentlemanly way."